FIRE DOWN BELOW

When William Golding was awarded the Nobel Prize in Literature, the Nobel Foundation said of his novels that they 'illuminate the human condition in the world of today'. Born in Cornwall in 1911, Golding was educated at Marlborough Grammar School and Brasenose College, Oxford. Before becoming a writer, he was an actor, a lecturer, a small-boat sailor, a musician and a schoolteacher. In 1940 he joined the Royal Navy and saw action against battleships, submarines and aircraft, and also took part in the pursuit of the *Bismarck*.

Lord of the Flies, his first novel, was rejected by several publishers and one literary agent. It was rescued from the 'slush pile' by a young editor at Faber and Faber and published in 1954. The book would go on to sell several million copies; it was translated into 35 languages and made into a film by Peter Brook in 1963. He wrote eleven other novels, *The Inheritors* and *The Spire* among them, a play and two essay collections. He won the Booker Prize for his novel *Rites of Passage* in 1980, and the Nobel Prize in Literature in 1983. He was knighted in 1988. He died at his home in the summer of 1993.

www.william-golding.co.uk

Books by
Sir William Golding
1911–1993
Nobel Prize in Literature

Fiction
LORD OF THE FLIES
THE INHERITORS
PINCHER MARTIN
FREE FALL
THE SPIRE
THE PYRAMID
THE SCORPION GOD
DARKNESS VISIBLE
THE PAPER MEN
RITES OF PASSAGE
CLOSE QUARTERS
FIRE DOWN BELOW
TO THE ENDS OF THE EARTH
(comprising *Rites of Passage, Close Quarters* and *Fire Down Below* in a
revised text; foreword by the author)
THE DOUBLE TONGUE

Essays
THE HOT GATES
A MOVING TARGET

Travel
AN EGYPTIAN JOURNAL

Plays
THE BRASS BUTTERFLY
LORD OF THE FLIES
adapted for the stage by Nigel Williams

WILLIAM GOLDING: A CRITICAL STUDY OF THE NOVELS
by Mark Kinkead-Weekes and Ian Gregor

TO THE ENDS OF THE EARTH

Fire Down Below

WILLIAM GOLDING

faber and faber

First published in 1989
by Faber and Faber Limited
Bloomsbury House
74–77 Great Russell Street
London WC1B 3DA

This paperback edition first published in 2013

Typeset by Faber and Faber Ltd

Printed and bound by CPI Group (UK) Ltd, Croydon, CR0 4YY

A CIP record for this book
is available from the British Library

ISBN 978–0–571–29855–6

FSC
www.fsc.org
MIX
Paper from
responsible sources
FSC® C101712

Introduction by Victoria Glendinning

If you have not already read the first two novels of
Golding's trilogy *To the Ends of the Earth*, the early
pages of *Fire Down Below* may seem a bit confusing. One
is plunged straight away into a scene of action on shipboard with characters who are not explained. But if you
persevere with the voyage, then, like the narrator, young
Edmund Talbot, you will be drawn into the relation-
ships between crew-members and passengers, and be as
overwhelmed as he is by the dangers and dramas of this
calamitous journey from England to Australia in 1813.

The first volume of the trilogy is *Rites of Passage*, which
won the Booker Prize in 1980. The second, *Close Quarters*,
was not published until 1987, after which he began *Fire
Down Below* straight away. It took three years, with three
or four drafts and rewritings, which was Golding's usual
way of working. He was at the height of his renown; he
had been awarded the Nobel Prize for Literature in 1983,
and received his knighthood during the proof-correcting
of *Fire Down Below*.

It was *Lord of the Flies* (1954) that had made his name,

and it remains his best-known novel. The themes and structure of that book – with characters isolated from the world in a way that allows or forces the revelation not only of their true natures, but visceral issues of domination, cruelty, shame, and extreme humiliation – are echoed in the sea trilogy. In *Fire Down Below* the ghastly fate of the Reverend Colley (from *Rites of Passage*) and the horrific suicide of his servant Wheeler (from *Close Quarters*) are fresh in the mind of Edmund Talbot. In the trilogy Golding also touches on homosexual desires and behaviours among men cooped up together on shipboard, with cross-currents of both excitement and disgust. Talbot in *Fire Down Below* is preoccupied by his feelings for a crew-member, Charles Summers, while professing his consuming passion for Miss Chumley, whom he encountered in the previous volume.

Talbot is an immature sprig of the English upper class, who sets off on the voyage with a haughty assumption of entitlement which antagonises everyone on board. But in this last volume he, like everyone else, undergoes a 'sea change'. He serves in emergency as a midshipman, and wears 'seaman's slops', startling young Mrs Brocklebank, with whom he has some rather ambiguous sexual contact. He himself is startled by the appearance of the ex-governess Miss Granham, also in seaman's slops, i.e. in trousers. 'Costume was proving to be a test of society.' Mr Prettiman, a visionary radical, dreaming of establishing a utopian community, seemed a ludicrous figure to Talbot at first, but by the end of *Fire Down Below* he finds him an inspiration. In the course of the novel Mr Prettiman marries Miss Granham, whom Talbot despised but whom he now learns to revere. There are times, writes Talbot in the journal he is keeping, when it seems 'I threw off my upbringing as a man might let armour drop around him and stand naked, defenceless, but free!'

Readers of Patrick O'Brian's sequence of Aubrey–Maturin novels, set at sea in the same period – towards the end of the Napoleonic wars – will find themselves making comparisons between O'Brian and Golding. One difference is their sense of humour. There is humour in O'Brian, but in Golding the humour has a lunatic quality, often in this novel based on physical indignities, on the instability of the decrepit ship in bad weather, and the ensuing slipping, sliding and staggering of the passengers and crew. There is a schoolboy slapstick about it, mingled – in a way that is quite disconcerting, and characteristic of Golding – with real passions and real danger to life. The ship is falling apart, its timbers strapped together; it is leaking; and the foremast is splitting at its base. How to secure the mast, by means of hot iron which contracts and holds the wood fast as it cools, is one strand of the plot-line, as is the problem of calculating longitude. But what you remember long after finishing the book are the two great dramatic high points: the great storm which all but reduces the vessel to splinters (just reading this makes you seasick), and the terror of the ice cliff against which it is nearly smashed to bits. Golding's powers of description are awesome, and include some lyric evocations of the beauty of moonlit nights on a quiet ocean.

Patrick O'Brian reviewed *Fire Down Below* when it came out (*London Review of Books*, 20 April 1989), and criticised it for its inauthenticity. The internal geography of the ship was confused, the language and technicalities wrong, the history inaccurate. Golding, he wrote, obviously did not care about any of this, and he concluded that the novel was 'a truly noble achievement'. Golding's biographer John Carey (in *William Golding: The Man who Wrote Lord of the Flies*, 2009) confirms that Golding did almost no historical research, and relied on his imagination, even though he was an experienced sailor. In the introduction he wrote for the revised single-volume edition of the trilogy (1991), on which this text of *Fire Down Below* is based, he concedes that a novelist generally finds research 'such a bore!' He corrected some mistakes he made about historical fact and nautical terms, but left in anachronistic language in conversations: 'But a novelist will claim – must claim – that any word must be in use for at least a generation before a lexicographer pinned it to his page.' That will not work for his use of 'intellectual snobbery', not recorded in the OED until the 1900s. Golding put the phrase in inverted commas in the novel, perhaps wilfully reinforcing the fact that his nameless ship is sailing in a world of the imagination.

Talbot feels the voyage has been something more than

just 'a simple adventure'. It was a voyage towards self-knowledge. 'We all change,' Mrs Prettiman says. 'It is danger, I suppose, which shows us all in our true colours.' But then Golding cancels out any thematic pretensions by having Mrs Prettiman tell Talbot later that the voyage 'is no type, emblem, metaphor of the human condition', but just a 'series of events'. Talbot himself suddenly throws everything, even the events, into doubt, as he thinks up different possible endings for his account – finally awarding himself a romantic happy ending, which we want to believe. Golding, though he trained as a scientist, is drawn to the irrational. He, like his novel, is ambivalent, unresolved, walking a tightrope between reason and spirituality and between tragedy and comedy. That is what makes *Fire Down Below* so compelling and disturbing, and much more than just 'a series of events'.

(1)

Captain Anderson turned away from me, cupped his hands round his mouth and roared.

"Masthead!"

The man who was straddled there next to the motion-less figure of young Willis held up a hand as a sign that he had heard. Anderson lowered his hands from his mouth and "sang out" in what for him was more nearly a normal tone of voice.

"Is the boy dead?"

This time the man must have shouted back but his voice was not like the captain's and what with the wind and sea, let alone the ship's unsteady motion, I could not hear it. Thirty or more feet below him in the fighting top Lieu-tenant Benét—in a voice loud as the captain's but a tenor to his bass—repeated what the man had said.

"Can't rightly tell but he feels main cold."

"Get him down then!"

Now there was a long pause and what looked like a wrestling match going on at the masthead while yet another seaman ascended, taking a tackle up with him.

Willis lurched, so that I gasped as he swung free. But he was made fast in a kind of seat. He was lowered down, turning and twisting on the end of the rope, now swinging out as we rolled and now coming in to thump the mast itself. Lieutenant Benét shouted.

"Bowse the man in there, you idle bugger!"

Willis was held and passed from one guiding hand to another. The duty watch or part of the watch who had stationed themselves in the rigging of the mainmast handled him as carefully as a woman with a baby. Lieutenant Benét slid all sixty feet down a rope from the fighting top and landed lightly on the deck.

"Handsomely does it!"

He knelt by the boy. Captain Anderson spoke from the forrard rail of the quarterdeck.

"Is he dead, Mr Benét?"

Benét swept off his hat with an elegant gesture, revealing what I had come to regard as far too much yellow hair as he did so.

"Not quite, sir. All right, lads. Get him down to the gunroom and roundly now!"

The little group disappeared down the ladders—or stairs, as I was more and more determined to call them—with Lieutenant Benét after them as confidently as if he were expert in medicine as in all else.

I turned to Mr Smiles, the sailing master, who had the watch.

"He looked dead to me."

There was a fierce hiss from the captain. Once again I had violated his precious "standing orders" by speaking to the officer of the watch. But this time as if he was conscious that he was to blame in prolonging the boy's punishment to the point of danger he turned with a grimace, which on the stage would have had a snarl in it, and went to his private quarters.

Mr Smiles had looked all round the horizon. Now he examined the set of our few sails.

"It is a time for dying."

I was at once irritated and appalled. I believe myself to be wholly devoid of superstition but the words were—uncomfortable when spoken in a crippled and quite possibly sinking ship. I had been cheered by an improvement in the weather. For though we were now standing inexorably southward towards the polar seas, the weather seemed no worse than it might have been in the English Channel. I was about to differ with the man but my friend the first lieutenant, Charles Summers, appeared from the passenger lobby and climbed to the quarterdeck.

"Edmund! I hear you rescued young Willis!"

"I, Charles? Never believe such a story! I am a passenger and would not for the world interfere with the running of the ship. I merely told Lieutenant Benét that I thought the young fellow looked deucedly comatose. Benét did the rest—as usual."

Charles looked round him. Then he drew me to the rail away from Smiles.

"You chose the one officer who could venture a difference of opinion with the captain and not be rebuked for it."

"That was diplomacy."

"You do not like Benét, do you? I too have differences with him. The foremast—"

"I admire Benét. But he is too perfect."

"His intentions are good."

"He is nimble in the rigging as a midshipman! But, Charles—do you realize that after all these months at sea I have never climbed a mast? Today, although the motion is unsteady it is slight compared with what it has been!"

"Is it? I am so habituated to the motion of a ship—"

"Oh, I am sure you could walk up the side of a house and not lose your balance. But the wind will get up, will it not? Now is perhaps my only chance of finding out what it is like to be a common sailor."

"I will take you as far as the fighting top."

"This will be a most valuable experience. Suppose me—as may befall—to be a Member of Parliament. 'Mr Speaker. To those of us who have actually climbed into the fighting top of a man of war at sea—'"

"The Honourable Member for Timbuctoo should pipe down, lay hold of the ropes and swing himself round. Gently! You're not a midshipman playing tag through the rigging!"

"Oh my God, this is no place for seaboots!"

4

"Feel the rung with your boot before you put your weight on it. Don't look down. If you were to slip I should catch you."

"'Safe in the arms of the Lord.'"

"Your casual blasphemy—"

"I beg your pardon, Bishop. The exclamation was forced from me. It was my seaboot swore, not I, as Euripides might have said but did not. It missed a rung."

"Now then. No nonsense about climbing out round. Up through the lubber's hole."

"If I must indeed choose the easier path—you insist?"

"Up with you!"

"Oh, God. It is commodious. Half a dozen good fellows might live up here provided they only used the vast hole I climbed through for purposes of necessity. 'For sale a villa. Luxuriously fitted, wooden construction, sea view—and a nautical gentleman with his eye sweeping the horizon!'"

"Fawcett. Now that Mr Willis has—vacated the masthead you may resume your lookout at that position."

The seaman knuckled his forehead, shifted his quid from one side of his mouth to the other and clambered out of sight.

"Well. How do you find it?"

"Now I dare to look down, I see that our ship, though she is a seventy-four, has shrunk. Really, Charles! Monstrous timbers such as this mast should not be stuck in such a rowboat! It is impossible that we should not be overset! I will not look—my eyes are shut."

5

"Inspect the horizon and you will feel more the thing."

"My hair is so erected it is pushing off my beaver."

"It is no more than sixty feet down to the deck."

"'No more!' But our yellow-haired friend slid all that way down on a rope."

"Benét is an active young man, full of spirit and ideas. But how would you go on if you was mastheaded?"

"Like poor Willis? Die, I think. Smiles said it is a time for dying."

I sat up cautiously and held on with both hands to the comforting ropes which stayed the fighting top. The sensation was agreeable.

"That is better, Charles."

"You were worried by what Smiles said?"

"Did he mean the Pikes' little girls?"

"They are somewhat better in fact."

"Davies, that poor, senile midshipman? Mrs East? She must be better, for I have seen her with Mrs Pike. Does he mean Miss Brocklebank, I wonder?"

"Mr Brocklebank says she is very poorly. A decline."

A thought occurred to me which set me laughing.

"Does he mean Mr Prettiman, our testy political theorist? Miss Granham told me that her fiancé had suffered a severe fall."

"You find him comic?"

"Well. He cannot be entirely despicable or an estimable lady such as Miss Granham would not have consented to make him the happiest of men. But comic! He is wicked!

6

Why—he is ill-disposed to the government of his own country, to the Crown, to our system of representation—in fact to everything which makes us the foremost country in the world."

"He is in a bad way none the less."

"No great loss if he leaves us. I am only sorry for Miss Granham, for though she has bitten my head off on several occasions, I repeat, she is an estimable lady and seems genuinely attached to the man. Women are very strange."

Someone else was climbing the rigging. It was Mr Tommy Taylor, who appeared with a monkeylike dexterity, swinging himself over the outer edge of the fighting top instead of coming the easier and safer way up through the hole in the middle.

"Mr Benét's compliments, sir, and Mr Willis seems comfortable. He is asleep and snoring."

"Very good, Mr Taylor. You are the watch?"

"Yes, sir. Mr Smiles, sir. His doggy, sir."

"You may return to the quarterdeck."

"Excuse me, sir. Watch changing now, sir."

Indeed the ship's bell was ringing out the time.

"Very well, you are off watch. Come and be a schoolmaster. Mr Talbot here is by way of thinking he would like to learn everything there is to know about a ship."

"No no, Charles! *Pax!*"

"For example, Mr Taylor, Mr Talbot would be interested to know what kind of a mast this is."

"It's a mainmast, sir."

7

"Are you trying to be witty, Mr Taylor? What is its construction?"

"It's a 'made' mast, sir. That means a mast which is all separate bits. Not 'bitts' of course. Bits."

Mr Taylor laughed so loudly I concluded he intended a witticism. Indeed, the boy was always in such high spirits I believe he found our desperate situation in a crippled and possibly sinking ship a joyous experience.

"Name those bits for Mr Talbot, Mr Taylor."

"Well, sir, the round bits on either side are the bolsters. Then there's the trestle trees which hold us up. Under them there's the round cheeks to keep the trestle from sliding down the mast. Mr Gibbs, the carpenter, he said—"

The boy broke into a loud laugh at the memory.

"He said, 'Every made mast has two lovely cheeks, young fellow, which is two less than what you've got, innit?'"

"After that sally, young man, you may take yourself off. You have a dirty mind."

"Aye aye, sir. Thank you, sir."

The boy departed with an offhand agility very suitable to his age and sex. The sight of him *diminishing* down the same rope which Mr Benét had used made me giddy. I looked up, fixing my eyes for security on the foremast which stood up between us and the bows.

"Charles! It is moving! There—see! No, it is still again. The top, I mean—there it goes, it is making a small circle, an uneven circle—"

"You knew that surely? We had thought it was sprung—a kind of greenstick fracture, but in fact the foot of the mast has broken the shoe and we have had to take measures. Come, Edmund! There is nothing to be done."

"It should not move like that!"

"Of course not. It is why we have spread no sail on the foremast or the mizzenmast since they are supposed to balance each other. Do you see the wedges where the foremast passes through the deck? No, you cannot—but they keep being forced out by the movement. We have made the mast as secure and motionless as we can."

"It makes me sick."

"Do not look then. I should have remembered how obvious the lurching is from up here. Oh no! Look! not at the mast but past it at the horizon! The wind, the south wind, the one we did not want!"

"What will it do?"

"Cold weather. We shall be able to haul round to the east, which of course is where we want to go, but we also want to get far south where the constant strong winds are. We must go down. Come. I will go first."

We climbed down to the deck and I stood in the lee of the starboard mainstays to watch as our old hulk lumbered round on the starboard tack when the south wind reached us. It had none of the softness which we associate with "south" in happier climes. Charles stayed on deck to watch Mr Cumbershum and Captain Anderson achieve the change of course. He was about to walk off forrard when I buttonholed him again.

"Can you spend another moment or two with me? I know how busy you are and do not want to interfere in your scanty time of leisure—"

"A first lieutenant is more at leisure in the middle of a voyage than at either end! But I must be seen about the ship and detect such awful crimes as a hammock left slung or a rope uncheesed—*that* is a properly cheesed rope, for your information. Well. Let us walk up and down in the waist as we used to."

"With all my heart."

Charles and I proceeded then to pace briskly back and forth in the waist. We stepped over the taut cables of his frapping, strode past the mainmast with its white line, its complication of wedges, ropes, blocks and bitts, on towards the break of the fo'castle before which the stripped foremast described its almost invisible circle in the sky. The first time we reached it I paused and looked. The complication was as great here as at the mainmast. The foremast was no less than three feet in diameter and where it passed through the deck it was surrounded by a collar made of great wedges. As I watched I saw them move, slightly and unevenly. A seaman stood by the mast and leaned on a huge maul. He saw the first lieutenant watching and shouldered the thing, waited for a few moments, then let it fall on a wedge which was standing a little *prouder* than its fellows.

Charles nodded. I felt his hand on my arm as he drew

10

me away and we resumed our walk.

"Is he doing any good?"

"Possibly not. But the appearance of doing good is better than nothing. At least it comforts the passengers."

"That is *à propos*. Charles, I am deeply sensible of the courtesy you officers have extended to me in allowing me the use of one of your hutches—cabins, I would say! But all good things have an end and I must return to the passenger quarters, in short, to my cabin off the passenger lobby."

"Did you not know? Miss Brocklebank has appropriated it! I have said nothing, since the poor lady is so sick. Surely you have not the heart to displace her?"

"She has squatters' rights. I mean my other cabin."

"Where Colley willed himself to death and where Wheeler committed suicide? You must not sleep there! Is our company in the wardroom—my company—become tedious to you?"

"You know it is not!"

"Well then, my dear fellow! A roughcut piece of nautical timber like I—such as me—might reasonably sleep there! But you—the place is dirtied."

"I do not relish the idea, it is true."

"Why then?"

"It is a case where I think I may say I have considered more deeply than you—indeed more deeply than you need, for it is wholly my affair."

"I beg your pardon!"

"Oh no—I mean I alone am responsible. I do not in the least mind telling you everything. The fact is, you see, I shall be stuck for some time in the administration of the colony. What sort of reputation should I bring with me if it were known that I had been scared out of a cabin by fear of a haunting? You see? It is a form of service which I propose to myself just as you have promised yours to the King."

"That is a proper attitude and does you credit."

"I think so too."

Charles laughed.

"All the same, you must not return there for a day or two. I am having the interior of the cabin cleaned and re-painted and so on."

"So on?"

"Come, Edmund—when a man has blown his head off in such a confined space—"

"Do not remind me!"

"You have a day or two to think it over. Well. This wind in the beam means the motion is easier, do you not feel? It also means the old tub takes in less water, which means less pumping."

"One thing I cannot understand. Why with this wind do we not simply go about and sail north to Africa and the Cape? We could replenish our food and drink and other stores—get our foremast fixed, land our sick—most of all, we could stretch our legs on lovely, dry land! How I long for it!"

"This wind will not hold. It is too light and unseasonable. To sail before it would be to do what is called 'chasing the wind'. A ship doing that may well go back and forth, round and round, and never get anywhere, like the *Flying Dutchman*. Take comfort in the three and a half knots we are making towards our goal. It is better than nothing—what is the matter?"

"Excuse me. It's this damned itching. As a matter of fact I have a rash between my legs."

"A rash. We all have them because of the salt."

"My clothes are gradually becoming impossible to wear. Phillips took my shirt away for a wash and though I was fierce with him in the end I had to put it on damp."

"Ah. That's rainwater."

"I thought rainwater was fresh."

"What do they teach young men nowadays? Of course it isn't. Well—rain may be fresh where you come from if you live far enough from the sea. Out here it is never less than brackish. Have you not been washing in it like the rest of us?"

"Of course I have, but the damned stuff will not lather. It gets covered in scum."

"What soap are you using?"

"My own, of course!"

"Has Webber not given you the ship's issue?"

"Good God, can that be soap? I thought it was a brick. I thought it was pumice or something for shaving in heavy weather like the ancients!"

"Trust you to know what the ancients used for shaving! But it is soap, my boy, saltwater soap!"

"I did not detect any scent."

The first lieutenant's laughter was almost as loud and prolonged as Mr Taylor's would have been. Then—

"I suppose you think soap is naturally scented."

"Well, is it not?"

But Charles was suddenly abstracted. He had his ear cocked. He wetted his thumb and held it up.

"What did I tell you? That wind has not even held for a dogwatch! Here we go again!"

(2)

I was still a guest of the wardroom when the next gale
arose in the middle of the night and it woke me with a
sense of the ship in ampler if not more violent motion.
I lay for some time calculating the direction of the wind
from the movement of the ship under me. She was over
to starboard mostly and never came over to the larboard
more than about to an even keel. Every now and then
she bucked like a horse. Now and then she jibbed like one
too—but not as she would have done with a wind over the
bow. I reasoned sleepily that the wind was on the larboard
quarter and we were moving in a southerly direction with
increased speed. In a ship there is nothing which pleases
so much as movement in the right direction! Our right
direction was east, but southeast in search of the westerlies which are said to circle the earth in the high southern
latitudes was a good second best. I lay awake therefore,
thinking of our crew, one part of the watch pumping, one
on deck with their eye on rigging and canvas, a lieutenant
and a midshipman standing as officers of the watch—our
moody captain emerging now and then from his quarters

15

to survey the whole—and our blunt bows dividing the billows faster than a man could walk! We were getting on. Life would have been more than tolerable had it not been for the itch—and my hand reached down hardly with my volition. At times the itch seemed worse than our dangers.

The ship pitched heavily, a ninth wave perhaps. I sat up in my bunk with a jerk, for the movement had been followed by a cry from above me—from one deck higher towards the open air, up in the passenger lobby or from one of the cabins ranged along either side. I waited for a repetition but it did not come, so I lay down once more. But the touch of cooler air outside my bedclothes now made the damp heat beneath them less tolerable. I was itching again.

I swung my legs out of the bunk and stood reeling in the near-complete darkness. A faint snore came from the cabin next to mine where Mr Cumbershum was sleeping after his turn at the middle watch. I felt round and got on my greatcoat—the one with three capes and now by no means the elegant garment in which I had begun this seemingly endless voyage. A nightshirt and a greatcoat! I pulled on woollen socks, then thrust my feet into seaboots. I got out into the wardroom. The dim horizon slanted across the great stern window at an angle. The dawn itself was not visible and a more diffused light allowed me to do no more than detect the line between sea and sky. We pitched again—a little more violently this time, as if our ship had come across a wave left from a wind in some

16

other direction. It was followed again by the cry from above me—a cry of anguish, there was no doubt about that. Scarce knowing what I did—hardly awake—perhaps connecting the anguish with my own itch—yet one woke unwillingly and half one's mind was always tending bed-ward—I clambered up the stairs into the passenger lobby. But I had scarcely grabbed the rail outside our cabins when we pitched and the cry came again, and came from the cabin of our comic philosopher, Mr Prettiman!

Now the next door, Miss Granham's, his fiancée's, opened and the lady appeared. She held the rail, opened his door and disappeared inside. I hastened across the lobby—a feat helped by the ship which tipped to starboard again and set me for a moment or two positively tripping downhill! What had begun with a spontaneous attempt to offer help became a run at the end of which I thumped loudly into Mr Prettiman's cabin door and only just con-trived to heave myself off before Miss Granham herself opened the door from inside. She stood there, looking at me. She wore a white nightdress. Her hair was decently concealed by a night-bonnet, or whatever it is called, and a large shawl hung over both shoulders. Her face was not welcoming.

"Mr Talbot?"

"I heard him cry out. Can I—that is—"

"Can you be of assistance? Thank you, no."

"A moment, ma'am. Paregoric—"

"The purser's laudanum? I have it."

She paused. I became conscious suddenly of my half-naked legs and of my nightshirt, which was showing between the open skirts of my greatcoat. Miss Granham smiled glacially and shut the door in my face. Another lurch sent me reeling along the rail and wincing as the cry burst again from the poor devil. Comic he might be—but the comic are able to suffer as much as the rest of us! I moved along the rail to the entry to the lobby and stood looking out at the waist in an effort to put some distance between me and his cries, but it was not far enough. I moved out into the cold dawn air and light and huddled under the larboard mainstays. Above me they were casting the log, for I heard a voice give the order.

"Turn!"

Then after a long pause:

"Five and a half knots, sir."

"Make it so."

There came the squeak of chalk on the traverse board. Five and a half knots! More than a hundred and thirty land miles to the southeast in twenty-four hours—and all from the sails on the one mast. Soon, surely, we should find those westerlies and be blown all the way to Sydney Cove!

Men were mustering forrard. There was a period of casual ritual as the watch changed. Mr Smiles and young Tommy Taylor handed over the watch on the quarterdeck to Mr Askew, the gunner. It was eight o'clock in the morning and the dawn bright all along the east. Then I saw my

18

friend Lieutenant Summers, and Lieutenant Benét come to the top of the stairs from the quarterdeck and it was plain that there had been a disagreement between them. Charles, mildest of men, looked stormy. Mr Benét on the other hand seemed even more brisk and cheerful than usual. Behind them appeared Mr Gibbs, the carpenter, and Coombs, the blacksmith. This was something new! Benét stood back with what looked like courtesy to allow the first lieutenant precedence down the stair, but in his grin and in the moody face of my friend was neither friendship nor consideration. There was no doubt about it. Clever young Mr Benét was triumphing. He carried a small and rather complicated object in his hands. It appeared to be made of wood and metal. Charles strode into the lobby and down the stairs without looking at me. Mr Benét and the blacksmith stood in talk with Mr Gibbs, who knuckled his forehead, then followed the first lieutenant. Mr Benét thrust the model into the blacksmith's hand and waved him forward.

It was too much. I had to be informed: and besides—

"Good morning, Mr Benét. There is something afoot."

"There is indeed, Mr Talbot."

"May I be told? Shall you celebrate it in verse?"

"I am not sure that you should be told, Mr Talbot. After all, you are of the first lieutenant's party, are you not?"

"Party? Do you mean 'faction'? What is all this?"

"We are absurd, you know—but the thing has happened. Ever since my success in getting weed off her

19

bottom with the dragrope and against the advice of the first lieutenant—"

"You pulled a baulk of timber off her keel!"

"And added more than a knot to her speed."

"Just one knot, the first lieutenant said."

"Whatever it is, we are now fated, he and I, to be on either side of the fence, backed by those who think I am saving our lives on one hand and those who think I took too big a risk on the other."

I was loath to quarrel with the man. He was, after all, in some sort the only connection I still had with a certain young lady.

"But 'faction', Mr Benét! As if the ship were a country in little!"

"Well, is it not?"

"He is your superior officer. What is more, these cables stretched across the deck—his frapping, as he calls it—are what stands between us and the ship's falling apart!"

"An idea old as St Paul, Mr Talbot. You credit the first lieutenant with too much invention."

"That object you gave to Coombs. Has it anything to do with the argument?"

"Everything. It is a model of the keelson, the shoe of the foremast and the lower part of the foremast itself. Seeing is believing. I have thought out a scheme not just for securing the mast—for you know it moves no matter what we do—but also for bringing it back to its former state. If I succeed we shall be able to spread sail on it again and therefore balance it with sails on the mizzen. Another two knots, Mr Talbot, in a moderate wind!"

"You showed the model to Captain Anderson!"

"Seeing is believing. He is convinced."

"But Charles not! I have faith in him, Mr Benét!"

"Oh yes. But he is a—well. He is a friend of yours and I say no more."

As if to indicate his resolve to be uncharacteristically silent Mr Benét clapped one hand over his mouth, sketched a naval salute with the other and then ran off, skipping over the cables of the frapping, and disappeared into the fo'castle. I hurried away down the ladders to the wardroom. Charles stood there, staring out of our stern window with his usual indifference to our movement. He turned when he heard me open the door.

"What is all this about, Charles?"

He did not pretend to misunderstand me.

"This time Benét wishes to give us back a couple of masts, that is all."

"And the captain agrees?"

"Oh yes. Mr Benét is a most persuasive young man. He will go far if he lives."

"If someone does not kill him first! But what is this risk?"

"Briefly, the foremast has split the shoe—the block of wood on which it stands. So the foot of the mast is able to move. We have stayed the mast below decks, rigged tackles, used chocks, wedges and props and reduced the movement a little. Benét wants to reduce it altogether."

"Where is the danger?"

"Any mistake and the foot of the mast may slip and go through the ship's bottom. That is all."

"He must be stopped!"

"More than that, his method involves the use of fire, red-hot metal—you understand my objections? It is the dragrope all over again. The thing may succeed but the risk is too great."

"Who else is of your faction?"

"Is it come to that?"

"I am of your faction, too!"

"You must not say so. Do you not understand? You have no business to use that word!"

"Benét did."

"He should not have done so. Most of all he should not have used it to you. You are a passenger with no right to an opinion in the matter."

I had no answer. He sank into the chair opposite me. He smiled bitterly.

"You would make it a matter of public discussion."

"A rebuke from you—"

"I did not mean a rebuke, only a warning. The captain has heard our arguments over a professional matter and given his decision. We must abide by it."

"I smell trouble."

"Stay out of it."

"We are friends, are we not? I must help you!"

He shook his head.

"I believe I may go so far as to make a formal protest at the appropriate time. Coombs is setting about the iron-work now. It is two vast plates—for which we have barely enough metal—four iron rods with screw ends and nuts to screw on them—"

"Do not tell me more, for I see it all! He will do what my father made them do to the old cottages down by the river: iron bars made red-hot which pulled some bulging walls together! I remember it well, for I saw it when I was a small boy—how the crosses on the ends of the rods pulled in the walls as the hot metal cooled. It was exciting as a Fair Day!"

"Was the building made of wood?"

"Brick."

"It will not have escaped your notice that we are made of wood. His bars will extend, red-hot, through four solid foot of timber—I almost heard your jaw drop! Of course, he will have holes bored wider than the rods and swears the heat will produce nothing inside the shoe but a thin layer of charcoal. His model worked, I allow him that. It produced plenty of smoke too."

"But only a while ago Captain Anderson was praising Benét for having no ironwork, no chain cable, no steam about him! A proper rope, blocks and canvas man!"

The first lieutenant struck the table with the flat of his hand.

"Listen to me, Edmund! We are still in mortal danger

even if the mast should not go through the bottom! Have you watched a fireback as the fire dies down? How the sparks move through the layer of soot on the metal as if they were alive? Have you never seen a fire, apparently dead, brought to life again and flare up? It will be shut in there—in the shoe. We are to sail on gaily with that added to all the rest! Added to the cranky hull, the jury rig, the distance, the terrible weather towards which we are making our clumsy way and which we need because it is the only force which will get us to land and shelter before the fresh water and even the food run out—"

He paused for breath, and in that silence the sound of the water running and thumping on the outside of our hull was only too clearly audible.

"Forgive me, Edmund. That young man tries me beyond bearing. He thinks he can find our longitude by lunar distance—he thinks—oh, he thinks this and that! I should not have said so much. I have fallen into the error against which—"

"You can say what you like to me and I shall be honoured to guard your secrets with my life."

It made him smile.

"No, no. Just keep quiet, old fellow. Forget the whole business. That's all I ask."

"I will keep quiet. But I cannot forget it."

He rose to his feet and went to the stern window.

"Edmund!"

"What is the matter?"

"Do you trust me?"

"You sound excited—some more danger? Of course I do!"

He came back quickly to the table.

"Go and get into your daytime rig—no oilskins—then into the waist—stand there in the open—don't stir no matter what happens—hurry!"

I rushed into my borrowed cabin, tore off my greatcoat and nightshirt—huddled on my daytime clothing and was out again more quickly than I have ever changed in my life. I reached the waist thoroughly out of breath and had to hang on the mainstays to get it back. I saw Mr Brockle-bank gathering his decayed coach cloak about him and lumbering back into the lobby. There seemed to be nothing about the waist to cause Charles's excitement. I leaned on the rail and stared astern.

"Well!"

What was astern of us and up wind was the blackest cloud I have ever seen in my life. Here and there it was touched with sour grey, giving it just the appearance of dirty water when you have done your worst with it and the steward has come to remove it from your disgusted sight. Moreover, this cloud was coming rapidly nearer and bringing its own wind with it—as I now saw it did! For our sails thundered, then filled again as our bows moved along the horizon from starboard to larboard. The cloud seemed to reach right down to the water and in a second, it seemed, it had enveloped us. The water was deadly cold, hissing, constant as the flow of a river which fell on me and took away my breath all over again. It soaked and resoaked my clothing, so that I loosed my hold on the mainstays and stumbled towards the lobby—only to remember Charles's prohibition and stumble back again, for I partly understood it though I cursed him for the first and last time in my life. The torrent continued to fall over me and my soaked clothes clung to me and the water rushed out of my unmentionables as if they had been drainpipes. Suddenly the cold increased as a fresh wind pushed my clothes even closer against me. Then as by magic the water ceased to thunder on the deck. I lifted my head. The wind was fierce in my face and the sea and sky were both alike dark. Webber, the wardroom steward, stood in the entry to the passenger lobby. He was grinning like a gargoyle.

"Mr Summers's compliments, sir. You may come in now you've had your bath!"

(3)

"Bath!"

I stumbled into the lobby, slopping water out of my clothes, then slid through what I was spilling. I fumbled, cursing, at the door of my old cabin, remembered sick and silent Zenobia, reeled across the lobby to Colley's cabin, then remembered that I was still using my borrowed cabin in the wardroom. I picked my way more cautiously down the ladder. Webber had the door open.

"I'll take your gear, sir."

Phillips was there too.

"Compliments of the first lieutenant, sir!"

It was a huge towel, rough as a rug and dry as a bone. Naked, I wrapped myself in it as I stepped out of the squelching pile of my clothes. I began to laugh, then whistle, towelling myself round, under, up and down, from hair to feet.

"What's this?"

"First lieutenant, sir."

"Good God!"

Item: a vest, apparently made of string. Item: a rough

shirt such as a petty officer might wear. Item: a woollen overgarment of jersey worsted about an inch thick. Item: seaboot stockings almost as thick. Item: a pair of seaman's trowsers—not, I have to say, unmentionables—trowsers! Finally: a leathern belt.

"Does he expect me—"

Suddenly I was overcome with a great good humour and excitement! It looked very much like goodbye to my itching. It was like all those childish occasions of "dressing up", of wearing a paper cocked hat and carrying a wooden sword.

"Very well, Webber—Phillips—take this wet stuff away and dry it. I will dress this time for myself."

There was no doubt about it. A man had to get himself accustomed to the touch of this sort of material on the skin, but at least it was dry and, by contrast, warm. I had a suspicion that unless I regulated the number of layers I now wore, the warmth would turn into an uncomfortable heat. But by the time I was clothed in a complete costume I was wholly reconciled to the change. Of course, no man could be elegant in deportment when clad so! Such clothing would force on the wearer a decided casualness of behaviour. Indeed, I date my own escape from a certain unnatural stiffness and even loftiness of manner to that very day. I realized, too, why though Oldmeadow's soldiers always gathered in the straightest of lines and appeared to be held up by their own ramrods inserted in the spine, an assembly of our good seamen, though

28

mustered regularly and standing in approximate rows, could never imitate the drilled and ceremonious appearance of the soldiers with their imposing uniforms! This was naval rig—in fact, "slops"! The curves and wrinkles defied a geometrical organization.

I went out into the wardroom. The first lieutenant was sitting at the long table with papers spread out before him.

"Charles!"

He looked up and grinned as he saw me.

"How do you find your rig?"

"Warm and dry—but good God, how do I look?"

"You'll do."

"A common seaman—What would a lady say? What *will* the ladies say? How did you do it? In this soaked ship! Why, there cannot be a dry corner anywhere or a dry inch of cloth!"

"Oh, there are ways—a drawer or box with bags of a suitable substance. But do not speak of that. The same cannot be done for the whole crew and the substance is not for casual handling."

"I have not been so moved by a man's kindness—it is exactly like the story of Glaucus and Diomede in Homer. You know they exchanged armour—gold armour on the one side for bronze armour on the other—my dear fellow—I have promised you the bronze armour of my godfather's patronage—and you have given me gold!"

"The story has not come my way. I am glad you are pleased, though."

29

"Bless you!"

He smiled a little uncertainly, I thought.

"It is nothing—or not much anyway."

"Will you not accompany me to the lobby and give me countenance for my first public appearance?"

"Oh, come! Do you see these papers? Water, biscuit, beef, pork, beans—we may have to—And after that I ought to take a look at Coombs and his ironwork—then there are my rounds—"

"Say no more. I am on my own. Well. Here goes!"

I left the wardroom, went as bold as brass up the stairs and into the passenger saloon. Our one Army officer, Old-meadow, was there. He stared for a moment or two before he recognized me.

"Good God, Talbot! What have you done to yourself, man? Joined the Navy? What will the ladies say?"

"'They say—what say they—let them say'!"

"They will say that 'tars' should stick to the front end and not take up the room set apart for their betters. You'd best stay in this part of the ship or a petty officer will lay his rope's end across your back for idling."

"Oh no, he will not, sir! Gentlemen do not need a uniform to be recognized as such. I am comfortable, decent and what is more I am dry, sir. Can you say the same?"

"No, I cannot. But then I ain't as thick as thieves with the ship's officers."

"I beg your pardon?"

"Spend too much of my time looking after my men to

30

badger the Navy into dressing me up from the slop shop. Well, I must be off."

He made his way out of the saloon handily enough against the cant and reel. It did seem to me that he went in order to avoid an argument. He was, and perhaps is, a mild creature. There had been a note of asperity in what he said. But then, during the increasing decrepitude of our ship and more evident danger to our lives, there had been a corresponding change in the character of the passengers and change in the relationship between us. We, so to speak, *rubbed* on each other. Mr Brocklebank, who had once been an object of no more than amusement, had become an irritant as well. The Pikes—father, mother, little daughters—were, it seemed, divided among themselves. I and Oldmeadow—

"Edmund. Take hold of yourself."

I looked out of the great stern window. It was a different sea, starker now, right to the horizon but strewn with white horses which attempted to follow us but were outrun by their own waves and slid back out of sight. Gusts were whipping through the steadier wind, for sudden lines of spray crossed the direction of the waves which were being marshalled to follow and overtake us.

I gave an involuntary shiver. In the excitement of my shift into seaman's costume I had not noticed that the air, even in the saloon, was colder than it had been.

The door of the saloon opened. I looked round. Little Mrs Brocklebank stared, then bounced forward and stood with her arms akimbo.

"Where do you think you are?"

I rose to my feet. She gave a squeak.

"Mr Talbot! I did not know—I did not mean—"

"Who did you think it was, ma'am?"

For a moment or two she stood there, staring at me with her mouth open. Then she turned quickly and ran away. After a while I began to laugh. She was a pretty little thing and a man could do much worse—if it were not for, of course—Costume was proving to be a test of society.

I sat down again and returned to watching the sea. Rain lashed across the window and already the waves had taken up their new direction. The white horses were more numerous and galloped for a longer period on the waves which had engendered them. It seemed to me that our speed had increased. There came a tap! on the outside of the window. It was the log being lowered. The line stretched further and further astern of us. The saloon door opened and Bowles, the solicitor's clerk, came in. He shook the last traces of water from his greatcoat. He saw me but evinced no great surprise to see how I was dressed.

"Good morning, Mr Bowles."

"Good morning, sir. Have you heard the news?"

"What news?"

"The foremast. Mr Benét and the blacksmith are delayed in their preparation of the ironwork. So the perilous work of restoring the mast to its former efficiency must be put off."

"Believe me, I am thankful to hear that! But why?"

"Charcoal for heating the iron. The ship does not have a large enough supply. The first lieutenant happened to check that part of the stores and found more has been used than was thought."

"That might well be a good thing and give the captain time to think again. What will they do?"

"They are able to make more charcoal. I am told the shoe of the foremast is split and they wish to use the enormous power of metal shrinking as it cools to pull the wood together again."

"So Mr Summers told me."

"Ah yes. Well, you would know, would you not? Some people think that Mr Summers was not sorry to report how little charcoal was available. Mr Benét was not pleased and asked to be allowed to recheck the amount in case the first lieutenant had made a mistake. He was refused abruptly."

"Does Benét not realize how dangerous the attempt is? He is such a fool!"

"That is the trouble, Mr Talbot. He is not a fool—not precisely."

"He had best stick to his poetry which can harm no one except perhaps a sensitive critic. Good God, a cranky ship, a sullen captain—"

"Not so sullen, sir. Mr Benét, I think—speaking without prejudice—has brightened his life."

"Mr Bowles! Favouritism!"

"Without prejudice, sir. Cumbershum is not in favour of the red-hot iron."

"Nor is Mr Summers."

"Nor is our wrinkled old carpenter, Mr Gibbs. Naturally he is a man for wood and thinks red-hot iron should be kept as far away from it as possible. Mr Askew, the gunner, approves. He says, 'What's a bit of hot metal between friends?'"

"They speak each according to his humour as in an old comedy."

I was suddenly restless and stood up.

"Well, Mr Bowles, I must leave you."

I went away through the cold air of the saloon into the windy lobby outside it, then down the stairs again to the wardroom where the air was minimally warmer. Charles had left and Webber brought me a brandy. I stood, my legs apart, and stared out of the window. So soon one accepts as normal a state once desperately desired! I had forgotten what it was to itch!

There came a tap! on the glass. The log was being lifted out of the water.

"The man's a fool!"

It was Mr Benét speaking. He had entered the wardroom silently.

"The quartermaster?"

"He should pay the line out over the quarter. He will break every pane if he goes on like this."

"How is your charcoal?"

"So you have heard too! This ship reverberates like the belly of a cello! Coombs is seeing to it. I must wait. It is in his hands."

"Not yours?"

"I am in overall control. I am only thankful that Coombs knew exactly how much sheet iron he had before certain other people could measure the area."

"At all events you must be glad for a time of leisure with your many activities."

"Work enables me to forget my sorrow, Mr Talbot. I do not envy you, given twenty-four idle hours a day in which to feel the pangs of separation."

"It is good of you to remember my situation. But, Mr Benét, since we are companions in sorrow—you remember those too brief hours when *Alcyone* was compelled by the flat calm to lie alongside us—"

"Every moment, every instant is chiselled in my heart."

"In mine too. But you must remember that after the ball I was lying delirious in my cabin."

"I did not know."

"Not know? They did not tell you? I mean during that time when the wind returned and *Alcyone* was forced to leave us—"

"'Utmost dispatch.' I did not know about you, sir. I had my own sorrows. Separation from Belovéd Object—"

"And Miss Chumley too! She must have known I was—lying on a Bed of Pain!"

"The fact is, what with my sudden—departure—from

one ship and entry into another—my exchange with one of your lieutenants—"

"Jack Deverel."

"And what with my separation from One who is more to me than all the world—despite the warmth of your genial captain's welcome—"

"Genial! Are we thinking of the same man?"

"—I had no solace but my Art."

"You could not have known that there would be scope for your engineering proclivity!"

"My Muse. My poetry. The parting struck verses from me as quickly as the iron strikes a spark from the flint or vice versa."

Mr Benét put his left hand on the long table and leaned on it. He laid the other hand on that portion of the chest where I am assured the heart lies concealed. He then stretched that hand out towards the increasingly tormented sea.

> *The salutation which she cast*
> *From ship to ship had been our last!*
> *Her eye had dropped a winking tear*
> *Which I could see for she stood near—*
> *And standing did not smile nor frown*
> *As seamen drew the main course down,*
> *But 'twas a dagger at my heart*
> *To feel the two ships move apart!*

36

The tap of blocks, a loosened brail,
A breath of air, a filling sail,
A yard no more, of shadow'd sea—
But oh, what leagues it was to me!

"I am sure all the verses will seem very pretty, Mr Benét, when properly written down and corrected."

"Corrected? You find some fault?"

"I could detect little *enjambement* but that is by the way. She was with Miss Chumley. Did Miss Chumley not speak?"

"Lady Somerset and Miss Chumley were speaking together. They ran to Truscott, the surgeon, as soon as he came aboard from your ship."

"You could not hear what they said?"

"Directly *Alcyone* had cast off, Sir Henry left the deck and went below. Then Lady Somerset came to the taffrail and gestured thus."

Lieutenant Benét straightened up. He raised his cupped hand to his mouth and deposited something in it. Then with a female twist of the body he brought his right hand back over his shoulder and, opening the palm, appeared to throw something through our stern window.

"It seems an elaborate way of getting rid of her spittle, Mr Benét. Commonly people do what young Mr Tommy Taylor describes as 'dropping it in the drink'."

"You are facetious, sir. It was the Salutation!"

"But Miss Chumley—you could not hear what she said?"

"I had been below, stowing my gear. When I heard the pipes I knew the moment had come—thrust Webber out of the way—rushed up the ladder—it was too late. The springs and breast ropes were in. You, sir, I doubt you have the sensibility to understand the completeness of separation between two ships when the ropes are in—they might be two separate continents—familiar faces are those of strangers at once. Their future is different and unknown. It is like death!"

"I believe I have as much sensibility as the next man, sir!"

"That is what I said."

"But Miss Chumley did not speak?"

"She came to the rail, and stood there as *Alcyone* moved away. She looked woebegone. I daresay she was feeling seasick all over again, for you know, Mr Talbot, she was said to be a martyr to it."

"Oh, the poor child! I appeal to you, Mr Benét. I will not elaborate on the nights of tears, the yearnings, the fear that some other man, the need to communicate with her and the present impossibility of doing so! She is bound for India, I for New South Wales. I met her for no more than a few hours of that miraculous day when our two ships were becalmed side by side—I dined with her—later I danced with her at that ball aboard this ship—was ever such a ball held in mid-Atlantic? And then I collapsed

—concussion—fell sick—was delirious—but we had parted—if only you could understand how precious to me would be some kind of description of her time in *Alcyone* when you were—wooing Lady Somerset—"

"Worshipping Lady Somerset."

"And she, Miss Chumley, I mean your acquaintance, even your ally in that reprehensible—what am I saying—that tender attachment—"

"The love of my life, sir."

"For you know, that one day thrust me into a new life! The instant I saw her I was struck by, destroyed by lightning, or if you are familiar with the phrase, it was the *coup de foudre*—"

"Say that again."

"*Coup de foudre.*"

"Yes, the phrase is familiar."

"And before we parted she did declare that she held me in higher regard than anyone else in the two ships. Later still I received a *billet doux*—"

"A *billet doux*, for God's sake!"

"Was that not encouragement?"

"How can I tell unless I know what was in it?"

"The words are chiselled in my heart. *A young person will always remember the time when two ships were side by side in the middle of the sea and hopes that one day they may put down their anchors in the same harbour.*"

Mr Benét shook his head.

"I find no encouragement for you there, sir."

"None? Oh, come! What—none?"

"Very little. In fact it sounds to me uncommonly like a *congé*, if you are familiar with the word. You would probably call it a 'congy' or something."

"A farewell!"

"With perhaps an undertone of relief—"

"I will not believe it!"

"A determination that the affair should end as painlessly as possible."

"No!"

"Be a man, Mr Talbot. Do I whine or repine? Yet I have no hope whatever of seeing the Belovéd Object again. All that consoles me is my genius."

With those words Mr Benét turned away and vanished into his own cabin. A tide of furious indignation overwhelmed me.

"I do not believe a word he said!"

For she was there, vividly—not the Idea of a young person, the lineaments of whose face I could never bring together no matter how I tried as I writhed in my bunk—but there, breathing lavender, her eyes shining in the darkness and her soft but passionate whisper—"*Oh no indeed*!"

Benét had not seen her so, heard her so.

"She felt as I do!"

(4)

So I stared out at the waters of separation until my anger subsided—but my grief remained! I heard a door open and close behind me, the brisk steps of Benét and another door open and close as he left the wardroom. I did not look round. Clearly the man was inclined to taunt me, and besides he was of the other faction. Even if Charles forbade the word he should not prevent me using it on his behalf to myself. He needed my support. With that thought I called for Webber and had him help me into my oilskins and seaboots. I then made a laborious way up to the waist and looked for Charles, who was nowhere to be seen. But what was immediately evident was that we had passed some invisible boundary in the open sea. There was a clear green tone in the water rather than blue or grey. The air had indeed become colder and a few drops of spray which struck my cheek felt as though they had frozen there. The wind was from the southwest now and we were reaching towards the south-east. It was no longer a gale but a strong wind marshalling the waves on our beam. Under the low clouds strands of mist were beginning to stream past us from the invisible

41

western horizon. Our ship once again had begun that swift roll which was the result of our shortened masts and inadequate sail area. But at least she did not seem to pitch and the cables which Charles had passed round her belly remained taut and motionless. The crew were busy. I do not mean that part of the watch which stood by for sail changing and which supplied the lookouts and quartermasters for the wheel. I mean the other part, which was busily rigging life-lines from the break of the fo'castle to the bitts of the main-mast and then from there to the aftercastle and the stairs ascending to the quarterdeck. This was suggestive. As I watched, I saw Charles Summers come out of the fo'castle and stand talking with Mr Gibbs, who presently knuckled his forehead and went into the fo'castle again. Charles came aft to the foremast, examined the wedges and then talked with the petty officer who was directing the men at the life-lines. He then examined the lines, putting his weight on them here and there. There was an argument for a while about one point of attachment but finally Charles seemed satisfied. He climbed up and spoke to someone by the belfry on the fo'castle, saw me and raised his arm in greeting. I answered in a like manner but did not go forrard. Charles busied himself with some other people on the fo'castle. Then he turned away and came briskly along the waist to me.

"You are still dry?"

"As you see—and wearing oilskins as much for warmth as dryness. The air is much colder."

"The 'roaring forties'. We have found them at last but

distinctly farther south than they ought to be!"

"The change was sudden."

"It always is, we are told. Waters have their own islands, continents, roadways. This is a continent."

"The lifelines are ominous."

"A precaution."

"You seem cheerful."

"I ought not to be but am. For—may I whisper?—forrard there, below decks, Coombs is making charcoal, which will take him days. Add to that the weather which as it gets rougher will render far too dangerous any tinkering with the foremast—"

"Our faction is in the ascendant!"

"Do not use that word!"

"I am sorry. I forgot."

"What sort of reputation would you carry to the governor if Captain Anderson told him that you had made trouble in the ship?"

"He will not do that so long as he remembers my journal which will lie before my godfather!"

"I had forgotten. How long ago all that affair seems! But to please me, avoid words which might suggest a division among us. All I meant was that I am happy because an unnecessary hazard has been postponed."

"I own I was looking forward to an increase in our speed. But that was before I understood the possible cost."

"May I advise you? Only wear oilskins for their proper purpose—keeping yourself dry. Inside them you heat up and sweat. Then before you know where you are all the good work of your rare bath will be undone."

He nodded meaningly, then strode back along the deck and into the fo'castle. I muttered to myself.

"A nod is as good as a wink. I used to stink."

I became aware that old Mr Brocklebank was standing within two yards of me. He was in the shelter (for what it was worth) of the starboard mainstays and had his right arm hooked through a bight of rope. Somewhere he had found or been given a large coach cloak which was ancient, worn and dirty. He had arranged this round his body so that it presented a kind of sculptural effect. His beaver was tied on by some material passed over the crown and fastened under his chin. I believe it was a lady's stocking! His plump face was melancholy as he gazed at nothing or perhaps into himself. I decided that I did not want any conversation with him, for he, at least, was unlikely to be able to add anything to what I knew of Miss Chumley. I went past him, therefore, with no more than a nod and into the passenger lobby. The door of the cabin to which I had planned so nobly to return was open. As I approached, Phillips came out with a brush and bucket and went to the larboard side of the waist.

I had not entered that cabin since Wheeler had chosen the place for his last, tragic and criminal act. With a sudden determination to get on with the business I opened the door and stepped inside. All seemed as before, except that the place was cleaner and brighter. For the bulkheads, the ship's side and the deckhead—or better, the walls and the ceiling—were now covered, not with the dull mustard-coloured paint which seemed to be the best the Navy could do for passenger accommodation, but with glossy white enamel. That was cheerful enough. I touched it here and there and found it dry. There was now no excuse for not returning. I sat down in the canvas chair and willed the place to be ordinary and not connected to its history. I could not succeed. No matter how hard I tried, my eye would return to that eyebolt in the ship's side so near the head of the bed. There the rigid hand of the dead man had hung, his body dinted as if leaden into the furnishings of his bed! My mind flinched away from Colley, only to imagine at once Wheeler standing by me, his head raised, the golden goblet of the blunderbuss only an inch or two from his face—there was no flinching from that! It was as if the man's misdirected courage in facing the shot of self-destruction held me too, chin up, staring up, his last sight of anything my last sight, nothing but the massive and worn timbers of the deckhead.

I went cold for all my seaman's clothing and oilskins—cold with more than the weather. White paint however carefully applied can conceal a corner but not the shape of a deformation. The beam most central to the deckhead was deeply pocked above the place where Wheeler's head had been. Some brains and a skull are little obstacle to a charge propelled by gunpowder at a range of an inch or two. In one of those pocks into which the brush had worked white paint it none the less could not conceal the point of a small, knife-like object which projected from the bottom of the hole. The seaman who had busily worked his brush into the hole had therefore painted the surface of this hideous *memento mori*. There were other traces I now saw and soon my eyes supplied a detailed knowledge which I could well have done without. I became *seized* of the explosion and the trajectories, knew intimately how the head had burst. This was no place to sleep. Yet sleep there I must, or be laughed at throughout the ship and later throughout New South Wales!

The deck moved under me, a sinewy motion lifting one seaboot and sliding away from the other. There came a moaning cry from Prettiman's cabin. Anguished as the sound was, I was almost glad to be reminded of the world outside this hutch. Fool Prettiman! Philosopher so called! Well, thought I, turning my attention away from dead men, he is paying for his folly. To which faction would he and his fiancée, Miss Granham, belong? My thoughts became mixed between the two cabins. If so strong-minded a lady consented to make Prettiman the happiest of men—But then again, he was a man of substance and such are always in danger of being married for their money. At all events, if *she* had to sleep here she would do so and stand no nonsense! The thought braced me in those morbid surroundings so that I got to my feet and out into the lobby. Through the opening to the waist I could see that at least part of the deck had a sheet of seawater sluicing from one side to the other. We were beginning to get that weather we had looked for! This time I found myself walking splay-legged and glad of a hand on the safety rail of the lobby, let alone the rail of the stairs down to the wardroom.

"Webber, help me out of these oilskins if you please. After that you can get my gear back to the cabin among the other passengers."

"Sir, the first lieutenant said—"

"Never mind what the first lieutenant said. The paint is dry and I shall sleep there tonight."

There was a fierce slash of water across the panes of the stern window.

"Getting up, sir, an't it? Be rougher before it's done."

"Yes. Now do as I told you, Webber."

"It's the cabin where he done himself in, an't it? And afore him the parson?"

"Yes. Now get on."

Webber paused for a moment, then nodded more to himself I think than me.

"Ah."

He disappeared into the cabin which had been loaned to me. There was no doubt about it. All things were combining to make me uneasy. But relieved of my oilskins I decided to try the passenger saloon though the hour was early for eating. Who should I find there but little Pike slumped over the table? As the ship rolled, a shot glass clattered along the deck.

47

"Pike! Richard! What is this?"

He did not reply and his body rolled with the ship. I found his intoxication disgusting; for no one is as high-minded in the article of strong drink as a reformed drinker! But that is by the way.

"Richard! Bestir yourself!"

No sooner had I said that than I regretted it. The truth is that the job of intoxication once done, the poor devil was best left to the sad oblivion he had chosen. Who was I to decide whether he should sleep or wake? A clerk, somehow able to pay the passage for himself, his wife and two small daughters to the Antipodes—two daughters quite possibly dying and a wife who was turning, by all accounts, into a shrew if nothing worse! No. Let him be.

The door opened and Bowles came in.

"Well, Mr Bowles? What news of the foremast?"

"You should ask rather for news of the charcoal, sir. They can only distil or brew or reduce—or whatever one does to wood to make charcoal of it—in small parcels. The fo'castle resounds with argument for and against."

"You have been there, then."

"Believe it or not, I was asked to advise on the drawing up of a will. Then, I suppose as payment, I was taken down and shown the foot of the foremast in the broken shoe."

"The people are divided in their opinions?"

"Oh yes. The argument is high and not conducted with proper legal, or perhaps I should say parliamentary, propriety."

48

"Do you agree with the first lieutenant or Mr Benét?"

"With neither. I am astonished at the ease with which uninformed persons come to a settled, a passionate opinion when they have no grounds for judgement."

"I believe the attempt should not be made. It is far too dangerous."

"Yes. The first lieutenant does think so. You should see the shoe! It is gigantic. So, I am afraid, is the split, and frightening too. So is the groaning of the mast as it lurches and grinds into the wood with that small, irregular—unpreventable—circle. I do not know what they should do. The place, though, is a tangle of temporary measures. Some the layman can understand, some are quite inscrutable. There are beams jammed between the shaft of the mast and the thicker timbers of the ship's side. There are cables twisted about the mast so taut you would think them made of metal. Yet the mast moves, for all the beams and twisted cables, the blocks and tackles, crows, shores and battens. The sight is frightening. But then, when you see the small movement, the sight is more than frightening."

"Can there be more?"

"Dread."

He said no more but stared out of the stern window at the rising sea.

"Well, Mr Bowles, we have become a poor collection of mortals, I think. Here is Pike drunk and incapable. Oldmeadow is consumed with bad temper and chooses

the company of his men rather than us. We have become—what?"

"Frightened out of our wits."

"Prettiman keeps his bunk—"

"He does not. He is helpless in it. The fall was of extraordinary force. Since we have no surgeon aboard and only
the matron of the emigrants to minister to him—"

"I cannot imagine that doing him any kind of good!"

"Nor I. But the seamen and emigrants would have her
do what she could, which was confined, I believe, to the
muttering of spells and the hanging of garlic round the
poor man's neck!"

"The seamen and emigrants sent her?"

"Prettiman is much respected among them."

"Have I dismissed him as a clown too readily? Oh,
surely not!"

Bates, the steward, came to provide us with what food
there was for those who still had a mind to eat—salt pork,
cold since the fuel must be conserved for making charcoal,
soaked beans also cold and the notorious ship's biscuit,
which I herewith give my affidavit had no weevils in them,
small beer or brackish water ameliorated by a dash of
brandy. I ate and so did Bowles. Pike slumbered until Bates
called Phillips in and the two men carried him to his cabin.
Oldmeadow, I am told, ate a seaman's portion in the
fo'castle with his men. The sea got up and our movement
was more violent. The daily business of the ship which
must go on whatever else happened—the changes of the

watch, the bosun's calls, the bells, the tread above our heads of seabooted officers and the leathery slap of the seamen's naked feet on planking—this resounded about us, endless as the voyage, as time itself, while the anxious hours drew on. Bates—whether it was his duty or not, I cannot tell—took plates of food to the ladies in their bunks.

Bowles went to his cabin. Mr Brocklebank, wrapped in his coach cloak, came and sat by me. He gave me a description of the processes involved in engraving on stone, copper, zinc, together with the various difficulties attendant on these operations. I did not hear above the half and at last the old man heaved himself away. Every now and then a wave would strike the ship explosively.

At about nine o'clock of a dark night I got to my feet and walked with care to my newly painted cabin. Webber was there, pretending to straighten the coverlet but in reality waiting so that I should give him money for doing his duty.

"Thank you, Webber. That will be all."

To my surprise he did not go.

"This is where he done it then. I'm not surprised."

"What do you mean, Webber?"

"A place gets right greedy after the first taste and would have him, you see, once it knowed what he had in mind—"

"What are you talking about?"

"Wheeler. Joss, we called him. He was my oppo among the stewards."

"Be off with you!"

"Once they have it in mind there's no stopping them, is there? He told me it was like a kind of comfort. He was a queer one, Joss. I believe he must have lived among gentlemen before he came to sea. He had a way of saying things—said he had lived among collegers until he relinquished that employment."

"He never said anything to me! Now—"

"He said there's a hole kind of. 'It's always there, Webber,' he said. 'It's kind of a hole and you know that if the weather gets too rough you can use the hole, get into the hole, hide and sleep,' he said. 'It's always there. For I won't drown, not again.'"

"Good God! He said something like that—something—"

"But then, why here? The answer is the cabin drawed him. It knowed, you see."

"Get *out*, Webber!"

"I'm going, sir. I wouldn't stay here, not in the night, not if you paid me, sir—which you won't, of course."

He paused for a moment, still looking, but I gave him nothing and he left. Yet it was difficult after he had shut the door. I went out again and worked my way to the entry to the waist and peered round the edge. The waves were organized in lines that might have been ruled they were so straight. The light of a waxing moon lay along the completely marshalled crests and turned them to lines of steel.

(5)

"Mr Talbot, sir."

Phillips carried candles in one hand and a lighted lantern in the other.

"In there, Phillips."

"Will you be wanting a light now, sir?"

"Yes—no! Not yet. See here, Phillips. Never mind the candle. Leave the lantern."

"Oh, I couldn't do that, Mr Talbot, sir! You know the passengers isn't supposed to have lanterns but only candles because—"

"Because if candles are overset they douse themselves? Yes, I know. And you know me, don't you? Wait a moment. Now. This buys the lantern off you. I wish to keep a lantern as a memento of the voyage."

An expression of comprehension rearranged Phillips's customary wooden face.

"Sir."

"Hang the lantern on that hook. Turn down the wick."

Of course a ship never sleeps. There was always at least a part of the watch on duty, to say nothing of the officer of the watch and his doggy. I got into my oilskins and made my way through the moonlight to the quarterdeck. Lieutenant Benét was leaning over the forrard rail.

"Come up, Mr Talbot! How do you like this wind? It is bustling us along capitally, is it not?"

"How does the ship like it?"

"She is making more water, of course. That is to be expected. I have been thinking. We ought to rig up some kind of windmill to pump her out."

"Oh no! Not again! Do not terrify us with some new contrivance! Dragropes, ironwork, red-hot rods—Have a care of us, Mr Benét. We are precious!"

Mr Benét tore off his oilskin headgear and spread his arms wide.

"Look about you, Mr Talbot! Is the view not magnificent? The moonlight on these moving waters, the silvered clouds, the unguessable distances up there—those brilliant bodies sparkling above us all! Where is your poetry? Does not the danger, the fear we all feel, give a keener edge to this intoxicating delight?"

"If it comes to that, where is *your* poetry? In days past you have been only too anxious to stuff it down my throat!"

"You are a severe critic. Then take a utilitarian view. This moonlight means that we may well have a clear horizon at dawn and take helpful star sights."

"I thought there was some difficulty over the navigation—erratic chronometers or something."

54

"You do pick about, sir, do you not? But at least we may find our latitude, which is nearly half the battle though not quite."

"Is that Mr Willis there? I hope you are recovered, lad. Mr Benét—cannot Mr Willis assist you in navigation?"

"I take that as a pleasantry, sir. Will you excuse me now? I am occupied with an Ode to Nature, a subject of such amplitude and depth I can scarcely get into it—or out of it!"

"Better that than sink us out of hand."

"I suppose you are talking about the foremast. We shall commence the operation when we have enough charcoal and when this sea has gone down."

At this point the odd young man shook his long locks about his face and orated:

"Spirit of Nature—"

"Are you sure, Mr Benét? The last time—no, the time before that—it was *Spirit of woman*—you are thrifty."

Mr Benét ignored me.

"Spirit of Nature, warm or hot or cold. Solidity—"

"No, no, Mr Benét! I am unworthy of the treat—as is Mr Willis! Allow me to detach Mr Willis from you. He speaks prose."

"Take him. Do what you like with him. Oblige me by returning to me what is left. One never knows what will prove useful."

Willis followed me sullenly enough, up to the poop.

"Well, Mr Willis. Are you quite recovered?"

"I'm deaf in me right earhole where the captain clouted me. And if anyone tries to get me up a mast he'll have to carry me up screaming."

"Good God, lad, your voice has broken! I suppose I should congratulate you. Not climb the mast again? Where's your spirit, lad?"

"What's that to you? It's my business not yours and I'm minding it."

"I'd be obliged for a little more courtesy from you, young man!"

"Why? You're a passenger. What in the Navy we calls a 'pig'. I don't have to take lip from you. Mr Askew, the gunner, said so. 'They're passengers,' he said, 'nothing more. This ain't a company ship,' he said, 'and you need pay no attention to them, not even when they're as high in the instep as Lord Talbot,' he said."

"I'll still require a little civility from you, Mr Willis, on the grounds that I'm older than you if nothing else. I'm sorry to hear that you were deafened but guess that the faculty will return to you. Good Heavens! Young Tommy was a bit lopsided after I cuffed him. Boys must be educated, you know! We all suffer! I doubt there's a schoolboy or midshipman in the world who has not some temporary derangement of his faculties in one department or another. That's how we are made, young fellow, and you should be grateful!"

"Well, I'm not. I wish I was home. And I would be if Dad didn't have an account with one of the managers in the docks and wished to make a gentleman of me. I'd still be serving sugar and happy with the tally wenches in the storerooms. Now the war's over, they'll have to decommission this rotting old lump of wood and then you won't see my arse for dust."

The moon ducked into a cloud and by contrast the night seemed dark. Mr Benét sang out from the quarterdeck below us.

"Mr Willis, oblige me by having the quarter lanterns turned up. When you've done that, you can tell me what happens at a half hour before sunrise."

"Aye aye, sir. Bosun's mate—"

I twitched Willis by the sleeve and murmured to him.

"Half an hour before sunrise is the beginning of Nautical Twilight."

"Well, I know that! Did you think I was stupid?"

Clearly the boy was proof against the advances of social amiability. I was about to dismiss him, therefore, when a positive party of men came to the quarterdeck. Charles was with them. They brought a considerable quantity of gear up to the poop which seemed to include a sail triced up to a heavy yard, an enormous block of iron which needed three men to carry it, and coils of heavy rope.

"Edmund! You are not yet in your bunk!"

"Evidently. Do you never stop working? What is all this?"

"It is a sea anchor."

"This is new to me."

57

"In extremely heavy weather a ship may ride to such an anchor—"

"But this is our stern!"

"Our circumstances are unusual. That is all. We may need to stream the anchor over the stern to check her way and ensure that she does not drive herself under. Oh, of course, not in this weather—it is moderating! But farther south, where the really heavy weather is—it is a precaution."

The men were tricing the gear to the rails of the poop.

"The captain's orders?"

"No. I have sufficient authority for this myself. Mine is an ancient profession, you see, and the duties defined well enough. But the time is nigh on six bells in the first—Why are you not in your bunk?"

"I—explanations are tedious! I am happy in my dry clothes and there was moonlight, to say nothing of a slight decrease in our motion—and so forth."

Charles looked closely into my face.

"You have moved back to the passenger accommodation?"

"Yes."

Charles nodded and turned to his men. He went round, as I saw, and personally checked the security of the lashing that held all this heavy gear ready for use. If care and forethought could secure our survival he would provide it! I had a sudden awareness of the two of them, Benét and

Charles, the one brilliantly putting us at risk, the other soberly and constantly taking *care*!

Charles spoke again.

"Very well, Robinson. Carry on."

He turned to me.

"Are you going down?"

"Are not you?"

"Oh, I have more work to do. I suppose it will be the middle before I turn in."

"Well then—yes, I will go down. Good night, Charles."

I made my reluctant way down to the lobby. There was now a lantern fixed to the mizzenmast just above the copy of the captain's standing orders, in its glass-fronted case. Someone had left two huge piles of rope beneath it. I opened the door of my hutch and stepped inside. By holding it open I had enough light from the lantern in the lobby to allow me to find my way round. I fumbled in the top drawer, got out my tinderbox and contrived to light the lantern I had bought from Phillips. I shut the door and sat in my canvas chair. I have to confess that already I was feeling something like one feels when bracing oneself to leap into cold water—very cold water. I stripped off my oilskins and my seaboots more slowly than an ancient. I remember bending to my boots as if the effort were painful and the business impossibly long. But at last I was in my "slops". There was still a way of postponing the unpleasant moment. I went to our office of necessity on the starboard side, turned up the blue bud of the oil lamp fixed to the bulkhead, adjusted my trowsers and sat on the nearer of our two holes to the door. Scarcely had I settled myself when the door opened and a petty officer of huge dimensions edged himself in.

"Well, damn my soul!"

"Sorry, sir!"

"Get out!"

"First lieutenant's orders, sir."

The man inserted a rope's end into the farther hole and proceeded to pay it out. I pulled up my trowsers in a rage, buckled the belt and flung myself out. There were more seamen in the lobby. A rope was creeping from the pile past my feet. Another rope was creeping in a like manner into the "female" offices of necessity on the larboard quarter. The place had gone mad. A young seaman, clad as I was in nothing but slops, came quickly out of the larboard office and ran to Miss Granham's door! This was the outside edge of enough! I got to him in a stride or two and had him by the shoulder.

"No, you don't, my lad!"

I spun him round—good God! It was *Miss Granham*! Her face, even in the dim light from the lantern, was scarlet.

"Let me go, sir, at once, sir!"

"Miss Granham!"

My hand had sprung from her thin shoulder as if it had touched a snake. An unnoticed heave caught me off balance. Miss Granham grabbed the knob of her door handle. I somersaulted backwards and was only saved from mortal injury by those same coils of rope which though diminished were still enough to break my fall. I was on my knees and scrabbled back towards her.

"Pray, Miss Granham—pray, Miss Granham—forgive me—I thought you was a seaman who intended you some harm—allow me—I will close your—"

"I cannot close it myself, Mr Talbot, while you have your hand on the sill. You have an uncommon knack of falling about, sir! Far be it from me to offer advice—"

"I do not hurt myself on these occasions, ma'am. But I should value your advice on anything."

She paused, her back to me, her door half-open.

"Sarcasm, Mr Talbot?"

The fall had warmed my temper.

"Why am I always misunderstood?"

She turned back. I continued.

"You do not comment, ma'am. During this voyage, people's opinions of their associates and companions have been modified—must have been—modified! That is as true of me as of anyone. What I said was a simple expression of the truth of—of my respect and for your—your—"

"My years, young man?"

She had swung round completely to face me. In the dim light the ravages of time on her handsome face were not visible. She was smiling and a lock of hair had escaped from the scarf in which the rest was confined and lay across her face. She put it up, and some trick of the half-light made her look as young as I, if not younger! My mouth opened and shut. I swallowed.

"No, ma'am."

"Let us be acquainted all over again then, Mr Talbot. Indeed, it falls pat. It would perhaps make you less indifferent to where and how you fall—Now, do not pucker up, sir! Hear me out! You may take more care of yourself if you see what the result of a fall can be. Mr Prettiman wishes to see you. I—the fact is, I recommended him to ask someone else. I see that perhaps I was wrong."

I believe I laughed.

"Mr Prettiman wishes to see me? Good God!"

"So, if you agree, I will call you to him tomorrow morning."

"I do agree, ma'am. Nothing would give me greater pleasure!"

The lock of hair had fallen once again. She put it up, frowning.

"Why do you say that, Mr Talbot? Is it the kind of remark you scatter among the members of my sex?"

I made a gesture of dissent. But quickly the smile returned.

"You do not answer, Mr Talbot. Nor should you. You find me minatory. I see the thought which is forming at the back of your mind, 'Once a governess, always a governess.' I was at fault, sir, and curtsey as you observe like the veriest milkmaid."

With that she closed the door. I stayed where I was, holding on to the rail, and I was bemused. There was no doubt about it. Miss Granham had the capacity to reduce a person to his constituent parts, apparently without trying! But we were—she had said so!—acquaintances once more. I do not believe myself quarrelsome and the change filled me with unusual relief and pleasure. I went to the entry to the waist and looked out. The deck was moon-drenched, white. Those stars that the moon had not quenched swung in great curves through the rigging like silver bees. I stared up at them until I was dizzy. I blinked and looked down. Men were coming aft, working their way along a bouncing lifeline, for they carried a heavy burden which seemed to make them unhandy. They laboured up to the quarterdeck with what appeared to be the body of some recently killed animal and large at that. Charles came hurrying along, unburdened, did not see me and went rapidly up the stairs after the men. I turned away and went into my hutch and shut the door behind me. I looked at the freshly made-up bunk with disfavour. There was no doubt about it. Coming back to this hutch was going to be a trial. It was like the time when I was a boy riding by the churchyard in the dusk on a pony which took me indifferently too near the graves. So now. However I had supposed the world and human life to be arranged, I found an air, an *atmosphere* in this hutch to which I had condemned myself! I seemed to breathe unease. True, compared with the light of the candle to which

I was accustomed a degree of brilliance blazed from my oil lamp, which hung steady by the wall, while the wall moved and shadows drawn in black ink raced over me as the ship moved under us. I turned down the wick until only a glimmer of light was left. I told myself that I would not undress for a while but wait until familiarity had made the place a little more mine than—*theirs*. Is not a cure for a burnt finger to hold it next to a fire so that the heat is drawn out? Then Colley had sat here. His elbow, pen, inkwell, sander—here he had known the extremes of dread and sorrow, of humiliation, mortification—experience of a misery beyond the power of my imagination! If that misery, that whirlpool of human suffering had drained away without trace, as my reason told me, why suddenly was there a winter on my skin? Why was this cabin different from the last time I had slept here? I came up from that state, muttering something about a poor boy who had too much sensibility—or in other words too much blue funk! That made me grin but with what must have been little more than a grimace. To "share the common lot of the other passengers who would one day be part of my care"! That was a noble sentiment. I found myself speaking out loud.

"In future, my boy, avoid noble sentiments. They are like drawing a card blind. You may get anything from the joker to the—"

Nevertheless I am a rational man.

The day had been long. Sleep ought to have been easy.

Yet I did not chuse to throw off my garments and get at once into the bunk. A naked man is defenceless. He cannot run naked out onto a moon-drenched deck. Not unless he is delirious. Well, thought I, I will do myself the kindness of going little by little. I lay down, fully dressed in my slops, on the coverlet of the bunk. I lay on my back. The eyebolt was inches from my face. I shut my eyes but was provoked by the slight intimations of light and shadow passing over them. I opened my eyes, therefore, and determining to ignore the eyebolt, focused my eyes on the white-painted deckhead. I found myself examining in detail the wounded underside of a deckbeam, a hole with a pointed thing in the bottom.

I turned over and lay on my face, but the roll of the ship and the occasional pitch made me lurch uncomfortably. I fumbled for the side of the bunk with one hand and at the side of the ship with the other. My fingers took hold. It was the eyebolt, of course. The hair of my head sprang erect. There was an instant in which I might have flung myself from the bunk and rushed away to find Charles or someone, anyone warm and living who breathed and spoke! Yet in that fearful instant I made up my mind and stayed where I was, the fierceness of my clutch making my whole body tremble. Eyes shut, I stayed there, in the very position of the dying man, and was as cold as he.

The change was gradual. The petrifaction of fear diminished into unease, then into a greyness of consent. Thus it had been. Thus it was.

There was a moan from somewhere, from Prettiman in

his bunk. I let go the eyebolt and turned over on my back. The wounded deckbeam had less to say to me. I shut my eyes.

I did not experience the passage from waking to sleeping. But it seems that at some point before the coming of the light I must have fallen into a kind of sleep or trance or place.

He was saying something. His voice was far away. A familiar voice, choked with sobbing. I could not place the voice but knew I must. Who in the name of God? I was in a place lit by a savage light which leapt and sank, again and again. The voice drew nearer.

"You could have saved us."

The voice was my own voice. I was awake, the flame was leaping and sinking behind the glass of the lantern. I turned it out and lay back, waiting for the dawn.

(6)

When the dawn came I dressed thoughtfully enough. But life must go on and even the sadness of self-knowledge cannot come wholly between a man and his stomach!

The passenger saloon was deserted except for little Pike. He sat under the window, his arms folded on the table, his head on them. I thought he was drunk again but as I entered he looked up, smiled sleepily, then put his head down. So there was another cabin in which people found it difficult to be at ease! I got myself a mug of small ale from Bates—there was nothing else to have—and drank "breakfast" quite in the antique manner. I went back to my hutch and got into my oilskins and seaboots and was about to go into the waist but saw old Mr Brocklebank standing there in the shadow of the larboard main chains. He had usurped my place. I sat in my canvas chair then, all oilskinned as I was, and surveyed my few books on the shelf at the end of the bunk. I remembered Charles and his gift of the slops that I was wearing. I took down the *Iliad*, therefore, and read in book *zeta* the story of Glaucus and Diomede. They had exchanged armour recklessly, it seemed, trading bronze armour for gold. I could not decide whether my determination to see Charles promoted was gold or bronze—certainly his care of me, getting me bathed and changed as if he were my old nurse, was gold in the circumstances! I read on but soon found the words drifting apart. It had been a short and troubled night. I remembered that Charles had told me not to wear my oilskins except to keep myself dry so I put the book back and went out to the waist. Mr Brocklebank had gone. I stayed in the lee of the main chains to allow the wind to freshen me.

Mr Benét came briskly out of the lobby.

"Well, Mr Talbot, we get on!"

"This weather is still too lively to allow you to tamper—I should say to mend, the foremast?"

"For the time being. But the wind moderates. And fortunately the movement does not prevent Coombs from making charcoal."

"Stay, sir. A moment. I have heard that in an emergency masts may be cut away."

"You have been speaking to the first lieutenant!"

"Indeed I have, but he said nothing of that. It is my own idea—cut away the foremast and you save yourself the risk of mending the shoe! I do have occasional ideas, you know."

"I am sure you do, sir. But if we cut away the foremast we should probably have to cut away the mizzenmast to balance things. Nor do masts fall precisely where you mean them to. Imagine the foremast going over the side, still tethered to the ship, and dragging her round so she broached to! We might be overset and swamped in seconds. Bravo, Mr Talbot, but no, sir. That will not do. The moment it is possible we shall crimp the shoe and draw it together. Bite your nails a watch or two longer."

I did not like his tone but there seemed nothing I could do about that. However, we did have interests in common—

Benét was moving away. I hastened after him.

"I had meant to ask you, sir, to explain a certain episode in which you and Lady Somerset and Miss Chumley—"

"Later, Mr Talbot. Oh, this weather! It makes a man want to sing!"

He ran swiftly along the deck and vanished into the fo'castle between one roll and the next. Charles emerged from the lobby. A petty officer and two seamen came with him. He paused when he saw me.

"Well, Edmund?"

"A bad night, I am afraid."

"There is little colour in your face. Are you feeling the motion?"

"No. I have had a bad night, that is all."

"You could return to the wardroom."

I felt myself flushing, for it was evident that he understood something of my "bad night".

"And be laughed at? No."

"In discomfort and danger people are glad of something to laugh at."

"So we are still in danger?"

He turned to the petty officer and gave him an order. The man knuckled his forehead and the little party cantered—doubled, I suppose I should say—along the deck to the fo'castle.

"Yes, Edmund. We are in the same danger as before."

"At least the weather is improving."

"My dear fellow! This is a pause and will give Benét time to tamper with the foremast. I do not like the look of the weather. There is something big up there which will search us out. Well, I must get on."

"Let me come with you."

"No no. You cannot. My rounds are not for you."

He saluted in the naval manner and went forward along the deck. The lifelines were not so much bouncing now as vibrating gently. Charles ignored them.

"Mr Talbot."

I turned. Miss Granham, in slops and seaboots too big for her, was standing in the entry to the lobby.

"Good morning, ma'am. What can I do for you?"

"I wanted to call you to Mr Prettiman. Is the time convenient?"

"To visit him? Of course, ma'am, whenever you wish."

She opened his door a crack, looked in, then shut it again.

"He has fallen asleep again. It is the paregoric. Perhaps—"

She seemed doubtful. But I could see no reason for delay.

"May I not go in and wait?"

"If you wish."

I entered Prettiman's cabin and pulled the door to behind me. The cabin was like all the others, a bunk, a shelf for books, a canvas washbowl with a small mirror over it and, at the other end, a writing flap with the usual accoutrements. There was a bucket under the washbowl and a canvas chair before the writing flap. Mr Prettiman had signalled his eccentricity by sleeping the wrong way round—his head was towards the stern, his feet towards the bow. His head was, in consequence, just above the bucket, which may have been his original intention in sleeping that way round. Certainly I had vivid and miserable memories of our first weeks in the ship and the nausea which had overcome me and the other passengers.

Prettiman was so deeply asleep that it was hard to believe he had been awake that morning. The air was thick, as must be the air of all sickrooms, I suppose, since fresh air is so deleterious to a troubled body. Though it was not to be thought that our ladies, accustomed as they must be to the treatment of childish ailments, would leave the sufferer unwashed, there was a distinct odour emanating from the man which made a close approach to him distasteful. I realized with a resigned determination that I was *in for* an unpleasant enough experience. However, I daresay that the hardly describable events of the night had made me a little more aware of my offhand ability to spread destruction! I sat

71

down cautiously, therefore, with a vague feeling that as long as he slept I was doing what Miss Granham required by being present. The odour from his body strove with another which I had no difficulty in identifying as paregoric, or laudanum. No wonder he slept. The bedclothes were pulled up to his neck. His bald head was dinted into a pillow far softer than the one which had been provided for me. His face above the tawny beard and scanty fringe of hair was very pale. It was a face I had seen often enough comically reddened by passionate anger. This mask of flesh and bone on which his emotions were so often played out for all to see was irregular enough. The tilted nose was as far from his long upper lip as that of a stage Irishman, a *Paddy*. His mouth was wide and firm, so that the lines of determination as well as anger were engraved there. Sickness had wasted his flesh and removed a great deal of the comedy. Those eyes which could glare in all the madness of social bigotry were veiled by dark lids and sunk deep under the frantic eyebrows. It was perhaps possible to laugh at the waking man. But this effigy, stretched as on the slab of a tomb, had nothing of the laughable. Where was ludicrous Prettiman, opinionated, sometimes frantic, indignant beside his unlikely fiancée? But she had suffered a like sea change without the trouble of a fall, a severe spinster, now seen to be handsome, dignified and sensible—and feminine! Why, the man himself—there came a ninth wave in our diminishing weather, for the cabin lurched. That same cry which I had heard when I was awake in the cabin off the wardroom—that cry which had drawn me forth—the anguish—woe—I sprang to my feet. It was not to be borne. I saw myself condemned to sit in this stink and be exacerbated time after time as the man woke and that cry burst out! I seized the door handle—

"Who is it?"

That was a feeble voice behind me. I turned.

"It is Edmund Talbot."

The man was sinking down in stupor again. I was exasperated. And I had said I would wait. Yet only that night I had known, found out what I bore in my hands! I sank down into the canvas chair again. The bedclothing was massed about his middle and hiding the lines of his body there. Lower down, his legs and feet lifted the blankets. The odour of paregoric was more perceptible since his cry. The spirit which had half-awakened in the tormented body had sunk away again into the depths. The eyelids fluttered and were still. The mouth fell open, but this time a sigh was all the sound he made.

I leaned back and surveyed him as he lay in the bunk. Under their lids his eyes moved rapidly from side to side. His breath came unevenly, he panted. I thought his eyes would open but they did not. He muttered in his sleep or swoon. The words dragged out.

"—John Laity for the term of his natural life. Hamilton Moulting Baronet as colonel light dragoons emoluments

from clothing—expenses of the returning officer—
Mungo FitzHenry master in Chancery for life four thousand and six pounds—"

Good God—it was my cousin and that superb *plum*!
What the devil did this man mean by it? I leapt to my feet.
I seized the door handle—and felt it turn from the out-
side. Miss Granham looked in. She whispered:

"Mr Talbot? Not yet awake?"

"No."

That same feeble voice again.

"Letitia? Is that you?"

"It is Mr Talbot come to see you, Aloysius."

"William Collier fourteen years for illegal assembly—"

"It is I, Mr Prettiman, Edmund Talbot. I am told you
wish to see me. Well, I am here and waiting."

Behind me Miss Granham closed the door.

"Letitia?"

"Miss Granham has stepped outside. She supposed you
wanted to speak to me, though what I have done to deserve such an unexpected honour—"

He was turning his head restlessly and gritting his
teeth.

"I am not able to sit up."

"Do not incommode yourself. I am able to stand here
and you are able to see me."

"Sit down, boy. Sit down!"

The man intended an order, there was no doubt about
that. I wish I could say that I sat to humour a sick man but

74

the truth is my body sat itself down before I was aware of what was happening! A slight movement of the cabin made him grit his teeth again and audibly. His face cleared little by little. I spoke abruptly, annoyed by my involuntary obedience.

"As I said. I am waiting to hear what you want."

"You are aware that Miss Granham and I—"

He was silent again. I did not know whether he was interrupted by some pain or whether he felt a natural embarrassment at raising the subject with a stranger. I thought it best to help the sick man where I could, otherwise this irritating interview would be more and more prolonged.

"I am aware as everyone else in the ship is that the lady has consented to make you the happiest of men. I have already felicitated the lady, I believe. Permit me to congratulate—"

"Don't smother the thing in nonsense!"

"I beg your pardon, sir!"

"She has agreed to marry me."

"That is what I said!"

"*Now, I mean.* Where are your wits?"

"We have no clergymen!"

"Captain Anderson will perform the ceremony. Do you know nothing?"

I was silent. Clearly the shortest way to the end was to listen and not interrupt. Mr Prettiman passed his tongue over his lips, then smacked them.

"Would you like a drink? This water—"

Now he turned his head and looked straight at me, examining my face as I had examined his. A trace of a smile, wintry enough, deepened the creases round his mouth and eyes.

"Unfair, amn't I?"

I grinned, however ruefully, at this sudden turn round.

"You're having a devilish bad time, that's what it is. Anyone—perhaps when the weather is better you could get out—"

"I am dying."

"But, Mr Prettiman! A fracture—"

He shouted aloud.

"Will you abstain from this foolish habit of contradiction? When I say I am dying I mean I am dying and I am going to die!"

The end of this shouted exordium was confused by another cry from the depth of his agony, which I am persuaded that time he inflicted on himself by some forbidden movement. The cry was not only the expression of despairing anguish but of furious resentment.

"Mr Prettiman, I beg of you!"

Once again he lay silent, but perspiration trickled down his face. Behind me the door opened and Miss Granham looked in again. She stepped over the sill, reached under his pillow, took out a handkerchief and wiped his face. A smile returned to it. In a far softer voice than he had used to me he murmured, "Thank you, thank you."

As Miss Granham was withdrawing he spoke again.

"Letty, there is no need for you to stand on guard. I am well enough and the dose still gives me some relief. Please return to your cabin and try to sleep. I am sure you need to. It frets me to think of you keeping yourself awake for my sake."

She glanced at me, then smiled at him, nodded and closed the door behind her.

"Mr Talbot, I wish you to be a witness."

"I?"

"You and Oldmeadow. To the ceremony—the marriage."

"That is ridiculous! We have no official standing in the ship! Charles Summers, on the other hand, or Mr Cumbershum—I will give the bride away if you wish or—why anything!"

"You are not needed to give the bride away. Mr East will do that."

"Mr *East*? The *printer*?"

"Will you listen? Or do you propose to prolong this interview indefinitely?"

There were many replies I could have made to that remark but in choosing the best I missed the opportunity. He had closed his eyes and now went on speaking.

"The officers of the ship will be distributed round the world. Who knows where they will go? In any case, they are at risk. Certainly this old ship will carry them no farther. You and Oldmeadow will remain at Sydney Cove.

Do you not understand, Mr Talbot? Modest as it may be, Miss Granham will inherit my fortune. But without unimpeachable witnesses and at a distance of eighteen thousand miles from our courts, corrupt as they are—"

"No, they are not! That is outrageous! British justice—"

His eyes had snapped open.

"I say they are! Oh, in respect of money you may rely on them, but they are corrupt in all else by privilege, by land tenure, by a viciously inadequate system of representation—"

All this had been uttered on a rising note. But as if the man knew how close to him was the angel of the agony he lowered his voice suddenly in a way which might have seemed comic to me only a few minutes before.

"I need not go into all that, Talbot. After all, I am talking to a representative of—well, there. To resume: you and Oldmeadow will be guarantors of her inheritance by virtue of your position as witnesses of the marriage."

"I shall be happy to serve the lady in any way I am able—" It came to me, as I said that, that it was true! "Yes indeed, sir. But I trust it may be many years before—"

The trace of hectic had appeared in his cheeks.

"Do not talk nonsense! I have not many days or perhaps hours left."

"The banns—"

"They may be omitted in these circumstances. Let that be an end of the matter."

We were silent for a while. Then he stirred restlessly. I

had half-risen from my seat but he held up his hand.

"I have not finished. I do not care to ask for favours. But now—"

"You may, sir. For the lady's sake."

"Mr Summers told me that you claimed at least to believe in 'fair play'. The phrase is juvenile—"

"The phrase is a good phrase, Mr Prettiman. What is 'fair play' in the slang of schoolboys is 'justice' among adults."

"You believe in justice."

There was another pause. I glanced at the shelf of books above his head. They were severe.

"I am an Englishman."

"Miss Granham has reported favourably on your progress—"

"My what?"

"I do not know how civilized the *mores* of a colony may be but I suspect the worst. I fear civilization may be sadly to seek. I ask you to see that the lady is treated as she should be in a civilized society."

"I would count her friendship a privilege, sir. I give you my word I will use every endeavour to protect her."

He smiled wearily, for his strength was ebbing.

"There are many ways in which she does not need protection. But in some things a lady by the unfairness of Nature will always be at a disadvantage. I believe the colony may not yet have accustomed itself to the proper attitude to the female nature."

"I do not know."

"One other matter."

I waited for some time but he was silent.

"Another matter, sir?"

He said nothing but seemed in some discomfort.

"May I not move you to a more comfortable position, sir? This mass of bedclothes round your waist—"

He was moving his head restlessly on the pillow.

"It is not a mass of bedclothing but a gross swelling of the lower abdomen and the upper part of the lower limbs."

"Good God! Good God!"

"Must every other sentence commence with an imprecation? You cannot move me. To move my body even for the most necessary purposes is a torture which is wearing me out and down, down and away."

He was silent again for a while. Then—

"This other matter. It is confidential. I have searched my conscience and believe that what I do is right. Come close."

I took my staying hand off the bulkhead and hitched the canvas chair to the bunk. I leaned my head down to his. The odour of the bunk and his body was quite plainly unpleasant. Was this the awful beginnings of decay? I was not well informed in the matter.

"I have a paper for you."

"Oh?"

"It is a paper signed by me. You see what a case I am in, helpless and dying. People will contest the will—there are always such, relatives so distant they have never before made themselves known. They might well bring a case that the marriage was not—could not—be consummated, that it was void and consequently the lady entitled to nothing."

There ensued a long pause.

"I do not follow what I am to do, Mr Prettiman."

He seemed in much discomfort.

"I have written a plain declaration that I have had carnal knowledge of the lady during the voyage and before the marriage."

"Good—"

"You were about to say, sir?"

"Nothing. Nothing."

His voice was a shout.

"Do you think, boy, that a superstitious rite such as a wedding ceremony means anything to such people as I and she are?"

My mouth was opened to speak, though I do not know what I should have said. For his anger was such that he had hurt himself all over again. He positively howled with pain, as if he were being punished for his blasphemy! I find the recollection amusing enough. For I did not believe in any of the superstitious rites myself and regarded them as serving to keep order. Christening, marrying and burying—they are the marks which distinguish men from beasts, that is all.

But the man was recovering.

"There is a green leather case in the upper drawer. Give it to me, if you please."

I did so. He held it to his chest, took out a folded and sealed paper which he held up close to his eyes.

"Yes. This is it."

"Why is the paper necessary? I could as easily stand before a court and swear that you had told me how matters stood between you and the lady."

"I do not trust them—that is all."

It was on the tip of my tongue to speak like a moralist! I felt like saying with all the force at the command of a member of the society which he despised—"You should have thought of that before!" Or—"The superstitious rites are then of some value, sir!" But I did not. This was all the odder, since I felt myself more and more out of sympathy with him and her—with her in particular. A lady, and one whom I had held in some esteem to behave so, like a drab! I did not know whether to laugh or what to do. She was provoking. It was very sad. Her—lapse made me sad and angry.

"I believe, Mr Prettiman, we have no more to say to each other. I presume I shall be told when the superstitious rite is to take place?"

He turned his head and looked at me in what seemed to be surprise.

"Of course!"

I put the green leather case back in the drawer and stood up.

"I agree to guard this paper and produce it in the circumstances which you envisage. I have no desire to read it."

"Thank you."

My bow was hampered. I had not got the door open when he spoke again.

"Mr Talbot."

"Sir?"

"Miss Granham is unaware of the existence of this paper. I wish her to remain so for as long as possible."

I bowed again and stumbled out of that fetid hutch.

(7)

I found myself standing by the entry to the waist and staring at the tattered garment which Mr Brocklebank had drawn round him. I could not tell how I came to be there. The wind was cold and searched me out even through my seaman's clothing.

There was something particularly disgusting about this furtive, middle-aged sexual congress! He might well be fifty years old, and she—

"Filthy, beastly, lecherous!"

Apparently the old man did not hear but was deep in some contemplation which must have been melancholy, to judge from his expression. I began to reason with myself. Why should I care? I looked at the sealed note in my hand. That, at least, contemptible as I thought it to be, was a duty. I took it to my cabin, wrenched the door open and slammed it behind me. I thrust the document into my bottom drawer, then flung myself into my canvas chair with a force which, had I any of Mr Brocklebank's substance, would have split it completely.

There was a knock at the door.

"Come in."

It was Charles Summers.

"Have you a moment to spare?"

"Of course. Will you sit here? On the bunk if you like. I am sorry Phillips has not yet put the clothes together. Everything is so dirty, so foul, so vile! Oh, I am so tired of this voyage! So much water! I wish I could walk on it. Oh, sorry, sorry! Well, what can I do for you?"

He sat down gingerly among the rumpled bedclothes.

"I have a proposal to make. Should you care to be a midshipman?"

"Are you serious?"

"Half, shall we say. Let me explain. With only two other lieutenants, Cumbershum and Benét, and one warrant officer capable of discharging the same duties as they do—I mean Mr Smiles, the sailing master—"

"I have never understood his position."

"He is something of an—anomaly, would it be? He is the last of his kind, warranted by the Admiralty at a time when navigation was coming more and more into the hands of the King's officers. But he is only the third. Mr Askew will stand a watch occasionally. Now if I take a watch myself we can divide the watch-keeping between five and so benefit everyone—"

"Except you! Good Heavens, you spend all your time going about the ship! When do you sleep? I am sure your ceaseless activity cannot be necessary."

"You are wrong, you know. Is there not a saying

among farmers that the best dung is the farmer's foot? But to resume: if I stand the middle, which by now you must know is—"

"—midnight until four o'clock in the morning."

"Just so. An officer of the watch has a doggy. Would you care to stand that watch with me as midshipman?"

"Should you leave me in charge?"

"You would do better than poor young Willis. Well. Do you agree?"

"Indeed I do. But you have added four hours to your duties! It is too much. For all that you have cheered me immensely!"

"Why do you need cheering? Is it our dangers?"

"Oh, that! No. I have—been told things. There is a young lady in whom I—It had seemed that she knew more of a criminal connection than she should and—Today someone said something which has raised the matter in my mind with much pain—so. When do we start?"

"I will get the quartermaster to give you a shake at a quarter to twelve."

"To stand a watch! Will you give me responsibilities?"

"I might put you in charge of the traverse board."

"Really, I have not felt so excited since I left home! 'Mr Speaker. To those of us who have actually stood the middle in one of His Majesty's ships of the line—'"

"Suppose when on watch you commit some awful error? 'Mr Speaker. To those of us who have actually been mastheaded in one of His Majesty's ships of the line—'"

"I can see you are an awful tyrant when roused."

"Indeed."

"By the way, how is Coombs getting on with the charcoal?"

"They have enough. Captain Anderson is only waiting for the sea to moderate a little more and he will give the order for the shoe to be mended."

"I must see this foremast with its shoe."

"Now you will go wandering where you should not. Do you want a direct order?"

"That would tempt me. But do you expect the weather to moderate even further?"

"Yes. Now. During the day I recommend that you get at least four hours' sleep to make up for what you are going to lose during the night. In fact, I believe I shall make that an order."

"Aye aye, sir!"

He nodded, and went away. I sat for a while and was ridiculously excited. The prospect was like that of childhood, when the idea of *staying up all night* has a mysterious attraction about it—the experiencing of how one day actually changes into another. There was something—adult about it! There was an invitation to the world of men who are doing this strange thing not as a dare or discovery but because it is their duty. They are masters of the dark hours. It has about it something of the attraction of a secret society! Indeed, my main problem at the time seemed to be how to find occupation for myself between then and midnight. I ate a meal and heard from Bates all about the short commons to which we should soon be reduced. I smiled icily at Miss Granham in the lobby but she did not appear to notice. I "got my head down" since I was now a probationary seaman, as it were, with a prescriptive right to the language of the sea, and passed as much as two hours asleep of the four which Charles had stipulated. I settled down to write letters. I tried to compose one to Miss Chumley, the very sight of whom had turned my world and my future upside down, but could not say what I meant. For I could not say in so many words, "Are you corrupted?" Every time that lovely and innocent image came before the eyes of my heart, they refused to see what loathsome conjunction I tried to put before them. Besides, what was the use? There was no guarantee that the letter would ever be delivered. I abandoned the attempt, therefore, thought of writing verses instead, thought of Mr Benét's verses, thought of Glaucus and Diomede, looked through my books, found the spine of *Meditations among the Tombs* was cracked and wondered how it had happened. I read the *Iliad* until my eyes were heavy. Stretched out in my bunk, I fell asleep again, and woke only when a voice spoke in my ear and the quartermaster shook me. The lamp was low and I turned it down to the veriest bud—then went out.

The ship was a ghost, a spirit of silver and ivory. Before me the pool of the waist was full of light to be waded through. I went out, and as I turned to go up the ladders the waxing moon blazed in my face. The sails were unbearable, their whiteness seeming to invade the very apple of the eyes. I climbed up and was overtaken by men trotting aft to stand at the wheel or as messengers with the officers of the watch. Charles came up the ladder and took over formally from Mr Cumbershum. The ship's bell rang eight times.

"Mr Midshipman Talbot reporting for duty, sir."

"It is good to have you here, Edmund. We might read by this light, don't you think?"

"Easily. All the lanterns are out."

"The central lantern is out, the quarter lanterns turned down as far as possible. We must conserve oil, as we must conserve so many things."

I did not know what to say to this, for, as the illegal possessor and nominal purchaser of an oil lamp which at that moment was burning in my cabin, I felt the subject to be a delicate one.

"Where are we?"

"You mean our position? I wish I could tell you! We know our latitude if that is any comfort. It is all Columbus ever knew."

"The longitude?"

"The chronometers—I beg you will keep this to yourself—can no longer be trusted. After this length of time the accumulation of their rates is ridiculous. Besides, water has been clean over them."

"Did you not bring them up one deck?"

I thought Charles seemed a trifle uncomfortable at the memory.

"I—we—it might have been the thing to do. But it might have made matters worse. As far as the longitude is concerned we must consider it to be what you might call 'assisted dead reckoning'."

"With the accent on the 'dead'!"

He thrust out a hand and grasped the rail—then snatched his hand away as if the wood had been hot.

"I should not have done that! In a grown man it is a vile superstition!"

"My dear fellow, you are too scrupulous. If touching wood is any comfort, why not touch wood, say I!"

"Well, there it is. Navigation is still an inexact art, though it may be improved. I cannot think how, though."

"Could not the Admiralty co-opt Mr Benét? Or examine the works of Dean Swift a little more closely?"

"I do not know what Dean Swift has to do with navigation. As for Mr Benét, you are only too right. He believes he can find our longitude without relying on our three damp chronometers!"

"We are lost then!"

"No, no. We are somewhere in an area about ten miles broad and fifty miles long."

"I call that being lost!"

"Well, you would. You are just like me when I was first a midshipman and felt my foot was on the rung of however short a ladder—for to be a lieutenant at that time seemed to me a notable achievement—"

"So it is, so it is."

"My seamanship was learnt already, for there was little about the management of a ship I did not know. I am not boasting."

"It is what Mr Gibbs told me the other day. 'A son of a gun, every hair a rope yarn, every tooth a marline spike, every finger a fishhook and his blood Stockholm tar!'"

Charles laughed aloud.

"Hardly that! But I knew nothing of the theoretical and computational aspect of navigation. One morning the first lieutenant appeared with his own sextant. Mr Bellows, he was. We were in Plymouth Sound—this was before they built the breakwater, so we had a clear horizon to the south. Mr Bellows showed me how to handle the instrument. When he had done he said, 'Now, Mr Summers. Oblige me by using this sextant to find out where we are by the time of local midday.' 'Why, Mr Bellows,' said I, thinking he was having a game with me, 'we are in Plymouth Sound.' 'Prove it,' he said. 'There's this sextant, chronometers in the hold and Mr Smith will be kind enough to lend you his pocket watch.' 'But, Mr Bellows, sir,' I said, 'we're at anchor!' 'You heard me,' he said and went away."

"You are remembering word for word!"

"Indeed it is written on my heart. You cannot think with what careful hands I held that precious instrument—no, Edmund, you cannot! It was not just a sextant.

It was—I do not know how to say what I mean."

"Believe me, I understand you."

"I wonder. I am sure you try. But I took the height of the sun—oh, dozens of times, I think, both sides of midday. I am not a *tremulous* character, Edmund—"

"No indeed!"

"I believe I am rather stolid, in fact. But as the measurements increased then decreased, I really found it difficult to stop myself—crying, trembling, my teeth chattering or myself laughing out loud with whatever it was—No, you cannot possibly understand."

"You had found your vocation."

"There I was, picture me, taking the sun's height again and again and young Smith noting down the time of each shot by his pocket watch—seconds first, then minutes, then the hour: and after that, the angle—seconds, minutes, degrees. Then I—Why labour it? I searched through Norie's *Epitome of Navigation*. I revere that book next to the Bible, I believe."

"I am all at sea in every way."

"So I worked out our position, and yes, it was in Plymouth Sound! I laid it off on the chart—crossed lines, each about a tenth of an inch long and a circle drawn through them by means of the finest pencil in the ship. When Mr Bellows came aboard again I jumped out of the sailing master's cabin, stood to attention and saluted. 'If you please, Mr Bellows, I have worked out our position by means of the sextant, the chronometers and Norie.'

'Let me see,' said he, ducking into the cabin where the chart was spread out on the table. 'Lord, Mr Summers, have you a microscope? This is hardly visible to the naked eye. Spectacles will have to do, I suppose.' He put on his spectacles and had another look. 'That will be our quarterdeck,' he said. 'I shouldn't be surprised if you haven't nailed this cabin. Was you on the roof when you took the sight?' 'No, sir,' I said.

"Then he felt through his pockets and fished out a stub of pencil as thick as his thumb. He held it more like a dagger than anything. He scrawled a huge circle round my 'position'. 'Now,' he said, 'I think we can say we aren't up on Dartmoor nor more than five miles outside the Eddystone Rocks, but where we are inside that circle the Lord Himself only knows.'"

"He was unkind."

Charles laughed.

"Oh no. It was a lesson I did not like but I came to value it. I have passed the lesson on to young Tommy Taylor who stands in need of it and imagines we know latitude to the width of a plank, though otherwise he is your true 'Son of a Gun' and will do better than any of us in the service."

"The lesson stressed the necessity for caution, I suppose."

"Just so. And I have seldom found circumstances in the service where caution did not enable me to detect the correct line of duty."

"That is why you do not want the foremast restored to use?"

"But I do want it restored! And if the wind fell away little by little to a flat calm—"

"Why little by little?"

"A sudden fall leaves a wild sea with no means of managing a ship in it. That would be no time for tampering with the shoring and staying of the mast."

"This moonlight—one could bath in it—swim in it. Was there ever anything as beautiful? Nature is trying to seduce us into Belief in every possible way, into every possible philosophical anodyne."

"I do not know the word."

"When am I to learn celestial navigation?"

"That will have to wait, I am afraid."

"I will study it ashore. But then I should have no horizon. Well—I will ride down to the sea."

"You need not. You may take altitudes by measuring the angle between, let us say, the sun and its reflection in a bath of mercury."

"And halve the angle! How ingenious!"

"You saw all that at once?"

"Why, it is obvious."

"Young Willis does not find that sort of thing obvious, nor young Taylor, come to that."

"Mr Benét, of course, would hardly need a sextant. He would use dead reckoning or build a mercury bath into it."

"There is nothing wrong with dead reckoning if you

know what you are doing. Mr Bellows could talk like a book when he wanted to and he had a sentence for that. He made me write it down in my log and learn it by heart. 'More seamen have been surprised by the accuracy of dead reckoning than have ever been disconcerted by its imprecision.'"

"He could indeed speak like a book!"

We were interrupted by the necessity of having the log cast. This was done every hour and it became my duty solemnly to lift the canvas cover of the traverse board and write in the result. But now I took great interest in the process, though it soon became so habitual as to be unnoticeable. It was followed this first time by a long silence while neither of us felt any need to speak. Occasionally wide clouds obscured the moon but they were fleecy round the edges and gave us almost as much light as from the round of moon itself. I climbed to the poop and stared at our gentle wake. That "body", which I had seen so laboriously carried up to the quarterdeck, now lay triced to the rail on the starboard quarter. A rope was attached to it—two ropes, in fact: and they led over the taffrail and down under the stern. Of course! One was the rope in the office of necessity—the other opposite—it was very mysterious. Suddenly our gentle wake burst into a splendour of diamonds. The moon was gliding out from the farther edge of a cloud. I turned back and went down to the quarterdeck where Charles stood by the stairs up to the poop. I was about to question him when I was interrupted.

"Charles—what was that?"

"It is the duty watch."

"Singing?"

They were visible, not sheltering now under the rail or to leeward of a mast but grouped at the capstan on the fo'castle. They were leaning against it. The music —for such it was, harmony and all—drifted about us, gentle as the wake and the wind, magic as the moonlight. I went forward to the rail of the quarterdeck and leaned over it, listening. As if they had seen and were glad of an audience they seemed to turn—or at least I had the impression of many moon-blanched faces looking my way—and the volume of sound increased.

"What is it, Edmund?"

Charles had come and stood beside me.

"The music!"

"Just the duty watch."

They were silent. Someone had emerged from the fo'castle and was speaking to them. Evidently the concert was over. But there were still the moon and stars and the glitter of the sea.

"How awesome to think that we actually use all that up there—make use of the stars and refer to the sun as habitually as to a signpost!"

Charles spoke hesitantly and, it seemed, a little shyly.

"No man can contemplate it without being put in mind of his Maker."

A cloud was swallowing the moon again. The water and

the ship were dulled.

"The concept is naïve surely. When I consult my repeater I do not *invariably* think of the man who made it!"

He looked round at me. He wore a mask of moonlight as I suppose I did. He spoke with due solemnity.

"When I consider the heavens the work of Thy fingers, the moon and stars which Thou hast ordained—"

"But that is poetry! Milton could do no better!"

"The psalms are prose, surely."

"Yet why should putting something into poetry make it truer than if it was in figures, as in your Mr Norie?"

"You are too clever for me, Edmund."

"I did not mean to be—oh, what a gross impertinence! Forgive me!"

"Was I insulted? I did not feel it. There is a difference between the sky and a pocket watch."

"Yes, yes. That is true. I was making a debating point which I suppose is one of the more detestable results of a gentleman's education. Poetry itself is a mystery—so is prose—so is everything—I used to think of poetry as an entertainment. It is more, far more. Oh, Charles, Charles, I am so deeply, so desperately, so deeply, deeply in love!"

(8)

Charles Summers was silent. The masks of moonlight which were hiding our faces made the night-time confession inevitable. It had burst from me without my volition.

"You say nothing, Charles. Have I annoyed you? I beg your pardon for mixing what must seem a trivial matter in all this going on round us—mixing it too into talk of the religion which is your deepest concern. In fact I do not know why you should be so kind as to listen to me. But so you are."

The first lieutenant went to the wheel and talked with the men there. He stared long into the binnacle. I wondered if anything was wrong, but after a few minutes he came back to me slowly.

"It is the young lady you met aboard *Alcyone*."

"Who else could it be?"

He seemed to brood. Then—

"Who else indeed? I have no doubt she is as virtuous as lovely—"

"Do not make virtue sound so elderly! But is it to be joy or wormwood?"

"I do not understand."

"A certain person engaged in, in fornication with a certain woman—She, Marion Chumley, stood guard, must have consented, must have seen, must have been a part of—Oh, it squeezes my heart to think of it!"

"You cannot mean—"

"If she took however passive a part she is wholly unlike the person I saw, met, talked with. And on top of that I am bound for Sydney Cove and she for Calcutta! The world could hardly thrust people farther apart. You cannot know what it is like."

"I know the young lady, at all events. I saw her. You remember how, since I do not dance, I elected to take the watch for the period of the entertainment and ball? I saw you dancing together."

"Well?"

"What do you expect me to say?"

"I do not know."

"I saw her next day too, early. She had come to the starboard quarter of *Alcyone* and was staring through the side of our ship as if she could see what was going on inside. You were inside, unconscious or delirious. She was wondering about you."

"How do you know?"

"Who else?"

"Benét?"

He made a dismissive gesture.

"Not in a thousand years."

99

"Who told you?"

"No one. I know, you see."

"Oh, you are making up speeches to comfort me!"

There was a smile, as it were, in Charles's voice.

"This, then, is the young lady 'perhaps ten or twelve years younger than myself, a lady of family, wealth—'"

"Did I say so? Before I met her it is certainly how I used to think in my nasty, calculating way. You must despise me."

"No."

He walked to the rail and stood for a while, looking over the side. At last he came back and leaned against the break of the poop.

"The moon is going down."

There was singing again from the fo'castle, very soft. I spoke too, but as softly.

"You know, however long I live I shall remember the middle watch. I shall think of it as a kind of—island—out of this world—made of moonlight—a time for confidences when men can say to a—transmuted face what they would never bring out in the daytime."

He was silent again.

"Think, Charles, had Deverel not slipped below for a drink we should not have lost our topmasts and she would have spent her life in ignorance of me!"

He laughed abruptly.

"You would have been ignorant of each other! There I saw a glimpse of the old 'Lord Talbot'."

"Are you puckering up there in the shadow of the poop?

But it makes no sense. We might have met conveniently in a drawing room. Instead of which—Will she lapse once more into that dream of girlhood until some other—Oh no, it cannot be!"

"She will not forget you."

"It is good of you to say so."

"No. I understand women."

It made me laugh.

"Do you say so indeed? How can that be? You are a proper old tarry breeks, a son of a gun, a man master of an honourable profession and skilled in the way of a ship!"

"Ships are feminine, you know. But I understand women. I understand their passivity, gentleness, receiving impressions as in wax—most of all their passionate need to give—"

"Miss Granham, Mrs Brocklebank! And are there not bluestockings? This is no character of a female wit!"

He was silent for a while, then spoke heavily enough, as though I had defeated him in argument and dispirited him.

"I suppose not."

He walked away and presently the quarterdeck was concerned once more with casting the log.

"Five and a half knots, Edmund. Write it in."

"When I look back on this voyage—if I am alive to do so—I shall think that for all the danger there were compensations."

"Whatever they were, they have got you through the middle or nearly."

"Why so brusque?"

But he had turned away and was plainly more interested for the moment in the ship's affairs than mine. A pipe was shrilling and men were moving here and there. The next watch was falling in just aft of the break of the fo'castle. Mr Smiles, the sailing master, appeared with Mr Tommy Taylor who was yawning like a cat. Smiles and Charles performed their ritual exchange. The duty watch fell out and dispersed to the wheel, the quarterdeck and positions throughout the upper deck. The off-duty watch was now drifting away to disappear into the fo'castle. In the belfry on the fo'castle the ship's bell rang eight times in four groups of two.

Charles came back to me.

"Well, Mr Midshipman Talbot, you may go off duty until midnight tomorrow."

"Good night then, or good morning. I shall remember this watch for the rest of my life—fifty years or more!"

He laughed.

"Say that after you have stood a year or two of them!"

But I was right, not he.

So I went off watch, suddenly overcome with sleepiness at four o'clock in the morning and yawning like Mr Taylor. I opened the door of my hutch and found that the lantern had burned or blown out. But I seemed still to be in conversation with Charles. I got my oilskins and seaboots off somehow in the moonless hutch, tumbled into my bunk, struck some eyebolt or other and cursed it sleepily. Nothing could keep me from falling into a dream-less sleep.

It was many days before I in my ignorance realized what had happened. Charles in his care of me had taken on the burden of the middle watch partly, perhaps, to relieve the other officers, but mainly, I am convinced, to spare me the dark hours of that dreadful cabin! It was just like his pro-vision of dry clothing for me. The extraordinary fellow, where he felt himself esteemed, responded with such gen-erosity, such warm and manly thoughtfulness as I had not experienced since the days of Old Dobbie or even earlier! It was in him, so to say, a pedestrian care which con-trived much out of small things. It was a kind of science or study of domestic donation, trifles set aside, saved, little schemes, manoeuvres, which he would not for the world have known to others but which must at last come to be understood by the caring recipient. It was an odd trait in a fighting sailor, I thought—yet not so strange when you think of the greater part of his career as a ship's hus-band, who is a man either shopkeeper and agent for the "domestic" care of a ship in port, or the ship's officer most responsible for and attending to her internal economy!

So I slept and the moon set and the sun came up, though not in my dark hutch. I was positively shaken awake by Phillips. He would not let me go back to sleep but continued to shake me.

"Go away, man. Let me be."

"Sir! Wake up, sir!"

"What the devil is the matter with you?"

"You got to get up, sir. The captain wants you."

"What for?"

"They're getting married this morning."

A marriage at sea! For sure the idea does at once summon a variety of comments and did so in our ship, I believe. Comments! They had been varied enough at the engagement! But now—Had the reader himself received nothing but the merest intelligence of the fact, his first thought might be "Couldn't they wait?" His next would be the converse, "Oh, so they couldn't wait!" But the whole ship knew much more than the mere fact. They knew that a man (respected *forrard*!) was dying. His reason for marrying could not be one for jesting comment. But aft, opinions on the man I discovered to be neutral or a little on his side. Then again, the lady he was marrying had literally undergone a sea change. Miss Granham, brought up in circumstances which some would consider easy, had, by the death of Canon Granham, been forced to school herself into the behaviour and appearance of a governess, no more. Unexpectedly presented with the prospect of an alliance with a man of even easier circumstances than those of a canon of the Church of England, she had divested herself of both the appearance and the behaviour of a governess as quickly as she could. Or am I so certain where the behaviour is concerned? I believe she was by nature a woman of great dignity, intelligence and—austerity. She had also, as I was beginning to discover, a certain warmth, as unexpected as welcome. Given all this, that she had submitted to the man's astonishing advances wounded me more than I could understand! I believe she had been the first lady to present me with a proper view of the dignity possible to the sex and I was—disappointed. Oh, that young man! However, there could be little about the marriage for rejoicing. It might well call forth those tears which lesser females are ever ready to shed.

I will report what I can of the event. For sure it must be a report like Captain Cook's, though the participants were white people rather than black savages, and some of them were gentlefolk. It was as if the whole ship was determined to exhibit at least a little of human nature in the raw—its innate superstition, its ceremoniousness, its joy when forced by the necessity of procreation to celebrate the animal in man!

Let me be precise. There is rather more here of the woman than the man. Miss Granham was visited early by Mrs East, Mrs Pike and Mrs Brocklebank. I am told that she had had to be persuaded out of her seaman's rig, her slops. The whole female section of our company was determined that she should be properly dressed for the sacrifice! Yet this was make-believe! The man was dying and—though they did not know it—the sacrifice had already—but that is complicated. In any case there was an outbreak of the warm remark, the *risqué*, even the downright salacious, and some drinking to go with it, as is customary on these occasions. Inevitably it was young Mr Tommy Taylor who went far beyond what was proper, even at a wedding. For looking forward to an hypothetical, an impossible honeymoon, he remarked in a voice breathless and split with his usual hyaena laughter—I call it usual, but as the months passed it seemed to me that the boy began to disappear and the "hyaena" become customary—I have lost myself. He remarked, and in the presence of at least one lady, that Miss Granham was about to resemble an admiral's handrope. When rashly asked what the similarity was, he replied that the lady was about to be "wormed, parcelled and served". In sheer disgust I took it on myself to give him a clout over the head which must have made that organ ring and did, I was glad to see, leave him with his eyes crossed for as much as a minute.

The congregation which assembled in the lobby was gallant and pathetic. A procession of emigrants emerged the wrong, the way forbidden to them, up the ladder from the gundeck to the passenger lobby. They mixed, uninvited, with the passengers—Mr Brocklebank wearing a stock of pink material and divested of his coach cloak! The men wore favours, some, I thought, dating back to the "entertainment". The women had made efforts and were neat in costume if nothing more. Naturally enough, I changed into the appropriate costume. Bowles and Oldmeadow had never been out of it. Little Mr Pike was not to be seen. There was much chattering and laughter.

Now the most extraordinary change occurred, as if

"Heaven smiled" on the ceremony! For there came a new noise altogether. The watch on deck was dragging the canvas cover and then the planking off the skylight. The gloom of the lobby was changed so that for a time we were in the same kind of modified daylight as you would find in some ancient village church. I am sure the change caused as many tears as smiles, this reminder of distant places.

Six bells rang in the forenoon watch. The canvas chair was bundled out of Prettiman's cabin. The noise of assembly diminished suddenly. Captain Anderson appeared, glum as ever, if not indeed more so. Benét followed him, carrying under his arm a large brown-covered volume which I supposed rightly to be the ship's log. The captain wore the rather splendid uniform in which he had dined in *Alcyone*. I had a mental picture of Mr Benét (the image of a flag lieutenant) murmuring to him, *"I think, sir, it would be appropriate if you was to wear your number ones."* Well, for sure, Benét was wearing his and meditating, it might be, a polite, poetical tribute to the bride. The groom, of course, remained helplessly in his bed. Captain Anderson went into Prettiman's hutch.

Miss Granham appeared. There was a gasp and a murmur, then silence again. Miss Granham wore white! The dress may have been hers, of course I cannot tell. But the veil which concealed her was one which Mrs Brocklebank had worn to protect her complexion. Of that I am sure, for it had provided a provoking concealment. Behind Miss Granham and from her hutch—how had they managed to cram themselves in?—came Mrs East, Mrs Pike and Mrs Brocklebank. The bride moved the few feet from her hutch to the bridegroom's with a certain stately grace, not diminished by the fact that she kept a cautious hand near the rail. As she passed, the women curtsied or bobbed, the men bowed or knuckled their foreheads. Miss Granham stepped over the threshold and entered her fiancé's cabin. Benét stood outside. I and Oldmeadow pushed our way to the door. Benét was contemplating Miss Granham's back in a kind of trance. I plucked him by the sleeve.

"We are the witnesses. Oblige us by stepping back."

Benét obeyed at last and a murmur rose from the crowd and passed away. Miss Granham was standing by the bunk, level with Prettiman's shoulders, and all at once a simple idea occurred to me—so simple that it seemed no one had thought of it. Prettiman lay with his head to the stern!

Miss Granham put back her veil. It is, I think, unusual for the bride to face the congregation—but then, everything was unusual. Her face was pink—with embarrassment, I suppose. The colour did not look like fard.

I now have to report on a series of shocks which Edmund Talbot experienced. To begin with, after she had put back her veil, the bride shook her head. This set her earrings in motion. They were garnets. I had last seen them ornamenting the ears of Zenobia Brocklebank during that graceless episode when I had had to do with her. I remembered them distinctly, their little chains flying about Zenobia's ears in the extremity of her passion! This was disconcerting; but I have to own, and it may have been the influence of the general air of lawful lubricity, that I found the fact flattering.

Miss Granham carried a bouquet. She did not know what to do with it, for she had no bridesmaids and the only publicly *plausible* recipient was Miss Brocklebank, now declining in her cabin. The bouquet was not made of cloth as were the favours which some of the congregation wore. It consisted of real flowers and greenery! I know that. For in the absence of a bridesmaid, the bride looked round her, then thrust out her arm at me and forced the bunch into my hands! All the world knows what will happen to the lucky girl who gets the bouquet, and there was an exclamation from Oldmeadow, then a howl of laughter from the congregation. At once my face was far redder than Miss Granham's. I clutched the thing and felt the softness and coolness of real leaves and flowers. They were, they must have been, from Captain Anderson's private paradise! Benét must have induced the sacrifice. *"I think, sir, the whole ship would be gratified if you was to honour the lady with a flower or two from your garden!"*

The next and last shock was delivered by the captain to everyone who heard it. He raised his prayer book, cleared his throat and began.

"Man that is born of woman—"

Good God, it was the burial service! Miss Granham, that intelligent lady, went from pink to white. I do not know what I did but the next time I looked at my bouquet it was sadly damaged. If any words followed this awful mistake I never heard them in the shrieks and giggles of hysteria which were followed by a rustle as our Irish contingent crossed themselves over and over again. Benét took a step past me and I had to haul him back. Captain Anderson fumbled with his book, which he had opened so thoughtlessly or which had opened itself at the fatal page, and now he dropped it, picked it up and fumbled again. Even his hands, accustomed to all emergencies and dangers, were trembling. The roots of our nature were exposed and we were afraid.

His voice was firm and furious.

"Dearly beloved—"

The service had been taken flat aback and was some time in returning to an even keel. Mr East, muttering what may have been an apology, pushed in past me and Anderson and placed the bride's hand in his. Benét was trying to get in and I held him back, but he hissed at me:

"I have the ring!"

So the thing was done. Did I detect a faint trace of scorn in the bride's face as she found herself literally being handed over? Perhaps I imagined it. Everyone held their peace as far as possible. No objections having been raised, this spinster and this bachelor were now both of them cleared for the business of the world and might do with each other what they would or could. Anderson neither congratulated the groom nor felicitated the bride. There was a sense, I suppose, in which such an omission was proper, seeing how little joy the two had to expect of the marriage. However, he leaned down over the writing flap and fiddled with documents. He opened the ship's log, signed papers on the opened page, then held the book open over the sick man. Prettiman had a sad job of signing his name upside down. Miss Granham, not according to custom, signed her new name, Letitia Prettiman, firmly and legibly. I signed, Oldmeadow signed. The captain presented her "lines" to the bride rather as if he had been giving a receipt. He grunted at Prettiman, nodded round, and left with the ship's log which I have no doubt he felt had been rendered a little ridiculous by the unusual entry.

We had now to complete our business. I felicitated Mrs Prettiman in a low voice and touched Prettiman's hand. It was cold. Rivulets of perspiration coursed past his closed eyes. When I remembered my great idea to improve his situation I opened my mouth to explain it. But a hearty shove from behind told me that I was in the way of Benét and Oldmeadow crowding forward. I turned resentfully, hoping for a quarrel, though it is difficult to understand why. The congregation were trying to crowd in and I had some difficulty in getting away from the bunk. The people had no knowledge of the proprieties and seemed to desire only to press the dying man's hand. Indeed, the first one tried to kiss it but was prevented by a faint rebuke from him.

111

"No, no, my good fellow! We are all equal!"

I squirmed away. I needed air. I had the crushed bunch of leaves and flowers in my hand. One flower was strangely foreign—what they call an orchid, I think. I got into the open air to throw the thing away but could not. Phillips, my servant, was coming from Prettiman's hutch.

"Phillips. Put these in water. Then leave them in Miss—Mrs Prettiman's cabin."

He opened his mouth, probably to object, but I went past him into my cabin and shut the door. I changed back into my seaman's rig, then sat at the writing flap. I could not think what I was doing there. I leaned my head on it for a while, then reached out for a book, leafed it and put it back. I lay on the bunk, fully dressed, thinking of nothing and doing nothing.

I have just looked at those last two words. How strange they are, how foreign! They might be Chinese or Hindoo—doing nothing, doing nothing. Nothing, nothing, nothing. I laughed aloud. It was a genuine "cachinnation" which sprang of its own accord from my lungs. Charles had assured me that Miss Chumley would not forget me. Miss Granham—Mrs Prettiman—had given me the real omen. She had thrown me her bouquet! I should be the next one to be married!

Nevertheless, as I lay there on my back, slow tears ran from the corners of my eyes and wetted my ears and pillow.

(9)

And then I fell asleep! The reason was the wholly unexpected behaviour of our world. We lived with noise of one
sort or another. There was always the sound of the sea
outside the hull, ship noises, feet on the deck, pipes, somewhere a loud and male voice cursing, squeaks and knocks
from the rigging, groans from timber, sounds at that time
all too frequently of a quarrel from one part of the ship
or another—once, a fight. But what helped me into a deep
sleep was nothing more than silence! Perhaps in our part
of the ship people were exhausted by the wedding, but I
cannot tell that. Charles gave the crew a "make and mend",
keeping the very fewest number of the crew on watch. As
seamen do in these cases, the rest slept, I as well.

What brought me back to the real world was the sound
of Deverel being put in irons! I started up and then realized that this metallic banging came from right forrard in
the eyes of the ship and must be Coombs, the blacksmith,
at his forge! It was the moment! I was fully dressed and I
leapt out of my bunk, pulled on seaboots and hastened into
the waist. The sea was spread out like watered silk, light

113

blue, and a faint haze reduced the sun to a white roundel much like the full moon. There was not a breath of wind. Benét and the captain had found their flat calm! I fetched my lantern from the cabin and lighted it, then turned the flame down. I descended the ladders—past the wardroom and down again to the gun-room. Here for the first time I found it was empty except for the ancient midshipman Martin Davies, who grinned emptily at me from his hammock. I smiled back, since it was impossible not to, and then proceeded to make my way forward. At once I had to turn up the light. It was a dripping, a moist progress, but this time, mercifully steady. Why, even those balletic lanterns in the gun-room had hung still, and now what with my lantern and the flat calm I could have run along the narrow planking between the stacked stores. I saw things previously I had only felt or smelt or heard—a huge pillar which must have been the warping capstan, the dull gleam of twenty-four-pounder cannon, all "tompioned, greased and bowsed down" and beyond them again—for those were but iron barrels—the flat gleam of water and the gravel of our bilges. Two walls, wooden for the most part and irregular, packing cases, boxes, bags, sacks of every size, some seeming pendant above my head—but there is no way of describing that hold, half-seen, partly understood, with a narrow way of planking which led through it along the keelson! Here was a ladder on my right that Mr Jones had lashed in place as an entry to the kind of loft which he had taken over as his sleeping quarters, living

quarters and office! I chose to ignore it and made my way
onward to the vast bulk of the mainmast and the pumps—

"Stand! Who goes there?"

"What the devil?"

"Gawd, it's the Lord Talbot, Mr Talbot, I mean, sir.
What are you doing, sir? You nigh on got a baggynet in
the guts, sir, if you don't mind me saying so, sir."

"I'm making my way forrard—"

There came a thunderous banging from ahead of us. I
had to shout.

"I'm going forrard!"

The corporal had to shout back.

"Orders, sir. Sorry, sir!"

The banging ceased for a moment or two.

"Look—the first lieutenant must be forrard there. You
ask him!"

The petty officer seemed doubtful but the corporal with
him had a little more sense and sent one of his two men
to tell Charles that I had appeared. He came back with
word that I was to wait, at which I was not a little crestfallen but leaned against a convenient support—I do not
know what it was—and waited, looking as nonchalant as
possible. Casually, I blew out my lamp. The little party
ventured no comment.

Forward of us there was light and noise. Some of the
light was daylight, as if hatches and skylights had been
opened in view of the importance of the operation. Some
of the light was smoky and flared redly now and then. I

even saw a spark or two float across what I was able to see of the open space where the work was going on. The work became a steady beating with a hammer on iron as if the ship was being shod. What with the smoky light and the metal noises I was overcome with a sudden return to the world of stables and harness and horses and the heat of a smithy fire! But it passed quickly, for the work took on another sound—a dull thumping as of a maul on wood. Peering into the light, and foolishly holding up my extinguished lantern—it is impossible not to hold a lantern up when you look, if you are carrying one—I could now see some of the structures which had been erected to stop the mast from moving. Those huge ropes which led so stiffly from the mast to eyebolts in the side of the hold were *staying* it. The baulks of timber which spread out at an angle on either side were wedging it. As I watched, the dull thumping stopped suddenly, there was a shout and one of the baulks fell, with a thunderous reverberation. It frightened me and it frightened everyone who heard it, for there rose a sudden clamour round the mast, but it was simply overborne by the captain's famous "roar" which, to tell the truth, I was very glad to hear, for it suggested safety and awareness of what should be done. Presently—with a brighter flaring and more banging on iron then wood—a second baulk came down but was received this time on a soft bed, for it did no more than thump. After that I waited for a long time while the smoky light brightened, then dimmed, then was extinguished.

116

There came the groan and scream of metal on metal. This scream was repeated again and again. Then silence. The light was beginning to die down.

Bang! It was metal contracting, I think. It was followed by the shriek of metal again and then another bang!

There was a sudden clamour which was interrupted by another "roar" from the captain. He was there—I could see him, see his tricorned head! He was down at the foot, the shoe, the heel, tenon, or whatever it was, and once more as the last baulk fell his roar overbore the sound of it.

"Still!"

Bang.

Bang.

Bang!

Silence.

The captain spoke in his normal voice.

"Carry on. Yes, Mr Benét, carry on."

Benét's voice.

"What do you think, Coombs?"

"Lat'un boide a whoile, zur."

Silence again. The wail of contracting metal and a vast grinding and creaking from the mast.

Benét's voice.

"Water. Roundly now!"

A fierce and continuous hissing! Steam was rising in the open space.

There was another pause, seeming interminable as the

117

steam rose and cleared. The mast creaked and groaned.

"All right, lads. Carry on."

One after another the dark shapes of men climbed the ladders. The captain's voice could now be heard. It was loud and *meant* to be heard by all.

"Well, Mr Benét, you may congratulate yourself. I believe you was the originator here. You too, Coombs."

"Thankee, zur."

"I shall enter your names in the log."

"Thank you, sir."

"Mr Summers. Come with me."

I saw their dark shapes ascend the ladder just forward of the foremast. A seaman came peering for me.

"Mr Benét says you may come forrard now, sir."

"Oh, he does, does he?"

I made my way towards the mast, then looked about me. Benét was there. Even in that light I saw he bore such an expression of rapturous triumph as I never had seen on the face of any other human being. I gazed about me with profound curiosity. Evidently the operation had been successful. I could only examine and try to understand the method of it. The huge cylinder of the foremast came down through the deckhead and appeared to enter a square block of wood. Since the mast was a yard in diameter, the size of the wooden block into which it was set may possibly be imagined. I suppose it was something like a six-foot cube. What a tree! I had never seen such a block of wood in my life. This in its turn rested on a member

118

which ran the ship's length above the keel—the keelson. Facing me on the after side of the shoe was a sheet of iron with huge bolts projecting. These then were the bolts of iron which had been made red- or white-hot in the midst of all this *tinder*like wood at the risk of turning the whole ship into a bonfire! On the top surface of the wood the wide crack made by the leverage of the mast was no longer to be seen. It had, if anything, more than closed! Good God, the mere force of cooling iron had crushed the vast block of wood so that the surface had risen everywhere into parallel wrinkles! It was awesome. The words were jerked out of me.

"Good God! Good God!"

The expression on Mr Benét's face had not changed. He was staring at the iron. Only his lips moved.

> *Thy face is veiled, thou mighty form,*
> *The dry the chill the moist the warm,*
> *All modes—all modes—*

His voice died away. He appeared to see me at last and I do not think there had been any pretence about his abstraction. His face became that of a social man.

"Well, Mr Talbot. Do you understand what you see?"

"I suppose there is another plate like this one on the other side of the block—the shoe."

"And the bolts go through both."

"The wood must be on fire within!"

119

He waved a hand dismissively.

"For a little while, no more."

"Do you mean to burn us all before any of our other dangers finish us? Or do you propose that this one should be held in reserve in case our other perils are successfully surmounted?"

He was kind enough to laugh a little.

"Be easy, Mr Talbot. Captain Anderson was under the same misapprehension, but by means of a model Coombs and I were able to convince him. The channels are much larger than the bolts. Air cannot enter. When the air is depleted of its oxygen—its vital air, sir—it will start to cool and there will be no more than a layer of charcoal inside the channels. But do you see the degree of force we have at our disposal?"

"It is frightening."

"There is nothing to be afraid of. I have seldom seen anything so majestically beautiful. The mast was moved upright in a matter of minutes!"

"So we may now use the mast. And the mizzen. Our speed will increase. We shall get there sooner."

He was smiling kindly.

"It is beginning to penetrate."

A testy reply was on the tip of my tongue, for I began to resent his condescension, but at that very moment there came a sharp report from inside the iron or wood which made me flinch.

"What was that?"

"Something taking up. It does not matter."

"Was to be expected, in fact!"

My sarcasm missed its mark.

"The sound was the expenditure of moderate force. *Thy face is veiled, thou mighty form—*"

It was evident that Mr Benét was no longer disposed for conversation. Idly I laid my hand on the iron plate and snatched it away at once.

"The thing must still be on fire inside!"

"No, no. There is ample area. My first line is a tetrameter. How the devil did I come to think it was an iambic pentameter? We are lacking a foot! *Nature, thy face is veiled, thou mighty Form!* I shall have trouble with the rhyme now, because having personified Nature and mentioned 'Form' the whole thing becomes Platonic, which I did not desire."

"Mr Benét, I realize you are in the throes of seamanship, engineering and poetry but should be glad if you would kindly continue our previous conversation. I know that one should not pry into a gentleman's private affairs, but with regard to your time in *Alcyone* when you were acquainted with Miss Chumley—"

But the strange man was rapt again.

"Warm, swarm, corm. They would be an ear-rhyme. Or balm, calm, palm—cockney rhymes unendurably vulgar. The dry the chill the moist the warm—why not the moist the dry the warm the chill—"

It was no use. The ironwork *banged again*, to be echoed dully from above. I set myself to climb the ladders into

121

modified daylight, then out onto the deck where the sun was now completely obscured by clouds and the sea more than ruffled. The forrard part of the waist was crowded. Oldmeadow's soldiers were grouped there by the rail on the larboard side. They had their Brown Besses. Oldmeadow threw an empty bottle as far as he could into the water, whereupon a fellow loosed off with a prodigious production of smoke and noise and made a small fountain of seawater. This drew shrieks of fear and admiration from the young women who were in attendance while the bottle floated very slowly away. So we were moving! I stared upward and saw that the sails on the mainmast were rounded. Fellows were swaying a yard up the foremast. Oldmeadow threw another bottle, there was another explosion and fountain of water as the second bottle followed the other one. I suggested to Oldmeadow then and there that he should attach a string to the bottle and thus be able to make do with the one but he ignored me. Companionship with the common and ignorant soldiery was doing his wits and his manners no good whatever. There were no passengers about. They had evidently decided that the best way to spend that upright and untroubled period was asleep in their bunks.

A little wind breathed on my cheek. I went back to the lobby and looked into the saloon. There was no one at either table—not even little Pike.

"Bates! Where is the first lieutenant usually at this time of day?"

"Couldn't say, sir. He might have got his head down, sir."

I went down to the wardroom.

"Webber. Where is Mr Summers?"

Webber nodded to Charles's cabin and spoke in a whisper.

"In there, sir."

I hurried to the cabin and knocked.

"Charles! It is I!"

There was no reply. But what is a friend? I knocked again, then opened the door. Charles was sitting on the edge of his bunk. His hands on either side grasped the wooden edge. He was staring at or through the opposite bulkhead. His eyes did not blink or turn towards me. His face under the tan of exposure was sallow and drawn.

"Good God! For Heaven's sake! What has happened?"

Now his head did turn, jerkily.

"Charles old fellow!"

His lips quivered. I sat by him quickly and set my hand down on the back of his. A drop of sweat rolled off his brow and fell on my fingers.

"It is I—Edmund!"

His other hand came up and he smeared it across his face, then put it down again.

"Tell me, for God's sake! Are you hurt?"

Still nothing.

"Look, Charles, the news is good! They are setting sails on all three masts!"

Now he spoke.

"Obstruction."

"What obstruction?"

"Obstruction. That's what he said. I am to cease my obstruction."

"Anderson!"

He shook as if with cold. I took my hand from him.

He muttered.

"I can feel her moving. He was lucky, wasn't he? A flat calm for the work and now—the wind again. An extra two knots, Anderson said. He gave me reasons. Coldly."

"What reasons?"

"For his words. Obstruction. I am—I did not know it was possible to be so brought down. The dragrope—but it tore away part of the keel. Who knows? And now—for a knot and a half, for two knots, Benét has stuck red-hot irons through wood and left them there!"

"He says they will no more than coat the inside of the channels with charcoal."

He stared into my eyes.

"You saw the man? You spoke with him?"

"I have—"

"I must not obstruct him, do you understand? A brilliant young officer—and I! Dull, superannuated—"

"He could not say so!"

"In defence of his favourite he would say anything! He will take no action yet but I am to watch my step—" He paused for a moment, then hissed with a fury of which I should never have thought him capable—*"Watch my step!"*

"I swear to you he shall be brought down! I will—I will raise the whole government of the colony against him! I will—"

He drew his breath in sharply, then whispered:

"Hold your tongue. It is mutiny."

"It is justice!"

There was a pause. He put his face in his hands. I could hardly hear what he said for the grief in the sound of it.

"I do not desire justice."

For a while neither of us said anything. Then—

"Charles—I know I am a passenger—but this monstrous—"

He laughed, bitterly.

"Oh yes, you are a passenger, but you may still put yourself in peril! And if it were possible to do what you have just said, do you suppose I should ever be employed again, let alone promoted?"

"Bénet is a kind of meteor, a passing flash. Meteors always fall."

Charles sat up and hugged himself with both arms.

"Do you feel how she moves even in this light air? He will nigh on double our speed. And, mark my words, every knot he adds will double the intake of water!"

"He is writing an Ode to Nature."

"Is he so? Well, tell him Nature never gives something for nothing."

"I will tell him, though the statement will come oddly

from me. I believe he would recognize the source."

A trace of colour had come into Charles's lips.

"Bless you, old fellow—may I still say that?"

"Heavens! Whatever you like."

"You are a true friend. It is like you to come looking for me with what comfort you could when no one else—Well. Forgive me. I have been less than a man."

"You are worth a hundred Benéts—two hundred Andersons!"

"Is that my lantern?"

The question disconcerted me. I followed his eyes, lifted my right hand with the lantern in it.

"No. In fact—"

I did not feel like going on. After a moment or two Charles shrugged.

"Dockyard issue. Well, what does it matter?"

Suddenly he struck one fist into the other palm.

"It was such a humbling, such a shaming rebuke! It was so unjust—for all I did was differ in opinion from my subordinate!"

"Did anyone hear him?"

He shook his head.

"He observed the forms. I am helpless therefore, you see. When we reached the quarterdeck he addressed me formally. 'Oblige me by stepping into my cabin, Mr Summers.' There he faced me. He lowered up at me under his thick eyebrows and projected his jaw at me—"

"I know! I have seen!"

"'Sticks and stones may break my bones but hard words won't hurt me.' A rhyme for children. What he said tore at me like hooks."

"You are better for talking about it. It has been searing for you, I can tell that. But I have sworn to see right done, justice—fair play! You remember?"

"Oh yes! A long way back, in Colley's time."

"Now what is to be done at the moment? I believe you are able to smile!"

"Did you feel that? The wind is increasing. Well, the captain and the officer of the watch—let them manage between them. Only think, Edmund, if this wind had come a couple of hours earlier—I can hardly believe in my own iniquity! I found myself wishing—no, no. The mast is repaired, our speed is increased and I am glad of it!"

"We must all be glad."

"But I tell you, Edmund, with that fire in the shoe—I will have a watch kept there as long as there is a trace of heat left in the iron. Other than that, there is nothing to be done. I must swallow everything and live out the commission—why are we such creatures that a few sentences from an angry man should matter more to me than the prospect of death?"

"At all costs no one must know—"

"What—in this ship? I have never been in one that so echoed and resounded with rumour!"

"The thing must be forgotten."

"The voyage will surely be remembered, for it bids fair

to be the longest in history."

"Well, you, at any rate, must not go down as anything but the lieutenant who by and by was Captain Summers and, after that, a famous rear admiral!"

Charles had coloured deeply.

"That is a dream and I fear must remain so."

"When you saved my reason by providing me with dry clothes—did you know I itch no longer?—I spoke of Glaucus and Diomede. I doubt the story will have come your way any more than the parts of a mast or the niceties of stellar navigation have come mine. Well. There was a battle and in it these two enemies found they were related—"

"So you said. As I told you once, I have no relatives at all and prefer that to being related to Benét or Anderson!"

"Come! That is better. That is humanly bitter. What a turn up for the book it would be if you found you as well as Benét was a frog! But these two warriors I liken to you and me."

"Oh! I am sorry."

"They stopped fighting and exchanged armour for remembrance. The gods took away their wits so that they never noticed that bronze armour was being swopped for gold! I used to take that as no more than story for the sake of story—but do you know, Charles, I now understand it as a profound allegory of friendship! Friends will hand over anything that is needed and think nothing of it!"

"Yes indeed!"

"I *think* your gift of seaman's slops was golden armour! Now here is my bronze! The first ship that returns from Sydney Cove shall carry not just my journal in which you are described with such admiration but a letter to my god-father giving reasons and declaring that you deserve to be made 'post' on the spot!"

The colour came and went in his cheeks.

"I thank you with all my heart. Of course, it is impossible. Luck and promotion have passed me by. *Can* you do so?"

"Exactly as I have said."

"Well—I will try to believe it. I *will* believe it! You see, I am so unused to—what? To privilege—to—"

"To getting your desserts."

He stood up.

"It is like that time when Admiral Gambier had me made midshipman!"

He stretched out his hand to the shelf and touched a book—a prayer book by the look of it.

"I do not think I can face my fellows just yet."

"What will you do? Oh, I see! You wish to, to meditate."

"And you, Edmund—will you stand the middle?"

"Of course, I shall. Why, I have already slept in preparation!"

Suddenly I reeled and fell on the bunk. He laughed.

"We have the wind, you see! This will test his foremast!"

"I think—yes, I think I had better get out into the open."

(10)

I went cautiously out into the wardroom. Webber was pol-
ishing the corner of the long table with unwonted and indeed useless industry, for the wood was much too stained
and hacked to take a polish. I clambered up to the lobby and
was glad to get into the waist and hang on by the mainstays. We were indeed making way. Things must have been
even more propitious while I had been down below with
Charles, for stuns'ls were being struck on the mainmast
in preparation for a further increase of wind. I could see
quite a spread of light before our bow, but astern of us huge
crenellated clouds seemed to be not so much sweeping forward towards us as towering upwards into preposterous
castles of storm. I might have taken another bath but did
not. I kept under shelter but looked out until I saw the first
savage lash of rain beat along the decks and leap back from
it. This was followed in what must have been less than a
minute by hail, so that the duty part of the watch huddled
in what shelter they could get or cowered with arms hiding
their heads. One man I saw had climbed into the belfry and
crouched there laughing at the others. The hail vanished

even more quickly than it had come. It was followed—as if a curtain had been drawn back in some theatrical presentation—by wind, not rain. In only a few minutes the world was darkened and the sea dirty grey. Then, astonishingly, all this was wiped away and we were in wind and sun, bright sunlight, evening, sunset light, a hard, bright yellow sun shorn of its beams and lying down on the horizon like a golden guinea. But this faded as it dropt, thin clouds coming up between us and it, so that staring back along the ship's side at the break of the aftercastle I saw that the sun lay out to the north at an angle as it set. I was aware of thin cloud, high at the zenith and appearing to move forward slowly while the wind was moderate but constant, seeming made whole with a great deal more to come.

The bell rang for the end of the first dog. The ritual completed itself in the wind and newly rocked ship. Mr Smiles and Mr Taylor came down from the quarterdeck.

"Well, Mr Smiles. What have you to say about the weather?"

But apparently Mr Smiles had nothing to say at all. I went, as by habit, to the passenger saloon.

Bowles and Pike were sitting at the long table under the great stern window. Through long custom the central position looking *forrard* had become my own, I cannot tell why. I had sat there at the beginning and it had been so ever after that. Bowles in a somewhat similar way sat at the starboard end of the table and faced along the length. Pike, on the other hand, was a movable object and sat

131

where he could. Just now he was sitting in *my* seat!

"Move up, Mr Pike."

He had his elbows on the table and his chin in his hands. His beaver was on the back of his head. When he heard me he began a kind of shuffle on the bench, his elbows still on the table. His whole body moved unhandily towards Bowles.

"What's the matter with you, Pike—Richard, I mean?"

Bowles answered for him.

"Mr Pike unfortunately indulged too freely last night, Mr Talbot."

"A thick head, eh? Good God, you was not used to drink at all! Well, we have taught you something! Bunk is the best place for a thick head, Richard—"

But Mr Bowles was shaking his.

"What is the matter, Bowles?"

"The moment is not propitious. What do you think of our weather, sir?"

"Mr Smiles, if you are able to believe me, had nothing portentous to say."

Mr Bowles shook his head moodily.

"I did not think I could be so hungry and yet accept the fact! I did not think I could come to terms with a settled state of dread!"

"Like Wheeler."

"I do not envy you your cabin, sir."

"I do not chuse to be separated from my charges by pandering to superstition."

"Insensitivity must be of assistance. What charges?"

"Insensitivity? Allow me to tell you, Mr Bowles—"

The ship heeled suddenly and as suddenly came back again. Mr Pike's beaver fell off the back of his head. He made no attempt to retrieve it.

"What charges, Mr Talbot?"

"That is my affair, Mr Bowles!"

After that we were all three silent. The only movement was made by little Pike. He closed his eyes.

Bates came in, splay-legged against what was now the constant movement of the vessel.

"What do you think of the weather, Bates?"

"It'll be worse before it's better, sir."

He collected the two lanterns and disappeared with them. There was a rattle of rain or spray across the wide window.

"That's what they all say."

"'They', Bowles?"

"Everyone—Cumbershum, Billy Rogers, now Bates."

"So we are in for it."

There was a long pause. Bates came back with the two lanterns. One of them was lighted.

"Which side will you have it, gents?"

Bowles had one elbow on the table. He pointed upwards with a finger of that hand. Bates brought the lighted lantern to the starboard side and hung it up, then took the other and hung it opposite. Our shadows began their merciless movement on the unfestive board. It seemed as if the movement was amplified moment by moment.

"At least the masts—"

"—are firm. Yes, Mr Talbot. It was a brilliant concept and a brilliant piece of execution on the part of a young officer. I believe we passengers should ensure that it does not go unrewarded."

"Let us leave the Navy to look after itself, Mr Bowles."

"Has that always been your opinion, Mr Talbot?"

The ship bounced. Bates reappeared.

"I have to serve the ladies in their cabins, gents. Would you be having your pork and beans in the ordinary way?"

"What do you think, Bates? Bring it here!"

I turned in my seat, shielded my eyes from the lantern and tried to make out the shape of the sea. There was a great deal of white scattered over it. None of us had anything to say.

Bates came back with plates of pork and beans. Pike staggered up, went reeling and fell on the bench which was set aft of the smaller table. He put his elbows on it and sank back into the position he had previously endured. I examined my portion with disfavour.

"This is confoundedly small, Bates!"

Bates did a little dancing step which maintained him upright in the same place.

"Ah, but then, sir, it's very hard, sir, and will take you twice as long as the same quantity would at home, sir."

"Go to the devil!"

"Aye aye, sir. What is it, Mr Bowles?"

"You had better take the pork away again, Bates. I am not equal to it."

"Beg pardon, Mr Bowles, but you better, sir. It's what we got, sir, and so long as you can keep it down, you better."

"Brandy for me, Bates."

"The brandy is all right, sir. We have plenty of brandy. The ale is gone though and we have to make do with the small beer, sir. Would you want the brandy to improve the water, Mr Talbot?"

"Can anything?"

"Mr Cumbershum uses the brandy to improve the small beer, sir."

"I'll try that. Good God! This pig must have been made of iron!"

Bates, to my astonishment, ran backwards! At the end of his run, being now a little higher than those of us seated at table, he ran forward again. Bowles clapped his hands over his mouth, stood up, then sat down again with a thump.

"Are you all right, Bowles?"

Bowles snarled.

"What a damned silly thing to say!"

He stood up again and staggered away. Bates opened the door for him.

"I think, Bates—"

I too stood up, then worked my way carefully to the door. I managed to get to my cabin without vomiting but then changed my mind and staggered to the entry to the waist. I held on to the mainstays—I call them mainstays and sometimes I call them the chains, both terms being inaccurate though not contradictory. I never bothered to understand the complexity of that part of the rigging except to say that it held the mainmast up and to some extent could be adjusted to circumstances. I used to hold on to anything available. This time it was a huge wooden thing with a hole in it, called a *deadeye*, I think—or perhaps not. I hung there and saw a dim horizon ahead of us tilting now this way, now that. The wind had increased but not to any great extent. It had now been increasing for hours but slowly: and I began to feel in this inexorable approach the reason for the moody and apprehensive answer to that question we passengers were asking.

It'll be worse before it is better.

Once again it is a matter of Tarpaulin, that economical and expressive language! A man may say, "In for a bit of a blow!" or "It'll make her bounce a bit!" But in the foreboding phrase there is an admission of ignorance as though these salted creatures are admitting that the sea can always do more than you expect and is in train to do it.

I turned round, and squinted aft past the break of the fo'castle on the larboard side. What was to come lay there, over that already invisible horizon. The wind was steady as the flow of time itself and as inexorable. Suddenly I felt a great weariness. It was not hunger, not seasickness. It was a dreary awareness of our peril and the greater test which our crazy old vessel was about to face. I desired nothing so much as oblivion, and there was only one place to go. I reeled back, tottered *down* the lobby and fell into my bunk.

I woke with my nausea gone, but stayed where I was, for the movement was much increased. At last I gathered myself together, went to the passenger saloon and crammed down a meagre offering. I was alone. I did not venture into the waist, for I could see the water running on the deck. At a few minutes to midnight when I made my way up to the quarterdeck I had recovered from my threatened nausea. I suppose the very few hours of motionlessness or comparative motionlessness, if such a thing can be, had reminded my limbs too much of the land and they had to readjust to the melancholy facts of our situation. The night was not dark, for although the moon was hidden the clouds were thin enough for that luminary to shed her light dimly everywhere. This was not a white night such as had preceded it but a light night! That solid wind blowing endlessly from the west had increased in power and the successive waves were outlined at their crests with foam. Charles was before me and I stood aside while the little ritual of the changed watch was performed. When we were settled Charles hunched himself in the shadow of the poop. I went and leaned against the ladder up to the poop by him.

"Are you feeling more the thing?"

For a time he made no answer. He was looking in the direction of the bows, but I do not think he saw the ship at all.

"Be a good fellow, Edmund."

"Surely! But how?"

"Leave the subject alone. Entirely alone. It is painful to me and dangerous to us both."

"But how can I—"

"Leave it alone!"

"Oh, all right. If you wish."

The ladder was convenient to my feet. I went up slowly to the poop. That diffused brightness now lit our cloud of sails on all three masts. There was no doubt that our old ship was doing her best to get us to Sydney Cove. There was a wave thrown out from her bow and another from about level with her mizzen. Her wake was visible, smoothed and swirling water which blunted the top of each wave as it reached us. Below me Charles moved out from shelter and went to the forrard rail of the quarter-deck. He stood there, his hands driven deep into the great pockets of his tarpaulin, his legs wide apart. Evidently this middle watch was to differ from the one before in more than weather. It seemed to me that Charles needed cheering up.

"How fast is this, Charles?"

He had not heard me approach, for he started at the sound of my voice.

"I do not know. Seven knots. Perhaps seven and a half."

"About one hundred and eighty land miles in the twenty-four hours. Are we taking in more water?"

"The well fills in an hour. Nature is hurrying us along

and presenting us with a bill for her assistance."

"Should we not reduce sail then?"

"Are you not hungry like everyone else?"

"I see. Of course. What a devil of a fix to be in."

"You have seen nothing yet, Edmund. There is something at the back of this wind."

"How can you tell?"

"I mean a matter of scale. The time the wind is taking to increase—and the quality of the wind."

"Now you are really worrying me."

I said that to give him a chance of forgetting his own troubles in cheering me up. But I was not successful. Still looking away from me at bows which as far as I could see stood in no need of his attention, he nodded merely. It was uncommonly like what Mr Benét would call a *"congé"*. I went to the traverse board and examined the figures written there. Eight knots, seven and a half, eight and a half, seven and a half. Below decks they would be pumping, not on the watch but on the hour. As if reminded by my thought, the personnel of the quarterdeck performed the ritual of casting the log. Eight knots. The quartermaster reported his findings to me! I solemnly repeated the figure to Charles who must in fact have heard it as plainly as I did.

"Make it so, Mr Talbot."

"Aye aye, sir."

On the fo'castle the ship's bell rang out twice and once!

"Charles! He has it wrong! It should be one bell!"

139

"For Heaven's sake, man—have you never heard of 'easting'? We gain an hour for every fifteen degrees of longitude we make to the east. About once a week we miss out one bell in the middle but start the watch off at three bells instead."

"I suppose the people there in the fo'castle think they lose a piece of their life, just as when the Julian calendar was replaced by the modern one."

"I am not interested in what they think. Let them do their duty and think what they like!"

"Mr Summers! Charles! This is not like you! Oh, come! Do not disappoint me, old fellow! I think of you as the personification of equanimity!"

For a while we were both silent. Then he heaved himself away from the rail and stood upright.

"The ironwork is still hot."

It was my turn to fall silent, for it was plain that he could not get his mind away from the foremast and Benét. I did not know what to do and took to wandering round the quarterdeck aimlessly to pass the time. On the hour the log was cast again and everything repeated itself except that the ship was now making slightly more, the man said, than eight knots, but not enough to count! I chalked in eight knots and leaned against the poop ladder again. This watch was three hours long instead of four. Charles spent most of it without speaking and without even looking at me. So vexed and anxious was I at this that when we were coming off watch and descending from the quarterdeck I taxed him with it.

"Silence I can endure, Charles. But an averted face—what have I done?"

He paused at the top of the ladder down to the wardroom, face still averted.

"You have done nothing. I have been shamed, that is all."

He went away, down, heavily. As heavily as he, I made my way to my bunk, but sorrow could not keep me awake.

It was nearly midday when there came a tap at my door and I woke, to find myself in my bunk and fully dressed, oilskins and all! I had but put my head on the pillow!

"Come in!"

It was Charles—but a happier man, with a cheerful morning face.

"Rebuke me if you choose, Edmund! But I have been round the ship staring people in the face, looking them in the eye. Anderson, Cumbershum, even Benét! But you are only half awake! Come! I have something to show you."

I was about to express my surprise when we were interrupted by a terrible cry from Prettiman. Even Charles, inured as he must be to other men's suffering, winced as he heard it.

"Let us get on deck. Come, Edmund! You will need care. The weather has worsened, as I thought."

He led the way to the waist, where water foamed about my knees, then sank away.

"Good God!"

"Up with you!"

Now at last I did begin to understand about the Southern Ocean. We had no more than a scrap of sail set. Our roll seemed slower. I laboured up the stairs against the wind, and when we came into the open space of the quarterdeck I experienced what I should not have thought possible. The wind, which on other occasions I had thought severe enough in seeking to blow my mouth open, now did the same to my eyes, and no matter how I screwed up the lids the wind forced them open, a crack, through which I could see nothing but blurred light. I got into the lee of the poop and learned how to make a shade of my hands, which enabled me to see more or less clearly.

"Up on the poop. Are you man enough?"

He laboured up the stairs with me behind him. Now this was the open air. The very lanterns on their painted ironwork vibrated. We crept round the rail and then with eyes blasted open turned sideways and squinted for glimpses but could see nothing. It was not surprising. There seemed nothing to distinguish wind from water, spray from foam, cloud from light, small shot from rain! I bent my head and examined my body. I had a shadow. But this was not the absence or diminution of light, it was the absence of mist, of rain, of spray. Charles had the same shadow; and now as I looked sideways across the wind I saw that every element in the rail, the turned uprights, the rail itself, had the same shadow.

"Why are we here? There is nothing to see! Is not the middle enough!"

He did not turn nor reply but made a dismissive and perhaps irritable gesture. The seamen were dragging and lifting those same curious, wobbling sacks that had looked so much like bodies in the semi-darkness. Now I saw that they were full of liquid and attached to ropes. Charles had a large sailmaker's needle in his hand which he stabbed into the bags several times.

"Over with them!"

The men toppled the bags over the rail and into the sea. A wave rose up, a whole plateau of moving water. A secondary wave appeared on its surface, was torn off by the droning wind and hurled at us like a storm of shot.

"Belay!"

I turned and looked forward in time to see the bows slide back down from the plateau which had outsped us. I felt our stern rise. I turned to see other plateaux following us, the one partly hiding the next, a monstrous procession marching endlessly round the world and creating a place which surely was not for men!

"What have you done?"

"Look."

I followed his pointing finger. A plateau had heaved up slowly with every complication of tormented water on its surface as shot to strike us. Then, at the very farthest edge of what was visible, I saw a gleam of silver. It was spreading, drawing out into a kind of path astern of us not unlike that path of light which we see in water beneath the moon or sun. But this was very mild silver, glossy and unblemished. It was definite as a lane in chalk country. It shone beneath the fits and whirls of spray, the waves on waves which flew into the air like nightmare birds.

"Oil!"

A place for no man: for sea gods perhaps; for that great and ultimate power which surely must support the visible universe and before which men can do no more than mouth the life-defining and controlling words of the experience of living.

"Oil on troubled waters."

(11)

So it was. No matter how the waves pursued us and threatened to overwhelm us, when they reached that streak of silver it subdued them more thoroughly than a great rock or—if it were possible—some breakwater or quay. It is a marvel in the physical world how a vegetable oil, expressed from the tenderest and most ephemeral of Nature's inventions, can yet subdue the rage of a tempest as Orpheus put Hades to sleep! I am aware that the fact is thought to be a commonplace—but only by those whose lives have not been saved by this thinnest and most fragile of threads! The silver pathway reached now to within fifty yards of our stern and in that unoiled fifty yards of water the malicious sea had no time to organize its fury. We still rose up and sank. Still the water welled over our flanks and made a bath of the waist where the black lifelines twitched and vibrated above it, but there was a saving smoothness in our motion!

"Charles! I would not have believed it!"

He beckoned me down from the poop to the quarter-deck. I came down and he drew me aside into the lee of the bulkhead.

145

"I wanted you to see that I too have my ideas."

"I never doubted that!"

He laughed excitedly.

"Normally we should heave to and spill oil over the bows, you see? Then the ship would be more or less stationary and we should make a wide area of oil to windward, but now we cannot afford the time. We must get on. I have to tell you that our supply of vegetable oil is limited; but so long as it lasts we may run before a following sea in safety—comparative safety."

"As long as the oil lasts."

"Just so."

"And the pumping?"

"Pumping will increase, naturally. But not too much."

He nodded, laboured away across the quarterdeck, spoke to the quartermaster, then, pushed by the wind, made a rapid and irregular descent to the waist and disappeared from view. I followed in my turn, ignoring the officer of the watch for once in a rare obedience to the captain's standing orders! I entered the passenger saloon and yelled for Bates who brought me beans and a small portion of pork.

"Brandy too, Bates."

He went off to get a drink and I sat, guarding my food but slewed so that I could see our oil, our silver snail trail. Far off I heard again that terrible cry from the dying Prettiman. He should have had the paregoric as a wedding present I thought. We should all have it. Oil or not, the best thing for us all would be unconsciousness. I sat for hours, numbed by the sea, until at last darkness drove me to my bunk. It now seemed as if the very regularity of our motion, immense as it was, gave us time to brood! I cannot say I slept. I was conscious that the ship still swum, and that we were alive. That was all. I believe lack of sleep came near to unsettling my wits.

Of the middle watch that night I remember little, although for me it was short. When the call came I huddled my way through solid wind to the quarterdeck and crouched in the lee of the poop. I do remember the light, for it was a storm light and not to be described—which is one reason why people who have never seen it do not believe in it. It seemed to inhere in the very atmosphere!

Presently Charles worked his way to me and crouched down.

"Get back to your cabin, Edmund. You can do no good here."

"When will it stop?"

"How can I tell? But you must go down. Cumbershum has fallen."

"Oh, that is terrible! If even Cumbershum—"

"He is not hurt. I mean if a man so used to this sort of thing—you see? Come. I will go with you to the break of the quarterdeck. Your best place is in your bunk. Stay there!"

This conversation was not in the heroic vein. I can only plead that if I dared the deck at all during that twenty-four hours it was more than any other passenger did. I doubt that they were more frightened than I. Possibly they simply had more sense. In the passenger saloon Bates told me that the emigrants and the off-duty watch had received permission from Charles to keep their hammocks slung and turn into them. I cannot think what the state of that overcrowded deck was, for occasional seas seemed to sweep the waist and run down off the fo'castle like a waterfall. We rolled a little but other than that the ship seemed to lift up and down without pitching at all, as if she were held in a narrow channel which denied her any other movement.

I got to my cabin at length, fell on my bunk and lay there exhausted, though I had done nothing. I even slept at last and woke in a grey morning light while the wind still droned. How that waking to a merciless noise and movement clutched at my poor heart! What must it have done to the children? Or could their parents and friends persuade them that all was well? Oh no! The pallid face, the quivering mouth had a plainer language than mere words. The voice which attempts to whisper, then finds itself suddenly and unexpectedly loud, the flashes of anger, the tears, the hysteria—no, I do not think the children were unaware, poor things!

It was the afternoon, with no change in our situation, before I pulled myself together sufficiently to get out of my bunk. The basest necessity drove me: after which, oilskins and all, I made my way to the saloon. Mr Bowles was there, sitting under the window and looking at noth-

148

ing. I sat near him and looked at nothing too, but there was a touch of comradely suffering about this nothing. After a long time he spoke.

"Pumping."

"Yes."

"Soon they will need us too."

"Yes."

"Frankly—"

There was another long silence. Then Bowles cleared his throat and spoke again.

"Frankly I ask myself whether I should give up hope, crawl away and huddle into my bunk—"

"I have done so. It is no help."

The door of the saloon burst open. Oldmeadow, the young Army officer, reeled in and flung himself on the bench facing us. He was breathing in gasps. His face was smeared with dirt.

"I suppose—you expect the ship to be run for your convenience."

"Is that intended as an insult?"

"How like you, Talbot! Talk when you have hands like these!"

He spread them before us. The palms were blistered and bloody.

"Pumping did that. He took my men without so much as a by-your-leave! 'Your men must pump,' he said."

"Mr Summers!"

"Your crony, Lieutenant bloody Summers—"

"Take that word back!"

"Gentlemen! Gentlemen!"

"I'm tired of you, Oldmeadow! You'll answer me for this!"

"Do you think I'm going to shoot you, Talbot, just to save the sea trouble? I said to Summers, 'Why can't you take the passengers, Bowles, Pike, Talbot, Weekes, Brocklebank?' Even that sodden old wreck would last a minute or two. I am—"

Oldmeadow collapsed over the table. Bowles got up and laboured round to him. Oldmeadow snarled:

"Let me be, curse you!"

He hauled himself upright and staggered away to his hutch. Bowles made his way uphill, then downhill, to his seat and fell into it as the ship came up and hit him. So we sat, the two of us, saying nothing.

Late that afternoon I left Bowles there and went to the necessity and sat by the humming rope which helped to drag our bags of oil. For all the snail-trail the place seemed as much under the sea as on it. When I came back to the saloon through a wash of seawater Bowles had gone. I had scarce reached my seat when the door opened and Pike came in. He had little enough to recommend him to the society of other men but there was no doubt about it—his dwarfishness was a positive help in preserving him from injury. Now he came skating or perhaps levitating across the uneasy deck and landed on the bench opposite me like a bird on a twig. He was pale but seemed sober.

"Good afternoon, Edmund. This is a fearful storm."

"It will blow itself out, Mr Pike."

"You were going to call me Richard, Edmund."

"Oh, God. Bowles, Oldmeadow—and now you! Richard then."

"It sounds cosier, Edmund, do you not find?"

"No, I do not."

"Friendlier like."

"Oh, for—how is your family—Richard?"

"Mrs Pike—you may have heard, Edmund, we have had words. It happens in every family, Edmund, between married people—"

"I doubt it."

"Well, you are not married, are you?"

"What the devil do you mean by that?"

"Married people understand. Since Mr and Mrs East took to helping Mrs Pike, our little girls have been better, there is no doubt about that."

"It is time we had some good news."

"Oh yes. Do you know, I am convinced that weeks ago when the dragrope pulled a piece off the keel—"

"You sound like a professional seaman, Mr Pike."

"—I was convinced that they were dying. But since we adopted Mr Benét's idea they have improved immensely."

"Another of Mr Benét's ideas?"

"He said they were getting weaker because of seasickness and the continual motion. He said that Nelson was the same."

"Oh no!"

"He said that Nelson had a cot rigged up for him so that it swung freely while the ship moved about it. He said—"

I was standing on my feet and fell sideways.

"But that was *my* idea!"

"He said that if we rigged hammocks for them the motion would be easier and they would think it a game—"

"But that was exactly *my* idea!"

"It doesn't matter whose idea it was, Edmund. It worked and they have been getting better ever since."

"I went there. I went to the cabin. I knocked and opened the door. Miss Granham was there. She looked at me as I opened my mouth to tell her this same idea but before I could get a word out, she—shut me up! Those stony eyes!—'Do not say anything, Mr Talbot. Just go!'"

"Like I say, Edmund, it doesn't matter whose idea it was, does it? They're better, you see."

"I will strangle that woman!"

"Who, Edmund?"

"Just because he has yellow hair and a face like a girl's—God damn and blast my soul to eternal bloody perdition!"

"Edmund! Edmund!"

I sat down with a thump. I was hot inside my oilskins and jarred from the seat. I cursed and tore my oilskins open.

"She has set out deliberately to put me down from the very first moment we met!"

"Why are you angry? They are better!"

"I am glad, Pike—"

"Richard."

"Richard then. I am very glad. Your little girls are better and that is all that matters. I will—"

"Mrs East is very helpful. She sings to them and teaches them songs. I do not think Phoebe is very musical but Arabella sings like a lark. I have quite a good voice, you know."

"I suppose so."

"You are talking very peculiar, Edmund. Have you been drinking?"

I suppose he went on talking. I did not notice. He was an unnoticeable little man. When I came to myself I was alone.

"Bates! Where the devil is my brandy?"

"Here, sir. I got it from Webber, sir. We got to go easy with it."

"Bring me some more."

"Sir?"

I held out the empty glass and he took it away.

This was the beginning of it all. The period is one of which I am still ashamed and shall always be so, I think. Rage fed on rage. It was Mrs Prettiman's fault, of course—but he, Benét, with his plain theft of my idea for helping the little girls—she had taken from him, accepted from him what she would not accept from me. *Say nothing, Mr Talbot. Just go away.* The two of them colluded—

There came a point where I found myself standing in the dim lobby with seawater cornering in diagonals and triangles which consumed themselves against the doors and bulkheads. I had some idea of confronting them—but where was Benét? I went looking for him, therefore, unhandily out into the open where the black lifelines shook above water and under it; and there, as Fate willed it, came the man himself, out from the fo'castle where he had been about some employment with or for his ironwork perhaps! He seemed not to see me but swept off his hat, shook out his yellow hair in apparent joy at release from the stench of below decks—and, just as I was about to accost him, dashed past me as if I did not exist! I followed him at once into the lobby. Benét was gravely examining the captain's standing orders as he yielded to the motion of the ship while seawater washed over his boots.

"Are the captain's standing orders not familiar to you, Mr Benét? You had best be about your business—stealing ideas, pulling pieces off the ship or sticking a mast through the ship's bottom!"

Mr Benét "looked down his nose at me". He was able to do this despite my height, since I was hanging on to the rail outside my cabin.

"A hole or two in a ship's bottom is of no consequence, Talbot. Pull out the bung in a ship's boat, stick your knife blade through and, provided the boat is making enough way, all the bilgewater will run out."

"Where did you steal that idea?"

"I do not steal ideas!"

"I am not convinced of that."

"Your convictions are irrelevant."

"The little girls were in peril. We are all in peril, you fool!"

"I am not a fool! Leave my name alone, sir!"

"I say you are!"

"That I will not allow! You will answer to me for that!"

"Listen, Benét!"

It was at this point that as far as I was concerned the whole conversation became incoherent. I do not mean unintelligible, for each separate remark or sentence made clear sense. But they added up to confusion. Mr Benét appeared to be giving me his family history with increasing acerbity while I accused him of dishonesty. He replied that I was perfidious *like all my race*! I replied with a threat of violence and made it the precise suggestion of pistolling a young gentleman of French extraction. This he countered with a brief description—

"Ah, the English! When one first meets them one dislikes them—but when one gets to know them, dislike turns to genuine loathing!"

The door of Prettiman's cabin opened and Mrs Prettiman looked out. She had changed back into slops. She saw who were standing outside and quickly disappeared again. Mrs Prettiman's ample hair was wholly undone. There had been little of her visible but her face and the hair. In the silence between Benét and me that followed her

appearance and swift disappearance we heard Mr Prettiman cry out. But the silence cleared our confusion and
deepened the quarrel.

Briefly then, Bénét and I had more words outside the
door. I taxed him plainly with stealing my idea for the
treatment of Pike's little girls—hammocks, à la Nelson.
He denied it, saying that he had arrived at the same conclusion as I but independently. He was more inclined to
believe that I had obtained the idea from him than the
other way about! We reached a foolish state of pushing
and shoving, during which I claimed to know how to help
Mr Prettiman; at which point I think he claimed the same
knowledge and had come to the lobby with that in view.
The brandy had much heated me. Perhaps I misunderstood him. At this point, Mrs Prettiman, her hair now
decently concealed, appeared at the door and rebuked us
in a way which would have sent us off had we not been
mad. Talking and doing at the same time, quarrelling and
thrusting, we entered the cabin. We told the man and
woman what we intended, but both talking at once. Prettiman shouted:

"Anything, anything to stop the agony! Yes! Turn me if
you will!"

Bénét got his shoulders up, Mrs Prettiman expostu-
lating. His legs were over the edge of the bunk and he
was trying not to cry out. I got an arm under his swollen
waist—the skin was disgusting to the touch, hard as a
board and burning as a dinner plate. Bénét thrust me,

156

shouting something, and I fell on poor Prettiman's legs. Had the edge of the bunk not held him I should have pulled him to the deck. Before my eyes the man's face drained of blood, went paper white. He fainted. Benét and I, now crestfallen and ashamed, got the helpless body round, replaced the pillows, exercised the most delicate care in the adjustment of the bedclothes—Mrs Prettiman spoke in her stony, governess's voice.

"You have killed him."

Eyes really do flash. I saw them do so.

(12)

I was the first to leave the cabin. I stumbled out, not daring
to confront those eyes or what words she might speak to
me. As I left I did not see her face but only Benét's, appalled,
white and anxious. I got to my cabin and climbed into my
bunk as if it were a hole I could curl up in. I believe I had
my hands over my ears. *You have killed him.* It is useless to
try to describe the anguish I felt. During the voyage I had
received a few shocks and found out a few things about myself which I did not much like. But this new event was like
falling into the darkness of a measureless pit. The fact is
that, in the end, somewhere in the darkness, I found myself articulating spontaneous prayers which I knew as they
burst from my lips were useless, for they were made to
a God in whom I did not believe. It was thus I suppose
that gods were invented, for I found myself praying for a
miracle—*Let it not have happened!* I do not think anything
should be made of these "prayers" unless subjecting them
to ridicule should be thought the adequate response. There
was little consideration for Prettiman in them, some for
Mrs Prettiman, widowed even earlier than she had expect-

ed; but in gross those "prayers" were for Edmund Talbot! He even went so far as to glance at the law as it applies to such concepts as murder, manslaughter, bodily harm and *intent*! Only slowly as the droning wind sounded an ever lower note did I see that legally none of these applied and the deepest of penalties I should suffer would be the disapproval of the passengers and officers and the implacable dislike, the vicious, female enmity of Mrs Prettiman! Let this be a full account of my folly—I even saw myself, after the man's death, offering my hand, the ultimate sacrifice of all I held dear, to the lady! But even in my despair that would not fadge. She would be a widow of substance and could pick and choose where she would and her choice would not be Edmund Talbot. It might—and with a flash of positive insight I felt myself assured that it would be—Benét! She would buy Benét with his yellow hair!

It was evening when I dared to venture forth from my cabin. I stole into the empty saloon and went to look for Bates, found him and asked for water in a whisper. On the way back, having drunk, I paused furtively outside Prettiman's cabin but heard nothing. I had heard nothing from him, no scream nor moan since the fatal occasion. I went to my cabin and sat in my canvas chair. Truly, I did not wish to hurt the lady. However much I might disapprove of her morals I still did not wish her to suffer. Indeed, I told myself that those who live in glass houses should not throw stones, but this is only an indication of the confusion of thought and feeling in which I found myself. If I had picked "the odd flower by the wayside" it was no more than might be expected of a young fellow, whereas Mrs Prettiman—oh, how different that was!

Late that evening, towards eleven o'clock, I dared once more to venture out. There was still no sound from Prettiman's cabin. I tapped very gently but Mrs Prettiman did not come to the door nor did Prettiman answer. I went to the saloon, thinking I might get a drink which would in its turn make me able to face a meal, for I knew that I had to eat, however I felt and whatever happened. I opened the door of the saloon and stood, unable to move. Mrs Prettiman sat in my accustomed place at the great stern window. Bates was taking a plate and a knife and fork from her. He glanced at me as he turned but said nothing. Neither did I.

"Come in, Mr Talbot."

Bates shut the door behind me. I advanced carefully to the nearer table and sat on the bench facing her. Of the two lanterns which swung in time from the deckhead only one was lighted on the larboard side. It lit the left side of her face. She waited.

"I am desperately sorry, ma'am."

She was silent still.

"Ma'am—what can I say?"

She was looking at me and still saying nothing.

"For God's sake, ma'am! Is he—has he—"

She was motionless as a judge.

"He is breathing."

"Oh, thank God!"

"He is still unconscious. The pulse is hardly to be felt."

Now it was my turn to be silent, imagining the heart fainting in its work, the chest hardly able to rise to take in stale, shipboard air. Mrs Prettiman put her small hands together on the table before her. It was a posture of judgement rather than prayer.

"Mrs East is with him. I shall return now. Mr East has taken the news through the ship."

"The news, ma'am?"

"Mr Prettiman is dying."

I believe I moaned or groaned. No words.

Mrs Prettiman spoke again. But her voice had altered. There was in it the vibration of extreme and hardly controlled anger.

"You do not know, do you? You never have, have you? This voyage, Mr Talbot, will be famous in history—not for you, nor for any of them, but for him. You thought it was a comedy, Mr Talbot. It is a tragedy—oh, not for you!—but for the world, for this new world which we are approaching and hope to reach. Your concerns will be forgotten and vanish as the wake of a ship vanishes. I saw you come aboard with your privileges about you like a cloud of, of pinchbeck glory! Now you have trodden with your clumsy feet into a place which you do not understand and where you are not welcome. He will regard you indifferently, not as a man but as an agent of his death, as it might

161

be a spar fallen from the mast. He will be above forgiving you. But I am not above it, sir, and I will never, never forgive you!"

She stood up, swaying. I scrabbled round to stand but she stopped me with a gesture.

"Do not insult me by standing in my presence. Once, I remember, when the movement was too much for my weak limbs, you assisted me to my cabin. Do not stand up, Mr Talbot. Above all, do not touch me!"

This last was said with a positive venom which made my hair lift. She went away quickly. I heard the door open and close but did not look round. I sat huddled at the table—not even my usual one—crushed by humiliation and grief. All the things I might have said, the excuses, the pleas, even perhaps the bravado of carelessness, had fallen round my "clumsy feet".

I cannot tell how long it was before I felt a touch on my shoulder and a familiar voice in my ear.

"Here you are, sir. Brandy, sir. You need it."

The man's sympathy was too much for me. Hot tears fell on the table between my hands.

"Thank you, Bates—thank you—"

"Now don't you take on so, sir. She's a right terror, isn't she—I wouldn't like to be a nipper when she was around!"

That made me laugh, though I choked on it.

"Nor I, Bates. But she made me feel like a nipper, I can tell you!"

Bates answered me in tones of dark dislike.

"That's ladies for you, sir. Women is different. You can hit a woman if she gives you too much lip."

"You sound as if you know all about it."

"Married, sir."

"Thank you, Bates. You can go now."

Once more I was alone and cradling my glass. It seemed to me that the motion was if anything a little more noticeable but I did not care. I can honestly say it was a point at which I was indifferent to whether we sank or not.

Somewhere a bosun's mate was piping a call. It was my watch to muster, time for me to stand the middle with Charles in the islanding darkness. I took the glass to the shelf and put it in an appropriate hole, then went to the lobby. There were people about but not the duty watch. Four emigrants—three women and a man—were waiting outside Prettiman's cabin. I saw what it was. They had come, so soon after greeting him as a bridegroom, to say farewell to a dying man! It was too much. I felt my way into the waist, then burrowed up into the wind. There were others doing the same thing, Charles among them. He took over on the quarterdeck from Cumbershum. I stood against the bulkhead under the poop. Presently Charles came and leaned against it by me.

"We have a very slight decrease in the wind. It will lessen gradually, I think. But it may take a long time."

He heaved himself away from the bulkhead, went to the side of the ship and stared back at our wake. There was a little less storm light. He came back again.

"Our oil is holding up. Indeed, I think at this moment we hardly need it. But I daresay if we got the bags in, the wind would get up and we should have to put them out again. It is vexing. The great thing, other than keeping the crests of waves down, is to make sure the oil does not come aboard. That's why I insisted on this elaborate way of hanging the bags of oil under the stern rather than over the bow. If we had hung them over the bow every time we shipped green water—and even white, come to that—we should have left a film of oil on the deck. Imagine in the weather we have had trying to keep your footing with oil to tread on!"

He was silent for a while, went to the other side of the ship, looked aft and forrard, then came back again.

"At least we are making famous way for a ship under bare poles. Nigh on five knots! I should be happy with that—but you know all this as well as I do. Well, let us be cheerful until something happens."

The bosun's mate approached.

"A message from Mr Cumbershum, sir. There's a lot of movement on the gundeck, sir. It's people trying to get aft to see Mr Prettiman and they can't hardly do it for the hammocks which is slung. Mr Cumbershum requests to forbid the waist to all but the duty watch in case these people take it into their heads to come that way, sir."

The man stopped talking and blew out his breath.

"You got that very well, bosun!"

"Yes, sir. Thank you, sir."

"Tell Mr Cumbershum I agree. We don't want any more men topsides than is necessary in this weather."

"Women too, sir."

"Even more so. Carry on."

The man hurried away with the message. For a while the waist foamed white and the safety lines were visible, blackly stretched along it.

"You are silent, Edmund."

I swallowed but did not speak.

"Come, Edmund. What is it?"

"I have killed Prettiman."

Charles said nothing for a while. He worked his way forward, stared into the binnacle, went to the side and stared back at our glistening wake, then came back to stand by me.

"You are talking of the quarrel between you and Benét."

"There is death in my hands. I kill people without knowing it."

"That is too much like the theatre."

"Colley, Wheeler and now the third—Prettiman."

"You have killed no one to my knowledge. If you had really killed someone the way a seaman does, you would not talk about it."

"Oh, God."

"Come. Do you know he is dead?"

"He is unconscious. His pulse and breathing are weak. The people are crowding to see him. She—"

"Were you drunk? Or 'disguised', as you call it?"

"I had had a couple of glasses of brandy. Nothing out of the way. I was turning him end for end—"

To my astonishment Charles burst out laughing. He quickly controlled himself.

"I beg your pardon, old fellow, but really, 'end for end'! Your grasp of the language of the sea is far firmer than a sailor's! Now be a little easier. You have killed no one and must not make a tragedy."

"They—the emigrants and, I think, the seamen—are flocking to bid him farewell."

"They are just as previous as you are. As far as my information goes you were trying to help—"

"How did you know that?"

"Good Heavens, do you suppose the news of your quarrel and its outcome were not immediately known throughout the ship? At least it took their minds off our situation."

"I fell on him."

"You do really find it difficult to know where your extremities are, old fellow. I daresay you will learn to control them when you are—older."

"How long will it be?"

"Before what?"

"Before he dies."

"I am moved by your faith in me, Edmund. We do not know he is going to die. The body is mysterious. Would it make you easier if I sent to find out how he is?"

"Please."

Charles called the bosun's mate and sent him below. We waited in silence. Charles stared critically into the rigging. Sails had appeared there since I had last been on deck. There was even a tops'l replacing the one I had seen blown out of its boltropes. There was also a difference in what I could discern of the water round us—the shapes of waves where, before, the surface had seemed to be planed off and blown flat.

The bosun's mate came trotting back, leaning into the wind.

"The lady says there is no change, sir."

"Very well."

The man went back to his station by the forrard rail of the quarterdeck. Charles turned to me.

"You heard? So we must not worry before we need to."

"I cannot help it."

"Now what have I done! My dear boy, you have been foolish, impulsive, clumsy. If he dies, or rather when he dies—"

"So he will die, then!"

"He was dying before you fell on him! Good Heavens, do you suppose a man can live in our circumstances with his body swoln like a melon and the colour of an overripe beetroot? He is smashed up inside where I doubt a surgeon could do anything. You may have hastened the process, that is all."

"It is bad enough. She hates me, despises me. How can I stay in the same ship!"

"You cannot do anything else. Be sensible. Good Heavens, I wish I had as little to be sorry for as you have."

"That is nonsense. I have never known so good a man."

"Do not say it!"

"I can do so and have. I have found that the middle is the time for confidences between man and man. I believe that when I look back on this voyage these middle watches will be precious memories, old fellow."

"For me too, Edmund."

For a time we said nothing after that. At last Charles broke the silence between us.

"All the same we have lived in such different worlds it is astonishing that we have anything to say to each other."

"I have recognized your quality, which is independent of 'worlds'—though why you for your part should be willing to make one in a conversation—"

"Oh, that. It is even more mysterious than the body, I think. Let us say no more about it. Besides"—there was a smile in his voice—"'who would not be a friend with a young gentleman who promises him the moon and the stars?'"

"Promotion is much more down to earth."

"How would you define my promotion—for so it seemed and indeed was—from seaman to midshipman? It was all through getting into trouble."

"I cannot believe you were ever in trouble!"

"How dull you make me sound! Well, perhaps I am."

"Tell me."

His face glimmered towards me in the gloom.

"You will not laugh?"

"You know me better than that!"

"Do I? Well—you see in a fo'castle there must be live and let live, since there is hardly room to swing hammocks. No one minds a man reading a book, whatever it is. Are you listening?"

"I am all ears."

"We were at anchor. It was a make and mend but I was one of the anchor watch. There was no harm in my reading but the divisional officer caught me at it. He rebuked me at some length to show how strict he was, when suddenly he and everyone else was called to attention. It was Admiral Gambier."

"Dismal Jimmy?"

"Some people called him that. Now he *was* a good man. He asked me what I had done wrong and I told him I had been reading on duty. He told me to show him the book so I brought it out from behind my back and he looked at it.

"'There's a time and a place for everything,' he said and went away. The divisional officer told the petty officer to give me some cleaning to do during the make and mend as a punishment. But before the day was out I was sent for by Captain Wentworth.

"'Summers, that was very clever,' he said. 'Get your gear together, you're going to the flagship to be a midshipman. I'm disappointed in you, Summers. Don't come back.'"

"But what was the book? Oh, I see! The Bible!"

"Captain Wentworth was not a religious man."

"And that is how you got a footing on the ladder?"

"Just so."

I was confounded. Miles separated the two of us! I could think of nothing to say. It was my turn to work my way to the rail and stare at the wake. I came back and pretended to look critically at the set of our sails.

"You are right, Edmund. We can shake out a reef."

He called to the bosun's mate who piped the order from the forrard rail of the quarterdeck, then lumbered forrard by way of a safety line, the water washing round his knees, and did the same thing on the fo'castle. The black shapes of men moved up the ratlines and along the yards.

"Is it giving us more speed?"

"No more than we had before."

I was silent again.

"At least you did not laugh, Edmund."

"It does not match you. You do not do yourself justice!"

"Oh yes. I owe everything to that good man—after you, that is!"

"Gambier? Will you think me cynical, I wonder. But I believe the account of Captain Anderson's strictures and the story of why Gambier had you made midshipman had best be kept between us."

"The first yes. But why the second?"

"My dear fellow! Dismal Jimmy's recommendation might have helped you had you chosen the Church—what is the matter?"

"Nothing."

"But it will not see you very far in a fighting service! Good God! It would be about as much use as a testimonial to your courage from poor Byng."

"That is a sad comment on the service!"

"No, no!"

"Well, at least we have made you forget your miseries for the time being. Go off watch now, and sleep."

"I must see the watch out with you."

He seemed surprised at my serious and determined tone and even laughed a little. As I have said, I think, I had not then understood why he had got me an excuse to be out of my cabin for four hours of the night and I did really believe I was useful! Now I laugh a little as he did then. But in fact the watch changed soon after he had spoken. I went to my bunk, wading through water which coursed and *cornered* from side to side in the lobby. The wind howled but at least it did not drone. I cannot say I slept, for I lay listening for Prettiman who I thought must have been in a drugged sleep, for he did not cry out.

The rest of that night was a bad one for me. I went off to sleep at last but in what must have been broad daylight outside. I woke, nevertheless, with the determination to stay where I was and where it seemed I could at least do no harm to anyone else. I felt that I could have cried out now in a way which Prettiman did not.

171

(13)

When at last I tried my repeater I found it was already a quarter to ten! I took the instrument out from under my pillow and examined it with some incredulity, but sure enough, the hands confirmed the message of the chimes. I came to the conclusion that I had indeed slept but could not think how or when. Nor did I feel the benefit of sleep. I was fully clothed and reproached myself for this decline in my own standards. Once a man will turn into his bunk "all standing", as it were, there is no knowing where the thing will end! It is the next way to decline into Continental standards or lack of them. However, the omission was not to be repaired. I stood out of my bunk into the seaboots which were ready and made my way, first to the necessity, then to the passenger saloon. Early though it was in the forenoon, little Pike was there with a glass of brandy in his hand. Indeed, it soon became evident that as far as he was concerned the time was not early but late. I learnt later that he had been dismissed from his cabin by his unloving wife—though it seems far more likely that he had dismissed himself—and he had roused Bates to provide him with liquor at what was really an unsuitable hour. He was elevated indeed and careless of the booming wind and sea. He offered to "buy me a drink" which I declined with point, asking him at once how his family did.

"Family, Mus'Talbot? I 'ate families."

He peered at me, blinking the while.

"She 'ates me."

"I think, Mr Pike, you are not yourself and should not say things you will come to regret."

But Mr Pike had looked away and appeared to brood. Then as if he had come to a satisfactory conclusion he turned back to me, helped by a movement of the ship.

"Well, thass awri, innit? I 'ate 'er. I 'ate 'er. Sodder. Pardon my French."

"I think that—"

"I don' 'ate them. But they 'ate me, because she says—she says—"

I lost my temper and went blind. I say that advisedly. Then I saw, but it was red. I saw red. It was literally red. My mouth opened and I shouted at him. I heaped on him every contumely, every insult my tongue could find, and when I had done I could not remember what I had said. It left me weak though, for the time being. I could hardly cope with the ship's movement though I was sitting. Pike was leaning his elbows on the table and sniggering and laughing weakly. He pointed at me with his right forefinger, his elbow still resting on the table. His hand was slack as though it supported a heavy pistol but was only just able

173

to do so. What with the motion of the ship and his drunkenness, let alone his silly, weak laughter, his finger circled like—like the hounds of a foremast broken in the step! I got my breath back. Far from feeling that I should apologize for my burst of rage I felt it was entirely justified.

"In fact, Pike, you are a disgusting little man."

But his sniggering, giggling laughter went on and on.

"Thass wha' she sez!"

More laughter. Bates, the steward, appeared loyally, my mug of small beer in his hand, a napkin over the other arm. He entered straddling, slipped in water, saved himself cleverly, then ran *down* the saloon under "*force majeur*" to end balancing the mug within my reach. I took it and drained it and would have had another but Bates had gone as cleverly as he had come. Pike was now screaming with laughter.

"Bates! Bates!"

Then as if he had changed his mind the silly little man laid his cheek on the table and appeared to go to sleep. His glass fell and went crosswise to the side of the saloon where it clattered for a while before shooting back. I tried to trap it with my foot but failed. It struck the other side of the saloon and at last shattered. The door opened. Bowles and the young Army officer, Oldmeadow, laboured in, followed by random wetness as a wave struck the outside of the chock in the doorway. Bates, as one having foreknowledge, came in with two mugs of beer in one hand and one in the other. He stood swaying and gesticulating by the

174

table as if about to perform a conjuring trick. Perhaps, in effect, he did perform one, for he got all three of us served and went away again without breaking a glass or his neck. Pike slid against Oldmeadow.

"Is this fellow dead?"

"Dead drunk."

Oldmeadow shoved the man away who moved a foot or two then came back again.

"I wish I was myself, Talbot, that's a fact."

"Oh no! We have enough trouble as it is. Cumbershum has fallen and I believe we should treat ourselves as precious objects and help each other!"

Oldmeadow gave Pike a positively vicious shove. It moved him to a position where one arm fell off the end of the long table and held him from returning with the roll.

Bowles looked up at me over his mug.

"According to Mrs Prettiman, Mr Prettiman is in a bad way. His condition is dreadful and he cannot last. He does not even cry out."

"He is dying peacefully then, Bowles. I am glad of that at least."

"Mr Oldmeadow—have you seen Mrs Prettiman?"

"No, I have not, Bowles. I've avoided her since she rigged herself out as a common seaman. It's indecent."

"Bates! Bates! Where the devil are you? Take these mugs away!"

"Go easy, Talbot! I have not finished with mine yet! Good God—as if Summers ain't enough!"

Oldmeadow at normal times is so mild-mannered I found it easy to forgive him his irritation.

"Why, what has Charles done?"

"Taken my men for good, that's what he's done. I said I didn't think it was proper to use my men when there were so many emigrants about. Why shouldn't he sweat the lard off that idle lot? He would have none of it. 'Your men are disciplined,' he said. 'They are young and strong and you have often bemoaned to me the difficulty of finding them employment to keep them out of mischief! I promise you that a few hours a day at the pumps and they will be as gentle as lambs.'"

"Was that the end of the argument?"

"What do you think, Talbot? I wasn't going to have a damned navy man taking over my command! I told him that I'd see him further first and that I proposed to get the captain to enter my protest in the ship's log."

"That is an awful threat to a naval officer! It might jeopardize his whole career!"

"Well, I know that! But I got no further, for he said as cool as you like, 'If your men do not continue to help with the pumping, sir, no one will ever hear your protest.' So it is as bad as that."

Bowles grinned round at us both.

"We often hear that danger brings men together. I see no evidence of it."

"We are civilians, you and I. Why should the Navy bother with us? This is not a company ship and the officers do not know quite what their attitude should be. Oldmeadow's men are not marines. Willis said to me—but I suppose I should tell you that I am a civilian no longer. Lord Talbot has been promoted to midshipman."

"You intend that as a pleasantry, sir."

"God, Bowles, a pleasantry! Colley, Wheeler and now Prettiman—oh well! To revert: the fact is, I act as the first lieutenant's midshipman during the middle watch. The middle watch is the one which—"

Astonishingly enough, Bowles, that quiet and composed man, positively shouted an interruption.

"Yes, sir, we do know what the middle is! God have mercy on us. Soldiers turned into sailors and now passengers put in charge of the ship!"

"After all, Bowles, he couldn't do much more damage to the ship than the new officer, what's 'is name—Benét. The man has lugged a lump off the ship's bottom and damned nearly set the front end on fire! Now he wants to find out where we are without using their clocks and things. I tell you what, Talbot. We should get all this raised in the House! My God, what a boat! There's that fool Smiles on the quarterdeck supposed to be in charge but simply grinning at the weather as if it were a friend of his, and that old fool Brocklebank standing outside the lobby door in the wind and rain, with seawater washing round his knees, and waiting for his morning fart to develop—"

"So that's why! I've wondered—Every day he stands out there in the waist, wind, rain or shine—"

"Well, that's what it is. The girls won't have him in the cabin until he's fired off a blank charge like a saluting gun!"

The very image set us all three laughing like jackasses.

"Did I hear someone mention my name?"

It was the man himself. The deck left us and he swung hard on the door handle. He was an old man after all. Old-meadow and I got to him before he fell and lugged him to the table, while Bowles heaved the door shut against the inclinations of the sea. I believe that the old man recovered his breath before any of us.

"I could not stand it any longer, gentlemen, that is the truth of the matter. Soaked above the waist, buffeted, nigh on washed away, this good old coach cloak, which has protected me so well, now as wet inside as out—"

"Why, Mr Brocklebank, you should be in your cabin—in your bunk if possible!"

"The fact is, I need the company of men."

"Good God, sir, anyone privileged to be the companion of Mrs Brocklebank—"

"No, Mr Talbot, it is not so. She endeavours to cheer me but the truth is, already she regards me with a widow's eye."

"Oh, come, sir! I have often seen Mrs Brocklebank about the ship and never less than smiling—never less than merry!"

"That is what I mean, Mr Talbot, though you exagger-ate a little. She may look merrily on you but not on me. I

178

do not like widows, sir, and have taken care to avoid them in the only truly logical way. But despite that, Celia, in the privacy of our cabin, has just that air of sad triumph, that almost holy smile with which a widow contemplates a *job* well done, an account paid in full: and that"—here the old man did seem passionate—"and that she is not entitled to!"

"Mr Brocklebank!"

"Now you are going to accuse me of conduct unbecoming to a gentleman, Mr Talbot. Be that as it may, I say no more under that heading. But I could not endure to return, you know, even though I had fulfilled Celia's stipulation. Yes, Bates! Good Bates, it is I! Have you put the brandy in it?"

Bates delivered the mug but looked conscious at Mr Brocklebank's words.

"Just a lick, sir, no more than a smell of it, you might say."

"Bates, you dog, you've been giving him brandy from the wardroom whereas I—"

"Your'n was mine, sir, Mr Talbot!"

"I would share my mug with you, Mr Talbot, but I am a martyr to fears of contagion."

"Devil take it! I believe the contagion would be the other way about!"

The deck fell away from us monstrously. I clutched at the table but found I had hold of Bowles. He struggled free of me just as the deck came up again and hit him. He swore in a way I would not have thought possible in such a man.

"And the food," said Mr Brocklebank, following a train of thought to which he had given no voice, "the food is just as bad. Why, only the other day when I tried to bite, or rather I should say *effect an entry* like a felon, into a lump of cold pork, what should ensue but this?"

The disgusting old man fished round in the many folds that clung about him and produced from some recess of his garments or person a blackened tooth.

"Oh my God, this really is the outside edge of enough!"

I leapt to my feet and went to the door, and was deluged with spray from the block which was supposed to keep salt water out of the saloon. Benét was there. Like everyone else in the ship he was holding on but with two fingers to the rail between the cabin doors. He was staring at Mr Prettiman's cabin. His lips were moving and I suppose he was in what are called the throes of composition. The sight maddened me. I still do not know why.

"Mr Benét!"

He seemed to see me but as a vexation.

"Mr Benét, I wish to have some plain answers!"

He was frowning and perplexed.

"Have I accepted your apology?"

"*You* should apologize! The relationship between you and a certain lady has caused a certain other lady—that is, has caused me—my opinion of her—I called your name—"

"Have you anything against my name, sir? Was that derision?"

180

"I called out your name—"

"Twice! I am proud of my name, Mr Talbot, and if my father used it ruefully as a reminder of his flight—"

"You are putting me off! I do not care about your name which is French, I suppose. I want a plain answer. What did she see? Was it a criminal connection?"

"Well really, Mr Talbot, after our late differences—"

"I wish to understand clearly the relationship between you and a certain lady!"

"You mean Miss Chumley, I suppose. Oh dear. Well, as I told you she kept *cave* for us, or if the Latin tongue is unfamiliar to you—"

"It is not, I assure you!"

"Now you are going red in the face like poor Prettiman."

I fought down my rising irritation.

"I am more concerned with you and a lady of maturer years!"

"So you have found me out! She is—oh, she is—"

Mr Benét seemed uniquely bereft of speech. He closed his eyes and began to recite.

> *Since thou didst doff thy woman's weeds*
> *And loosed the glories of thy hair*
> *The eye that weeps, the heart that bleeds—*

"So you did have a criminal connection! Miss Chumley did indeed understand! She did indeed see!"

"What connection?"

"Lady Somerset!"

"The heart grows with understanding. Profound though my esteem for the lady is—"

I shouted. It was fortunate perhaps that the words were audible in that weather to no one but him.

"Did you have her? Did Miss Chumley *see*?"

A look of compassionate understanding came into his face.

"I might resent your words, Mr Talbot, on her behalf and my own. Your mind evidently cannot rise above the farmyard level."

"Do not talk to me about farmyards!"

"You are passionately moved and hardly responsible for what you say. I knelt before the lady. She offered me her right hand. I took it in mine and dared to imprint a kiss on it. Then—and I beg you will understand what passionate chastity was implied in the gesture—remembering my childhood and dearest mama coming to say good night to me in the nursery, with an irresistible flood of emotion I turned the white hand over, dropped a kiss in the dewy palm and closed the slender fingers over it!"

"And then? Then? You are silent, sir! That was all? That was all, Mr Benét?"

"Once again you are not amiable, Mr Talbot. This is the second time, like your jeering use of my name!"

"A plain answer, if you please, to a plain question!"

"That was 'all'. Though to a man of any sensibility—"

"Explain why she took her clothes off. Explain that!"

"Lady Somerset took nothing off!"

"'Since thou didst doff thy woman's weeds'!"

There was an explosion of water. Spray drenched us. Benét dashed it from his face.

"I see it all. The coarseness of your mind has deceived you. The lady did indeed 'doff' her 'woman's weeds'—"

> *Since thou didst doff thy woman's weeds*
> *And loosed the glories of thy hair*
> *The eye that weeps, the heart that bleeds*
> *Has found a refuge in thy care,*
> *Letitia! Though thy hand be given*
> *The thought of thee is my delight,*
> *To dwell in the same ship is—*

"Miss Granham! Mrs Prettiman!"

"Who else? The lines are unpolished as yet."

"You are writing poetry to Mrs Prettiman!"

"Can you think of a worthier aim? She is all that the ages have looked forward to!"

"You wish to kiss her hand, sir, I have no doubt she would oblige. She has, after all, obliged gentlemen before—Mr Prettiman, her husband—but what has that word to do with poetry? He is in his bunk and cannot get out of it. I have no doubt that if you tapped on her door and asked nicely you might find yourself kissing her hand inside and out for a full watch by the sandglass!"

"You are nauseous."

I must have snarled.

"I believe I am, sir. But at least I do not drool round the oceans dropping kisses in the palms of women old enough to be my mother!"

That appeared to sting. He heaved himself away from the mast and stood rocking.

"You had best stick to schoolgirls, Mr Talbot."

"I resent the plural! For me there is only one lady!"

"You are loveless, Mr Talbot. It is your main defect."

"I loveless? I am saying 'ha ha', sir! Do you hear me?"

"You are not yourself. We will continue this conversation when you are sober. I bid you good day."

He vanished with what I might call an assisted celerity down the stairs to the wardroom, passing Mr Smiles as he did so. I shouted childishly after him.

"Mr Smiles, can you hear me? We are in love with our mothers!"

Mr Smiles came past me with a deft tread, neither looking at me nor speaking to me. He might have been a ghost with an appointment somewhere else.

I went to my cabin. Time, time itself was unendurable. I climbed into my oilskins and went out to stand on the deck. Immediately a wave lifted me up into the main chains and would have left me there had I not detached myself. It cooled my senseless rage. I stood holding on while the ocean performed. The crests of waves went past us, it seemed to me, at more than head height. Sometimes we bowed sideways into them so that the waist flooded deep, sometimes we leaned away and there was a gulf in which a solitary bird was suspended over darkness between hills of foaming green. Then horizontal rain and mist would blot out even the bird, and water would tumble down from the quarterdeck as from the guttering of a cathedral.

It cooled and calmed me. The ropes that bound us together and kept us from drowning were there before my eyes as a reminder of how and where we stood. I rebuked myself for my anger and for showing so much of my fear. It was not what I had expected of myself. I went to my cabin and at long last fell asleep.

(14)

What woke me from a dream of cliffs and slopes was a shattering blow. I was on the deck by my bunk from which I had fallen or been thrown, and as I scrabbled to get up, my canvas chair tipped over on me so that we went sliding together to thump the bulkhead beyond my writing flap. I got to my feet somehow and the angle at which my lantern with its loaded base now stood frightened me into a moment or two of near-immobility. I could only interpret the angle as information we were now sliding backwards—making a sternboard!—into the sea and should vanish there. My feet skidded from me and I was hanging from the bunk, the idiot lantern projecting above me as if the laws of Mr Benét's Nature had been suspended. From that moment, I believe, I did not know quite what I was doing. I had some idea that the ship was under water already and that at any moment all the orifices would start to squirt. Confused with this was the thought that it was now the middle watch, I was late for it and Charles without a midshipman. Nor, as I gathered my wits together, did things get any better, for it was plain that we were in some emergency. There were noises. The Pike children were screaming needle-sharp and so was another female—Celia Brocklebank probably. Men were shouting. There were other noises too, booming and banging of sails, batter of blocks—somewhere glass shattered and cascaded. I got out into the lobby and found myself hanging from the safety rail by both hands—literally hanging from it as though the ship had stood on its head. I took one hand off the rail and immediately a sudden tug tore my other hand from it. I went tumbling the length of the lobby head over heels and fetched up with a dizzying thud against the forrard bulkhead. Some force pinned me there for a while, so that I could see Oldmeadow fighting—and not succeeding—to get out of the passenger saloon. Then the pressure slackened a little bit and I used an interim to scramble into the waist and hang in my usual place—the larboard shrouds—as if for comfort in the familiar. But nothing was the same and what I could see held no comfort for me. Someone was cursing near me but I could not see who it was. Such sails as we had now glimmered into view as my eyes became accustomed to the dim light. It was that unearthly storm light again, which served not so much to light up the ship as illuminate what looked like solid walls of cloud surrounding us on every side and reaching up to a space in which stars swam erratically all together. The glimmering sails were empty! Below them the world of water made no sense, for there were dimly descriable mountains ahead

187

and astern of us—black mountains. Then, in the first few moments of my gaze, the one astern changed shape, sank down and perhaps vanished. I say "perhaps", for I did not see it go! As the mountain sank away I felt a stronger and stronger pull on my limbs, so that once more I seemed to be hanging, this time from the shrouds. The whole length of the waist sloped away from me under another mountain which had grown up before the bows—grown up and bid fair to fall on us. The tops'ls filled with loud bangs and the main course followed suit with explosions like cannon shot. We were lifted to the top of the world. I made a run for the stairs and got there, clinging to the rail. While the ship was upright I reached the top of the stairs and thrust my head above the level of the deck. I could see no one!

Was that the most terrifying moment of my life? No—there were others to come. But this, which might have been the prime contender, was muted and qualified by my sheer inability to believe in it! The quarterdeck deserted—oh, God, the wheel! I scrambled back down the stair which was suddenly flat and hauled myself—uphill? sideways?—into the steering space.

"Edmund! Oh, thank God! Help me!"

The need was plain enough. I trod on the body of a man, dead or unconscious. Charles hung from the starboard side of the wheel, bearing down on it.

"Starboard!"

That was the beginning of a period when I had no time to be frightened. For what was in fact minutes but seemed timeless, I put such strength as I had to aid and increase the efforts that Charles made to handle the wheel in that sea by himself. I did help. I felt the wheel move under my applications and often what Charles himself could only begin I helped him carry through to its conclusion. The beginning of a movement of the wheel is easy enough, the whipstaff sees to that! But then after your strength has been put into flexing it, there is always a moment at which nothing, it seems, but sheer blind determination to defeat some invisible monster will allow one's muscles to carry the thing through. I do not know how often the two of us moved the wheel. The movements were gross, for the ship was as near as nothing still since the puffs of air that filled her sails on the crests of these mountains were enough to give us only the merest token of steerage way. Presently Charles ceased to give me orders, for it was obvious that I could follow what he wanted without words. The requirements of the wheel spoke to me in their own language.

"All right, sir."

It was a seaman. There were two—taking the wheel from us. Someone was on his knees and shaking the unconscious body on which I had stepped. The captain was there in the waist. There was blood on his face and a pistol in his hand. He was hatless, staring up at the sails.

"Midships!"

And then in a calm voice:

"I have her, Mr Summers."

I crawled away from the wheel to the stairs. Mr

Summers joined me on hands and knees.

"I was not called for the middle!"

He spoke exhaustedly.

"It is not the middle. It is the morning watch. I cannot talk."

"What in the name of God—"

He shook his head. I fell silent, glad of a rail to hold on to.

"Are you all right, Charles?"

He nodded. The sense of usefulness, of being able to do more than cower in my bunk, was strong upon me.

"I will see what is to be done. There may be—"

I made my way up to the quarterdeck. The captain and Lieutenant Cumbershum stood by the forrard rail. I worked along it and shouted unnecessarily at Cumbershum.

"Can I help?"

His snarled answer was still in the air when some force tore me from the rail, held me suspended in a moment of positive flight.

"Stay out of trouble!"

I fell *on* rather than against the stairs up to the poop. I crawled up and entwined myself in the rails at this loftiest part of the hull. There was a faint wind, but just enough to fill the sails when it had the opportunity. For the rest, the sight was enough to send a man scuttling down to the bilges so as not to see the end which was coming upon him. Those waves which had been hidden or even beaten down by the smother of the storm had now come forth. The dying wind had allowed them to form in their ranges. I saw that our world was limited to three waves, three ranges, one astern of us, one ahead, one supporting us for the moment between them. Then, as our stern sank, dimension and direction fell into confusion. The bows towered above us and then fell until we seemed to hang above them. The sight was unbearable and I shut my eyes. I became therefore, as they say in books, "all ears". As the stern sank under me I heard the successive flap and clatter as one course of sails after the other lost the wind. The thunder as of great guns was our sails filling as we were lifted up again into the faintest of airs—bows first, stern first? The con must take such movements into account, for they might make the rudder work in reverse, a contingency for which the men at the wheel would not be able to allow. Yet a small mistake in these vast seas would allow the ship to broach to, be overset and sunk—This then was why an officer must stand, hour after hour, exercising his judgement and minute by minute hazarding us all on it!

I opened my eyes and found it just possible to keep them open. The faintest trace of wind breathed on my cheek. We were, I saw, on a crest, though in the darkness behind my eyelids I had thought us in a trough. Now we slid back and it seemed a gulf opened under the stern—there was no light in that abyss towards which we sped and I *clenched* my eyes shut as that blackness of water moved the ship on to an even keel, then tilted her, pitched her the other way until she was standing on her bowsprit.

At last I got my eyes open once more. The snail-trail of our oil glistened astern of us over one mountain range which was all that could be seen there even when we were on the crest of the next. These ranges made no spray, had no foam on them. They were a welter of black flint.

Time and again.

There were gleams and glitters now and then, either moon on water or some curious quality of the water itself.

Time and again.

There was a noise to be detected. It was not a ship noise, sail noise, wind noise. It was a *thump*, then a prolonged but diminishing roar to follow. I could fit the noise to nothing in my experience for all the time we had spent, all those months with the limited repertoire of the sights and sounds of water—

Of course! It was solidity! It was one of those horrible ranges striking rock! I was on my feet, my mouth open to shout—but my seaboots shot from under me and in a moment I had skidded the short length of the poop and crashed into the after rail under the larboard lantern! My mouth had been open to shout something or scream, for the inference of solidity in all this water was very terrible, but the breath had all been knocked out of me. I do not know how near I came to breaking the rail and ending my career hopelessly in a streak of oily water, but at least the upright I struck was not rotten whatever was to be said of the rest of the ship. I scuttled back to my previous place as if that were safer. This was panic which now knocked out of me all the honour and heroics together with my breath.

I stared round me. We were rising at another range—they must have been a quarter of a mile apart—and saw nothing but black, horrible flint with a sullen dawn sky over it, dully shining flint, liquid flint—how to convey the sheer horror of *size*? For after all, the three moving mountains among which we were now living were nothing but ripples—yet magnified, multiplied in size past the huge, the colossal, to the point where they were overwhelmingly monstrous! They were a new dimension in the nature of water. This nature did seem to allow us to live—just; was not inimical, would not, so to say, go out of its way to harm us. For a mad moment I felt that could I but lay my ear close to the glistening, mobile blackness I should be able to hear into its very being, hear, it may be, the fricative movement of one particle against another. But then I remembered how we were literally tied together by the undergirdings and my soul became nothing but terror. For I heard that same sudden *thump*, then grumbling diminution from somewhere over the larger horizon—that one which a man might see if he dared to climb the mast—a consideration which made me sick to think of—say then a horizon visible to some giant here who was made to the same measure as our watery ranges. Land, then, was within earshot?

The dawn was clouding over. Light lifted off the earth so that the sea itself collected blackness wherever there was allowed a temporary hollow. I will try to find the words which will describe what happened at this point of suspension between day and night. We were poised on one range when a new thing began to happen to the range which was pursuing us. I cannot tell even now what the cause was. We were not in shallow water, that is certain. Everywhere about us and for many hundreds of miles—perhaps thousands—the bottom, the solid globe was miles away down there under the majesty of the liquid element. Was there perhaps some confusion or even contrariety in that current with its endlessly marching billows, moving from one age to another round the bottom of the world? Whatever it was, the range pursuing us began to steepen and sharpen. Except for the trivial notch in which our oil lay, the whole wave—I call it "wave" having no better word—stood sheer. For a mile, it may be, on either hand it stood ready, then curved slowly and fell! I heard the hiss of the waters in the air even as they descended and then the strike of water on water, acres, miles of it, with a noise which went beyond noise. For that fall was a feeling, a stab in either ear, after which I could hear nothing. But I had my eyes still. At the moment of fall, as if the invisible air was a solid thing, a line of foam and spray flicked away across the sea. It *was* air, it was the air displaced by the fall of the mountain and thrust in every direction with the speed of a musket ball. But now on either hand the sea went mad, foaming past us higher than the waist, higher than the rail of the quarterdeck, the

194

rail of the fo'castle. The poop, with my arms wound in the rail, was all that stood above the water. But then, as if the oil had slowed it, the water which had lain in our notch of safety, though it did not foam, stood up and washed clear over the poop as well. I suppose it was a moment at which a seabird gliding over these sunless gulfs would have seen nothing but foam and three masts projecting. I stared forward as soon as the water left me and saw our ship begin to labour up, water pouring off the fo'castle before the waist had reappeared. Two more sails were in tatters. Was it that fearsome gust of air?

To remain alone was no longer possible. I moved and slipped. It was a new hazard and a ridiculous one. For all Charles's care, his hanging of the bags of oil under the stern rather than the bows, our oil trail had come aboard at last. I crept to the ladder along the rail, or crawled rather, for most of the way I slipped and slid on my knees. High above me the sails "spoke".

Captain Anderson had the con. He stood just aft of the wheel. Cumbershum lolled by the starboard rail, one arm hooked through it, his legs stretched along the deck. He looked across at the captain. He was speaking, for I could see his lips move. It was only then that I understood I had been literally deafened by the fall of the wave. I stayed in the shelter of the poop until little by little my hearing came back to me. Forrard I could see Mr Benét had men working already in the rigging among torn sails, though I did not think there was anything to be done. Had we not suffered a mortal blow? I did, I suppose, credit our ship with feelings and supposed that at any moment she might decide to give up this unequal struggle with an ocean never intended for ships—and particularly not for a superannuated hulk rendering like an old boot.

I glanced up at the sails. Those that had escaped destruction were full and Benét's men were working the yards round. There was wind—enough for steerage way, enough even for security. The ranges themselves as though the monstrous billow which had broken round us like some marine cataclysm had been the peak of all, a seventh wave beyond all seventh waves, was being succeeded by smaller ones.

I could hear Charles speaking thickly, as though his mouth had been damaged.

"Wind's moving on to the quarter, sir. We could set stays'ls."

The captain stared over the quarter, then back at Charles.

"Are you fit?"

Charles laboured to his feet.

"Think so, sir."

"Stays'ls then—" The captain turned to me and seemed about to speak but changed his mind and stumped to the forrard rail.

(15)

It took that day which was dawning and the next one too for Captain Anderson and his officers to restore some order and routine to the vessel. For one thing, getting the pervasive film of oil off required the whole crew, the soldiers and the emigrants!

The stuff was everywhere. It even reached some fifteen feet up the mainmast, or so Bates assured us. In the lobby it was smeared to a height of three feet along the bulkheads and doors through which it had effected some degree of entry to the cabins. Of sheer necessity the panic among the people which had gone near to drowning us all was ignored tacitly, though I am sure the captain was enraged at the situation in which he found himself. To abandon the post of duty was of course a fault which should have been punished with the utmost severity. I do not say this in indignation but from a cool sense of what some other ship might expect of her people with such an example before them! I repeat, there is no doubt that men abandoned their duty and tried to hide from the sea. As Charles once said, "Men, like cables, have each their breaking strain." Next to

197

open mutiny the crew had committed the blackest crime in a seaman's calendar.

Yet what was to be done about it? A minority, even one possessing the natural authority of office, cannot guarantee obedience in making the body politic punish itself! No one could deny they had been sorely tried. Apart from the weather, our outrageously lengthy voyage meant that the food was scanty and the drink almost gone. We had little firing left, so that hot water was a luxury no longer obtainable even for the ladies. The ship was labouring. The pumping, though not constant as in the heaviest weather, was nevertheless a sore trial to men becoming weak through exposure, toil and inadequate nourishment.

However, the thing was done. The ship was scrubbed, squeegeed, mopped and dried until at least a man with a seaman's sense of balance could keep his footing. Those sails which could be mended were attended to and others spread. Whatever else the ship lacked she was well provided with rope and canvas. A great deal of fishing went on in the easier weather which we then experienced though nothing that was caught came my way. Fish do not appear to be tempted to the line from a large vessel. Perhaps rumour of that strangest of fish, Man, had descended among the finny tribes! We did, however, see whales often enough and Mr Benét was said to have suggested a number of ways of killing them. The crew, though most crafts and skills were represented among them—particularly after they had heard his mad idea for a harpoon with an explosive charge of gunpowder attached to it—were not eager.

My own suggestion of using our great guns and firing, as near as we could, a broadside at the monsters met with no better success. We settled therefore to our short commons and were only consoled by the thought—the fact—that we were *getting on*. The foremast had passed the severest of trials triumphantly. When the light wind was broad enough on the quarter we spread not just stuns'ls, but stays'ls too—large triangular areas of canvas stretched between the masts rather than on them. For days I believe we never made less than six knots.

The reader who is not a seaman must accept my apologies for these lengthy divergences into a detailed account of their craft and skill! The fact is that I miss continually the point I am trying to convey. When your life depends on it there is a pleasure like no other in the movement towards your goal, in the chuckle of cleft water at the forefoot, the swell of sails, the movement night and day of a mass of cleverly constructed timber which must come close to totalling two thousand tons! The very seamen themselves walked with a more cheerful gait and a readier response to orders. Everyone seemed happy, even the officers—except perhaps Charles. He, I have to say, clung to the idea of a spark of fire burrowing in the shoe under the foremast! During another of those middle watches which I so enjoyed I taxed him with it.

"Confess, Charles. The mast is safe. You are hugging to

yourself the thought that Mr Benét might be wrong after all!"

"He cannot always be right. No man can. Since he is wrong in his proposed method of finding our longitude—"

"Wrong?"

"The theory is correct—but do you understand the difficulty, the near-impossibility of measuring the angular separation of two heavenly bodies—one of them at least changing shape all the time?"

"I asked the sailing master to explain Mr Benét's method to me but he would not."

"It is a question of parallax and so on. It seems to involve the moon, the sun, planets and even the moons of planets—a whole cobweb of measurements—the man is brilliantly mad!"

"Yet he was right before. Do not, I beg of you, Charles, let a habit of dislike blind you to the man's merits. I cannot endure to see you less than you are! Forgive me—I am now the one to preach."

"You may do so. My objection to Mr Benét's method of finding our latitude without reference to chronometers is based on reason not dislike. If the most learned and intellectual minds of our country have abandoned this method it is because the method is inaccurate. Is he mad or am I?"

"Not you, I beg—you are our prop and stay in informed common sense!"

"Well. We have a passage at least a hundred miles wide between the few islands of this ocean. Knowing the latitude is enough to keep us safely between them. We cannot yet be far enough advanced to risk running on our objective before we see it. That day must look after itself."

Mr Prettiman no longer screamed or roared when the vessel pitched. My simple plan of "turning him end for end" seemed successful. He might be dying but was doing so peacefully. I had tried to avoid Mrs Prettiman since the time when she had—oh, I felt it too deeply to play with the event in Tarpaulin!—when she had given her opinion of me in the measured tones of a judgement from the bench. Once, she came into the saloon when I was there but left before I had time even to get on my feet. Once, I detected her running *downhill* across the lobby at a roll of the ship, and after I had seen her arrive safely at the rail between the doors of the cabins I averted my face and passed on. She still kept to her "seaman's rig" and I could not but applaud her decision. Once you have accustomed yourself to a sight sufficiently shocking at first, there is little to disconcert you in the sight of a lady wearing "trowsers". Indeed, if you consider the possible inconveniences and *revelations* which the costume proper to a lady on shore might occasion in a pitching, tossing, reeling vessel, trowsers, or a cleverly made female form of them, might well be thought more appropriate than skirts. What is more, they are undoubtedly safer, since a lady has no longer to put propriety not to say decency at odds with safety and prefer death to immodesty like the girl in the French story.

All the same, I was fated to confront her again and in circumstances which were reminiscent—though she was de-
voting herself to the sick man—of high comedy. I had been
walking, or rather staggering, in the waist, for the weather
now seemed set so fair that where possible I had ceased
to make use of the lifelines. At times the dark and soaked
deck wore the dirty white of salt beneath which the ancient
wood showed mouldy splinters and here and there oakum
pushing through the tar of the seams like hair. It was not,
one might have thought, a place in which the human mind
could contemplate anything other than its latter end. Yet as
far as I could see no one did so. We were inured to danger,
some of us made indifferent to it, some of us—Bowles for
example—in a state of constant dread, some of us
coarsened by it and some finding in it a source of exhilara-
tion, like young Mr Taylor who sang, whistled and laughed
in a way that the more sullen of us, such as I myself, found
positively demented. One, at least, appeared to be above
such trivial matters as death. It was Mr Benét. As I
staggered back from a brief word or two with Mr East at
the break of the fo'castle I saw him coming off watch, down
the ladder from the quarterdeck. He had a paper in his hand,
his eyes which were wide open looked clean out of our dirty
world, and there was an ecstatic smile on his face. He ignored me as I approached, and rushed into the lobby. The
foremast being safe as far as anyone knew, I thought he had
turned his attention to his next craze, the foolish scheme
of finding our position without the use of a chronometer. It

was a scheme I thought I might well understand and hurried after him. I reached the door of the lobby just as he had knocked on Mrs Prettiman's door and evidently been answered, for he opened the door wide, stepped into the cabin and *pulled the door to behind him!* This was too much. If *he* had no care for the lady's reputation, *I* had! Though it was "uphill" for the nonce, I was three-quarters of the way to that door and so careless through outrage that a buck of the ship flung me face down on the slippery deck. I was stunned, I think, for a moment, for I was no more than on my knees when the door of her cabin burst open and with a positive clatter of his tarpaulin garments, Benét came staggering out. He had no paper in his hand. The door slammed shut behind him. The next roll to the one which had floored me sent him flying downhill in a most unseamanlike manner across the lobby. He was no longer smiling. He struck the great cylinder of the mizzenmast and stood rocking above me. Then with speechless care he went to the ladder down to the wardroom and disappeared.

But I had seen! On his left cheek there was a white patch, and in the few moments during which he remained in view, with the deepest satisfaction and indignation I saw that patch turn to the pink shape of a lady's hand!

However, my duty was plain. Mr Prettiman was in no state to defend the lady. The offer must come from me. I went to the door and tapped. After a few moments it was—I will not say "pushed" but flung open.

The fact is I was intimidated by that lady! Was it perhaps her years? I do not think so. She stood there now and glared at me as if I had been Benét. As the voyage lengthened towards a year, her own years had become less and less obvious to the casual beholder. True, the sun and wind had darkened her features to a uniform brown which was more appropriate to the peasantry than a lady from the Close! Her hair, which she commonly bound up with a scarf instead of the bonnet she had once thought suitable to her condition, had a habit of escaping—for it was abundant. It tended to catch the eye irritatingly. It hung now about her face and shoulders. Her person was otherwise quite unexceptionable.

I had no time to offer my services. The crimson of indignation suffused her cheeks despite the attentions of the sun.

"Are all the young men in this ship stark, staring mad?"

My mouth was open to reply when we were both interrupted.

"Letitia!"

It was Mr Prettiman calling from his bed of pain—and now repeating the call in tones not much like those of an invalid.

"Letty!"

Mrs Prettiman closed the door behind her and opened that of her husband's cabin. She spoke over her shoulder.

"Please remain, Mr Talbot. I wish to speak with you."

She shut the door behind her. So there I stood, and just as a schoolboy who does not know whether he is to run an errand or be punished for a misdeed but fears the worst, and he cocks his ear to find (if he can) a clue to his fate but is not able to translate the sounds that come so faintly to him from an adult world, so nor could I! For the first human sound I heard was surely that of laughter! He—a dying man! She—his devoted wife! I—

His cabin door opened and she came out. I got the door of her cabin open and held it for her. She passed inside and stood by the canvas washbasin staring into her right hand. With an exclamation of distaste she seized a scrap of cambric and scrubbed the palm vigorously. She caught my eye, stopped, then flounced herself down in the canvas chair in a way which had she been a girl I would have called pettish. She put some of her hair back with her right hand but quite without effect, for it fell forward again.

"Fudge!"

She caught my eye again and had the grace to blush a little.

"Oh, come in, Mr Talbot. Kindly latch the door back against the stop. The proprieties must be observed. We must not sully your reputation—"

I suppose my jaw had dropped, for she seemed irritated.

"Sit on the bunk, for Heaven's sake! I cannot be for ever staring up at the ceiling."

I did so.

"If you please, Mrs Prettiman, I had wished to offer my services. Believing Mr Prettiman incapacitated by his injuries—"

"Oh, he is, he is!"

"By good fortune I saw Mr Benét force his attentions—"

"Say no more, sir."

"Force his ridiculous verses on you—"

Mrs Prettiman sighed.

"That is the trouble, Mr Talbot. They are not ridiculous except in the article of addressing me as 'Egeria'. He is a talented young man. Mr Prettiman and I desire that the affair should be forgotten. Yet I blame myself in part. I am not usually an unreasonable woman, but to be addressed in such terms, to have my hand seized in such a manner—and all from a man young enough to be—a younger brother, Mr Talbot."

"He deserves to be flogged!"

"There shall be no violence, sir. Once and for all, I will not have it!"

"He should be ashamed—"

"*I* am ashamed. I am not accustomed to such feelings. I am happy to say I have not merited them."

I opened my mouth to agree—then shut it again. She went on.

"The extraordinary events—the fearful weather—the queue of simple souls doing Mr Prettiman reverence—your well-meant but clumsy action—"

She paused for a while.

"Pray continue."

"You see, he is not dying! Since you stretched his poor

torn leg the swelling has subsided. Perhaps he will not walk again. He is not out of danger. But the pain is becoming bearable. How can I be ashamed that he is recovering? I am delighted and ashamed! He too has owned that, in some ways, if it were not for the cessation of pain he would himself be ashamed of his recovery! He and I, you see—we are rendered *conscious* by the situation. This is all mad, you see. But true!"

"I understand, indeed I do! Not dying! For there is a kind of magical comedy about our situation. The intellect disdains what the heart knows feelingly! I *know* that!"

"Mr Talbot! This from you whom I have thought incapable—"

"Oh, I am, ma'am, wholly so. But, as you say, so much has happened; and after all, the world is upside down, is it not? We hang from it by our feet!"

"This is fanciful! We all change. It is danger, I suppose, which shows us all in our true colours, our grim captain, the right man to get us where we are going, our decayed vessel contriving to float and Mr Prettiman's careful plans all thrown into the melting pot."

"But he is recovering!"

"So he may be. But I cannot conceive of his leg ever being as serviceable as it was. How can he get about to examine the condition of the convicts? How can he endure the hardship of exploration, of leading a crowd of reformed criminals and settlers into the interior of this continent in search of his promised land?"

"I see."

"Aloysius Prettiman—who was to be to the Southern Ocean what Tom Paine was to the Atlantic—lamed and having to be helped where he had hoped to lead!"

My immediate thought was, *This is phantasy*, but I did not say so.

"I am sure our government will help, ma'am!"

She had been looking, as it were, through the bulkhead as if at some more distant prospect. Now she glanced at me and smiled—bitterly, I thought.

"To found the Ideal City? There is a refreshing innocence about you, sir. Mr Prettiman has revealed to me the elaborations and knaveries of the government! Be sure they will have known of his intentions even before we sailed. There is no harm in your knowing now what we may have concealed from them, but he—we—carry a printing press with us."

The air about me and particularly about my ears seemed to burn, but I did not know what to say. It seemed as if my whole interior self was suddenly spread out for her inspection. I was once more in the high-ceilinged office before the huge desk.

By the bye, Talbot. You will be going out in the same ship as Prettiman and his printing press. Keep an eye on him.

"You were about to say, sir?"

"I shall be a part, however small, of that government."

"My dear Mr Talbot! I was not thinking of you! We believe now that they will have put a spy to sail with us."

"Spy!"

"An agent of the government if you prefer euphemisms. Indeed"—here she glanced through the open door, then back at me—"Mr Prettiman believes that the accident which crippled him may not have been a simple accident."

"That is impossible!"

"Lean your head a little closer, sir. I wish to whisper. He finds Mr Bowles's masquerade as a solicitor's clerk transparent."

"Bowles!"

"Your astonishment is natural. Well, there it is. What are we to do?"

"You should both go home, I believe."

"You think it is only in England—in Europe—he would find the medical attention which might restore him to some degree of mobility? He will not be so easily deflected from his purpose!"

"Even so, it is good news that he is better. Now for Mr Benét. If he continues to plague you, you may call on me. I will take his verses and invite him to—"

"I wish things were as simple. As I said, his verses are not all ridiculous. This, though it addresses me as 'Egeria', is pompous but fluent and far above what might be expected from a naval officer. Put together with his two contrivances which are said to have saved our lives—"

"I would mention first the frapping invented by Lieutenant Summers! That above all has been the principal agent of our preservation. Why, even in the late tempest, it held the ship together! Believe me, Mr Summers—"

She held up her hand, smiling.

"I understand you. You need not continue. So believe *me* that at moments when your careless assumptions of privilege have been most provoking you have been rendered tolerable by your evident admiration for that worthy man!"

It was a backhander. But then, as I have said, Mrs Prettiman was an adept of the backhander. I was annoyed and should have said something like—"For a lady who indulges in premarital copulation", but I did not. As the words rang in my head I heard myself use other ones.

"Is it impossible that I should read the verses to Egeria?"

"Quite impossible. I am addressed in such terms as puts me to the blush."

Again the words in my head were pushed aside by others—

"I might agree with more of the verses than you think, Mrs Prettiman."

Oh, it was intolerable! She was looking at me with plain astonishment!

"One request, ma'am. May I visit the patient?"

"He is asleep, I think—I hope. Since we have no more laudanum sleep is precious and hard to come by."

"I would go in like a mouse and sit by him till he wakes."

She seemed doubtful. I pressed the point.

"Believe me, when I knew of him at first I made all the

assumptions about your husband which could be drawn from gross political caricatures. But my first presence at his bedside—well. Now I remember my stumble against his leg—though I may be the unwitting agent of his recovery—as a moment which will haunt me for ever, the moment when I inflicted on him such agony that he fainted away with it."

"And so?"

"I should be less than human did I not wish to offer him my congratulations on his partial recovery, my commiserations on his disability and my profound sorrow for the agony I caused him."

"No man could say fairer than that, Mr Talbot. Had you by any chance evolved and put by you those ringing periods?"

I was silent. Suddenly she started to speak, I know not what, for now it was my turn to hold up a hand.

"Say no more, Mrs Prettiman. I am fated by my nature to talk like that sometimes. Generally it makes people believe me older than I am."

"So I suppose. But you will grow out of it."

I was silent for a moment. Who was she to be critical of me? A lady, a woman who had behaved like a common trollop!

"I do not desire to 'grow out of it'. And now, ma'am, may I visit the patient?"

Her face was quite without expression as she bowed in assent.

(16)

I left Mrs Prettiman's cabin and closed the door behind me without looking back. I stood for a few moments in the rocking lobby and thought. I had meant to be uniformly dignified and stern with her—but there it was!

I remembered the letter which the man had given me when he thought himself dying. Would he not wish to have it back now he was on the mend? But I had not pockets in my seaman's rig in which the letter might be carried without crumpling and I did not wish to carry it openly in my hand. She might look out, see, and ask and so set in train endless complications and confusions. I therefore opened Mr Prettiman's door as quietly as I had shut hers—there was a thump and hiss beyond the wall as some point of cornering water struck our hull—and brought it to behind me. He lay, as I have said, turned end for end. His head was now next to the writing flap. I moved forward cautiously and sat in the canvas chair by him. There was no longer a mound lifting the bedclothes at his waist. The blankets were gone as well. A cotton sheet and a shawl of woven material were all that covered his body. The air was not balmy. Such an adjective would be out of place for any sickroom! But the scanty bedclothes gave me a sudden awareness of the other change in our circumstances. Water might still swill about our feet and legs—condensation might lie on and stream down any wall, any bulkhead, but we were at last approaching, if we had not reached it, the southern spring! If this continued, I thought, we should find ourselves wearing "doldrums" rig again!

Mr Prettiman's eyes were closed and he breathed easily. His face was still wasted and lined but there was now the faintest trace of colour in his hollow cheeks where before there had been nothing but shadow. His hands lay outside the sheet, one of them on an open book. I leaned forward with a natural curiosity but must have disturbed him somehow. His head turned on the pillow, his breathing altered—became laboured. I kept deadly still in a state of apprehension that I had injured him all over again! But then his breathing eased, his hand moved from the book and a page stood up so that I could see what it was.

"Good God! Pindar!"

His eyes opened and he turned his head.

"You. Young Talbot."

"Mrs Prettiman said she thought you wouldn't mind if I sat by the bunk until you woke, sir."

"Had to move, didn't you? Had to speak? Had to wake me?"

"No, Mr Prettiman! The word was—involuntary."

A trace of a smile appeared.

"What else did you suppose I meant? But never mind. You said 'Pindar'."

"Yes, sir. There, by your hand."

"When you have to lie flat, holding up a book makes the whole thing a trial. I was looking for a quotation and drifted off. It's somewhere in the sixth Olympian. It goes—'φύονται δὲ καὶ νέοις ἐν ἀνδράσιν πολιαί'."

The lines were very familiar to me.

"'Grey hairs flourish even among young men'—and it goes on—'here and there before the right time of life for it'. But that's not the sixth Olympian. It's the fourth, right at the end. May I—? There!"

"So you know!"

"Well, sir, we are all having a rough time of it, aren't we? I daresay I could find a grey hair or two if I looked."

"Not that, boy! The Greek! You've kept it up—Why?"

"I just liked it, sir, I suppose. I read it now and then."

"No boy of your age who keeps up his Greek can be entirely witless—silly perhaps—but with some inkling of a wider view."

"I'm not precisely a boy, Mr Prettiman!"

"You're not precisely a mature man either! Now don't answer back. I must apologize for not looking you straight in the face all the time but I have to lie flat, you see. This leg. Have to hobble for the rest of my life, I suppose. How is a man to get round like that? I suppose the surgeons will strap me up. Do you think I shall be able to ride?"

"I can't say."

"Might be able to ride side-saddle. Mrs Prettiman would ride astride, of course, in her trowsers"—a laugh began in his chest but never reached the surface except to give it a heave or two—"'Here come the Prettimans,' they'll say. 'Which is which?'"

"I came in to say, sir, that I congratulate you on your recovery, and apologize for my part in it."

The laugh was right there, loud and prolonged. Tears ran out of his eyes.

"'Apologize for my part in it'! Oh, my hip!"

"I see what you mean, sir, and it is indeed amusing—or I would have thought it so had I not said it myself. But I am sincerely sorry for the terrible pain I caused you."

"You certainly gave me a twinge, Talbot. But without it I should still be in a sad case. Having your own thigh bone rammed up into your body is no joke, I can tell you. Well. So you know more Greek than was beaten into you. Latin, of course. But let us say nothing of Latin. It is a language for sergeants. Why do you read Greek then? Come along!"

"I don't know. Amusement perhaps. No, that won't do. Glaucus and Diomede—"

"Intellectual snobbery? Being better than your neighbour? Belonging to a select few?"

"Yes, to some extent. But there is more, sir, as well you know!"

"Ambitious to become a bishop?"

"No, sir. But you must not be plagued with me, Mr Prettiman. I have said how sincerely sorry I am for the pain I caused you. And now I will leave you."

Good God, this was in the very vein of Parson Colley! But the sick man was making fretful motions of denial with his right hand.

"Don't go!"

"I believe I am not an adequate conversationalist for you, sir. And so—"

"My dear Mr Talbot!—does that form of address content you?—if you had lain for days in the forced contemplation of a white-painted ceiling only eighteen inches above your head, I don't know what seamen call it—"

"The Tarpaulins would call it 'the deckhead', sir. Well, I am flattered to be regarded as a little more interesting than white paint!"

"Your opinions interest me profoundly. Some of them have been reported to me while others I must confess I have overheard, for you know you tend to speak in a loud not to say authoritative manner!"

"As I am clearly—"

"I said 'Don't go!'"

"That was certainly authoritative!"

"So it was. We must be gentle with each other. Sit down again—please! There. Now. What is the purpose of your voyage?"

"I would have said a few months ago that it was to fit me for a position of responsibility in the government of my country. Now my ambitions are somewhat different."

"Since *Alcyone* drifted alongside us with her ladies—Oh, sit down! Do you think that sort of thing can be private? Marriage is a public declaration! I should know!"

"I could only wish it had indeed been a question of marriage—but I do not suppose our conditions are similar."

"I should hope not indeed! The considered alliance of two persons dedicated to the betterment of the human condition is not lightly to be compared with—"

"'Oh, she doth teach the torches to burn bright!'"

"You started your voyage with the objectivity of ignorance and are finishing it with the subjectivity of knowledge, pain, the hope of indulgence—"

"And you, sir, travelling with the avowed intention of making trouble—of troubling this Antipodean society is created wholly for its own betterment! It is a noble gesture which offers freedom and rehabilitation even to the criminal elements of our own society at home!"

"Do you know 'our own society'?"

"I have lived in it!"

"School. University. A country house. Have you ever visited a city slum?"

"Good God, no!"

"The cottages on your father's estates. Do the labourers sleep in beds?"

"They are accustomed to the ground. They are happy there. They would not know what to do with a bed stood on legs!"

"You know nothing."

"You are clearly seized of universal truths, Mr Prettiman. Some of us do not find them so easy to come by!"

"Some of us do not try to find them."

"The established order—"

"Is sick!"

This was a kind of cry which convulsed the man's body.
It was resumed—subsumed in one of those great cries
which had so disconcerted me. His body which had jerked
under the bedclothes now shook as with the extremity of
passion, but this was pain. His face had paled again. Sweat
coursed down it as he gritted his teeth. The door opened
and Mrs Prettiman hastened in. She looked quickly from
him to me. Then she pulled a large handkerchief from beneath his pillow and wiped his face with it. She murmured
to him. I could catch no more than the word "Aloysius"
and the word "calm". His anguish appeared to subside. I
was rising from the chair again to withdraw from this
private scene when his hand shot out and grasped my
wrist firmly.

"Stay, Talbot. Letty. We have a specimen. What do you
say? Shall we see if anything is to be done with it?"

The word "specimen" had a precise medical connotation
as far as I was concerned. But to my surprise Mr Prettiman continued to hold my wrist instead of allowing
my departure. Mrs Prettiman, on the other hand—and I
noticed that her hair was now properly confined and hidden—said nothing but nodded solemnly, then withdrew. I

feared that I might be about to be lured into some medical nastiness but the sick man simply continued our previous conversation.

"What *do* you know then, Mr Talbot?"

I thought.

"I know fear. I know a friendship which would exchange gold armour for bronze. Above all, I know love."

"Oh, do you? Do you not vaunt yourself? Are you sure you are not puffed up? Do you not seek your own?"

"Perhaps. But without it I am indeed become as sounding brass and tinkling cymbals. And long before St Paul, did not Plato claim that we may ascend from the one love to the other?"

"Well said, my boy! Well said indeed! There is a book above my head. The third along, I think. Please take it down. Thank you. Will you read it to me?"

"It is French."

"Do not speak so dismissively of the language just because you are acquainted with a greater one!"

"To tell you the truth, I have had such a dose of Racine from my godfather it has soured me with their whole literature."

"This is by a master who could stand with all but the very greatest of the ancients."

"Very well, sir. What do you want me to read?"

So, moving with roll and heave, with creak of timber and roar of wind, I found myself as we moved towards the unknown shore sitting by the bed of a man as strange

219

and unknown; and reading aloud with an accent which appeared to satisfy Mr Prettiman, though it was little like
Mr Benét's, from Voltaire's *Candide*! He had directed me
as I now see was inevitable, to the passages concerning
Eldorado. As I read, an astonishing change began to appear in Mr Prettiman. He nodded every now and then,
his lips moved, his eyes, as if they did not merely receive
light but could refashion it, seemed to shine with an interior source of their own. His face flushed, words moved
towards his lips but were never given air, he listened so
intently. When I read out the words of *le bon vieillard*: "We
don't pray to God, he gives us what we need, we are eter-
nally grateful—we do not need priests, we are all priests!"
he interrupted at last, crying out, "Yes, yes, that's it!"

It was my turn to interrupt.

"But, Mr Prettiman! This is no more than an expansion
of Pindar—the Fortunate Isles—you have it there under
your hand—allow me!"

I took the book, found the place and read it out to him.

"'ἀπονέστερον ἐσλοὶ δέκονται βίοτον, οὐ χθόνα
ταράσσοντες ἐν χερὸς ἀκμᾷ—', and so on."

When I had done he took the book back, glanced at the
text, smiling, and muttered a translation.

"'The gift of easy life they get, not irritating earth with
lusty hands, no, nor troubling salt water to scrape a bare
living—'"

"And the rest, sir! They rejoice in the *presence* of the

gods! There's the tower of Cronos—ocean breezes, flowers of gold blazing—"

"Yes, yes, I remember. I might as well tell you, Edmund, that I had to learn it all by heart as an imposition and even that did not entirely spoil it! It was—perceptive of you to bring it into the ring with Eldorado. You are well read, my boy—and you read well too! But don't forget the difference between Pindar and Voltaire. Pindar is talking about a mythological land—"

"So is Voltaire, surely!"

"No no! Oh, I have no doubt that literally speaking South America was much different from the country Candide discovered! How could it be otherwise in a country devastated by the Roman Catholic Church?"

"They had not reached it."

"But there was indeed an Eldorado, and there will be again."

"You are overexciting yourself, sir. Shall I—"

"It is what this voyage is about, you see. Do you understand? How can I—I am crippled. Not for me, not for me. I may see the promised land, glimpse a far peak of Eldorado, but the country itself will be for other men!"

"And *that* is what the voyage is about?"

"What else? We would have gone, a caravan of convicts released, our printing press with us, immigrants of goodwill, women convicts, or the poor young followers of their ignorant men—"

"You are feverish, sir. I will call Mrs Prettiman."

"Stay."

For a while he was silent. He lay quiet, then spoke with his head straight in the pillow and his eyes shut.

"It seems I shall—survive if we all do. A certain document which I entrusted to you—"

"I had wondered, sir. Shall I bring it to you?"

"Wait. Why will you always try to be one step ahead? I am confined to my couch. Mrs Prettiman devotes herself to me. She must not be troubled with the view of such a missive or *ever know* that I entrusted it to your hands."

"Of course not, sir."

"So do not bring it back to this cabin. Drop it in the sea."

"If that is your wish, sir."

"Wait again. This is—difficult. You must know, Edmund, that the lady is like the land we are approaching?"

"Sir?"

"Good God! Where are your wits, boy? Unpolluted, sir!"

"Oh, *that*! I—I rejoice to hear it, sir. Of course I—"

He cut me off, glaring at me with the anger which was so close to his heart and his lips.

"Rejoice? Rejoice? Why should you 'rejoice'? And there is no 'of course' about it, sir! Had I not had the misfortune to dislocate this hip the lady would not now be unpolluted—that is to say—"

"I understand, sir. You need say no more. I will do it immediately and with such a good will—"

"Not with a rush but casually, boy—man I should say, should I not?"

"I hope so, sir. But 'Edmund' would be better."

"We must not have a youth dashing through the lobby and waving a paper in the air as if he were, were—"

"Lieutenant Benét? I will be discreet."

"And, Edmund. You read well."

"Thank you, sir!"

"So does Mrs Prettiman. But of course she does not read Greek. It is too much for a woman's brain."

"I doubt that in the case of Mrs Prettiman, sir. There have been bluestockings! But I take the point. I shall be happy, indeed flattered, to read to you on your bed of pain. And now if you will excuse me—"

"Any time you feel like coming back—if I am not asleep—"

I went away with the most mixed feelings, happiness, strangely enough, being the uppermost. It was a feeling which I was, from that day forward, to associate with him and her. When the memory of Miss Chumley—most adorable and commonsensical of young persons!—returned upon me I felt no more than that she would have agreed that they were likeable but mistaken—whereas I—

What shall I say? No matter what nonsense Mr Prettiman talked—and I have never entirely convinced myself that it was nonsense—the listener came away with a sense of well-being, of enlightenment, of feeling that *yes* it was true, the universe was great and glorious and that these adventures of the mind and body were the crown of things—a feeling that drifted away naturally enough, of course, as other considerations supervened and hid them!

So this, then, was the beginning of what for me was the strangest adventure of our long voyage. Still battered but in weather that seemed never to rise above the level of a favourable gale we sped eastward towards our goal and life was *irradiated* by the nature of them both—for sometimes she would bring her canvas chair and sit by me while I read to him. They were quite unlike any people I had ever met before! He was donnish; but there was nothing laughable about him unless it was his capacity for explosive anger. Beyond that his mind ranged vastly through the universe of space and time as it did through the other universe of books! And she, following his lead but not scrupling to differ from him and sometimes leading us where we had not thought to go! The Crown, the principle of hereditary honours, the dangers of democracy, Christianity, the family, war—indeed there were times when it seemed to me that I threw off my upbringing as a man might let armour drop around him and stand naked, defenceless, but free!

Then after a doze in the evening I would spend the middle with Charles, bring ideas to him and test them against his absolute integrity. I found in truth that I had never examined an idea before! To have read Plato and not tested an idea! It sounds impossible, but it is not, for I had done it.

(17)

It could not have been more than a day or two after I had become acquainted with Mr Prettiman that I noticed a change in Charles. He was more silent than before. At first I thought that he was concerned with the state of the ship but it was not so. The fact was, he found my sudden esteem for the social philosopher strange, not to say incomprehensible. Charles did not generalize. He would not examine the ideas of liberty, equality and fraternity but dismissed that modern trio because of the way they had been applied among the Gallic Race by the medium of the guillotine and the splendid wickedness of the Corsican! Always his mind moved at once to the practical.

"You will do yourself no good with the governor of a penal colony, Edmund, by tossing such ideas about as if you approved of them!"

The truth is, Charles was well enough where he was. Unlike mine, his ideas had been tested in the fire of his religion, Prettiman's in the cruelties and torments of social condemnation, derision, dislike. It was not more than a very few days after I had begun to read and discuss with the Prettimans that I taxed Charles with his silences. His reply—if in unconscious sympathy with him I may revert to Tarpaulin—*brought me up, all standing*.

"You are moving away from me, Edmund. That is all."

I seized him by the arm.

"No! Never!"

But it was true nevertheless. I liked him as much, would do for him as much. But set in the foreground of the world which Prettiman was opening to me, Charles was—diminished. I understood his practical approach, his anxious grasp of his position in the ship, his battle with jealousy and spite, his devotion to the *customs of the sea service* which would not allow him to criticize his captain even when his captain was wrong! I saw, and admired, his simple goodness. Surely, I told myself, that is enough? I thought of the way he found me dry clothing at a time when it seemed a miracle in that soaked ship. Thinking thus, it was then I first realized how he had contrived to free me from my haunted hutch for four hours of every night. Then I would remember Glaucus and Diomede, the bronze armour Charles had given me and the gold armour I had sworn to give him! The only armour which Charles would find golden would be promotion to post captain.

Yet Charles? I had no doubt at all of his courage. His knowledge of the economy of a ship was complete. Yet *Charles*, a ship's husband, in command of a ship, a warship with the future of our world in his hands?

I did dare to put my problem before Mr and Mrs Prettiman. Prettiman bade me undertake the exercise of *un-twisting* the affair back to where it had started, and I understood at last that I had simply promised more than I could or should promise or perform. Mr Prettiman declined to help.

"You must, of course, do what you think is right. If you do not believe he is worth making post you must tell him so."

Of course I could not tell him! Who was I to do so? The result was there were now periods of silence from me during the middle watch as well as silence from Charles. Oh that voyage towards which I had looked as a simple adventure! What ramifications it had, what effects on the mind, the nature, what excitement, what sad learning, what casual tragedies and painful comedies in our rendering old hulk! What shaming self-knowledge! For brooding on my problem I even imagined one saying in the future—when my naval client had at last demonstrated his inadequacy as a post captain—*that was one of Talbot's recommendations, you know*. Sometimes I thought, and bitterly enough, that the only human quality to the depths of which there could be no limit was my personal meanness!

My broodings were interrupted by another twist in our society. It was the question of our longitude. I had known that Benét and the captain were immersed in some high theory of navigation but had not thought much about it. A glum Bowles brought me up to date. He illustrated in water spilt on the saloon table the problem before the captain. Sooner or later we must approach the new continent.

But though we knew where we were to larboard or starboard, so to speak, we could not define our position fore and aft! In a sentence, without an accurate knowledge of our longitude we might hit land before we saw it! The solution adopted by seamen in earlier days had been to heave to during the hours of darkness and only advance when there was light enough. Naturally, this was a luxury which our captain could not afford with a crew on half rations and only those with good teeth able to profit by what was left. Add to our uncertainty the circumpolar current which might or might not be helping us towards our destination and it will be seen what an added exacerbation was inflicted on me by Lieutenant Benét's confident assertion that he could find our longitude without a chronometer. I put aside my dislike of the man and, knowing the time of his watch, waylaid him from my usual position by the main chains.

"A word with you, sir."

"A challenge?"

"Not at the moment—"

"Ah! So we are back on conversational terms, are we?"

"This matter of the longitude and the chronometers—"

"I thought it was pistols. Good God, Mr Talbot! Do you suppose Captain Cook carried chronometers with him?"

"Of course!"

"Well, he did not!"

With that, he leapt away up the stairs as the duty watch set about its four-hourly dance during the minute or two before the bell rang out. I followed him but already he was deep in talk with Anderson. Even when the watch was changed and Mr Askew descended from the quarterdeck, Benét and Anderson talked on about the moons of Jupiter! They bandied astronomy as if it were a ball game—eclipses, parallax, perigee and apogee—I began to have an uneasy feeling that they were both aware of me and were deliberately keeping me out!

"Lunar distance, Mr Benét. Agreed. But the check—"

"The passage of Calypso. We shall present it to their lordships—the Anderson-Benét method!"

Anderson laughed aloud! He did!

"No no! It is all yours, my boy!"

"No, sir—I insist!"

"Well. You had better make it work first."

The message was plain. Even so, the contrast between this excited pair—whether their "method" was practicable or not—and poor dear, dutiful Charles was so clear as to be painful. I stood, ostensibly watching the waves, until I was heartily tired of it. But the two men continued to ignore me and at last there was nothing left for me to do but go away. It was one of those defeats which are so easy to describe in their outward event and so impossible to sum up in their total effect. I went below, knowing that I had been set aside in a matter which concerned not just the Navy but every man, woman and child in the ship. It would have needed more than all the assurance with which I had entered the ship to break in and interrupt them; but I could not think precisely why.

I went cautiously down the ladders, for the ship was moving more that day. Water was coming aboard even into the waist, which fact would once have seemed notable to me though now it was common enough. Clear water was running inches deep with every roll over the planking newly scoured from Charles's oil—planking from between which, as some unhandy configuration of the sea passed under us, the spewed oakum flopped this way and that like worms in a flooded field. I was making my moody way to the saloon when I saw old Mr Brocklebank open the door, his legs wide apart, his tall and portly figure wrapped in the dirty coach cloak, and I decided that I wanted no closer acquaintance with him. I went to Mr Prettiman's door therefore and asked if I might read to him. He was glad to see me, he said, for he had passed a wakeful night now that the paregoric or laudanum was exhausted. He was not in pain but ached, he said, which was wearisome. I thought he looked a little feverish, for there was colour now high on his cheekbones and his eyes seemed unnaturally bright. He would not have me read to him. He said he would be unable to fix his attention. He wanted instead to know what the state of the ship was. He said he could feel that the weather had worsened again. I told him that the water was indeed moving about a little more but that we were getting along capitally. I went on to say—and now Mrs Prettiman entered—that the great *political* point in the ship was Mr Benét's proposal to find the longitude without reference to the chronometers. I laughed as I said this and Mrs Prettiman agreed with me, saying that she understood the use of the globes, having had to instruct the young in their value. Without exact knowledge of the time at the Greenwich meridian no ingenuity on earth could discover our longitude.

"You are wrong, Letitia."

She was as disconcerted as I.

"Benét said that Captain Cook had no chronometer."

"He is right, Edmund. The angular distance between the moon and the sun was used to find longitude before the invention or the perfecting, rather, of the chronometer. The defect of the method was the skill required in making use of it."

"So Benét is right again!"

"Anderson took his proposal seriously?"

"Very seriously, I thought—even excitedly. But then, anything which our naval Adonis proposes is certain of an enthusiastic reception from that quarter."

Mrs Prettiman opened her mouth to speak but shut it again. Prettiman frowned up at the deckhead a few inches above his face.

"Anderson is no fool. I am told he is a complete seaman."

"So is Mr Summers, sir. Mr Summers says—"

I heard my voice trail off into silence. It was broken presently by Mrs Prettiman.

"We are all indebted to Mr Summers, Mr Talbot. His care of us and the ship."

231

"He is brave, too, ma'am. Why, in the last dreadful storm among those mountains of water he managed the wheel with his own hands and alone in the greatest danger! It might have killed him!"

Mr Prettiman cleared his throat.

"No one doubts that the first lieutenant is everything you say. But, you see, I do not think you have experienced the difference between a man who has a natural aptitude for the mathematics and one who has not. The difference is absolute—a matter not of quantity but of quality."

I had nothing to say to that. Mrs Prettiman spoke:

"I am told that you helped Mr Summers at the wheel, sir. It seems I am always, as a lady, in the position of expressing my gratitude to you."

"Oh, Lord, ma'am! It was nothing! Nothing at all—"

"Since there have been times when I have had to express other feelings and opinions I am happy to tell you that I believe your conduct was admirable and most manly!"

But Mr Prettiman was turning his head from side to side on the pillow.

"I cannot envisage the method—will he use the passage of a satellite as a check? But how? It is not so easy—"

"Aloysius, my dear, should you not try to sleep? I am sure Mr Talbot—"

"Of course, ma'am, I will go at once—"

"Stay, Edmund. What is the hurry? I am well enough in my mind, Letty, and see their Heavens as clearly as I see

232

you! A man is seldom better employed than in their contemplation!"

"I believe you should not excite yourself, sir."

"'*This majestical roof, fretted with golden fire*—'"

"If it comes to that, sir—'*The floor of heaven is thick inlaid with patens of bright gold.*'"

"Does Mr Benét see them so through his sextant?"

"The young man is a poet, Aloysius. Is that not so, Mr Talbot?"

"He writes verses, ma'am, as who does not?"

"You?"

"Only in Latin, ma'am. I dare not reveal my scanty thoughts in the nudity and plainness of English speech."

"I am really rather impressed, Mr Talbot."

"Since I have you at a temporary disadvantage, ma'am, may I beg you to follow Mr Prettiman's example and address me as 'Edmund'?"

I thought she looked disconcerted at the suggestion. I was bold enough to press her still further.

"After all, ma'am, it is not improper in view of your— that is to say, in view of my—your—"

She burst out laughing.

"In view of my age, you mean? Edmund, my dear boy, you are quite, quite inimitable!"

"We were having a rational discussion, Letitia. Where was I?"

"You and Edmund were exchanging quotations so as to get the universe on a proper literary footing."

"What could be better than ascending from the trivial matter of our exact position on this globe to a contemplation of the universe into which we have been born?"

"And which, sir, is more truly revealed by poetry than prose!"

"Aloysius may agree with you, Edmund, but I am a plain woman."

"You do yourself less than justice, Letty. But, Edmund—continue."

"It is only that—little by little during this voyage, for one reason and another, poetry—has become open to me not as entertainment, as mere beauty—but as a loftiness —man at full stretch—then at night, with the stars—with preposterous Nature—I am half-ashamed to admit it—"

"Oh, look, boy, look! Can the whole be less than good? If it cannot—why, then good is what it must be! Can you not see the gesture, the evidence, the plain statement there, the music—as they used to say, the cry, the absolute! To live in conformity with that, each man to take it to him and open himself to it—I tell you, Edmund, there is not a poor depraved criminal in the land towards which we are moving who could not, by lifting his head, gaze straight into the fire of that love, that χάρις of which we spoke!"

"Criminals?"

"Imagine our caravan, we, a fire down below here—sparks of the Absolute—matching the fire up there—out there! Moving by cool night through the deserts of this new land towards Eldorado with nothing between our eyes and the Absolute, our ears and that music!"

"Yes. I see. It would be—the adventure of adventures!"

"You could come too, you know, Edmund. Anyone could come. There is nothing to stop you!"

"Your leg, sir. You are forgetting it, I believe."

"I am not. It will heal. I know it will. The fire in me will heal me. I know it will! I *will* go!"

"But do as Mrs Prettiman wishes, sir, and keep your body still."

"But you will come!"

I said nothing. It was a silence that grew, lengthened until the very noise of the water hissing past our hull sounded like some wordless voice; and at last I knew that it did not need words and was something even closer to me than words themselves. It was the cold, plain awareness which we call common sense.

And yet I really had *seen*! For a time, in that increasingly fetid hutch, I had felt the power of the man, that attraction of his passion. I had even glimpsed, or thought I glimpsed, our universe as a bubble afloat in the uncommensurable golden sea of the Absolute, the myriad sparks of fire, each the jewel in the head of an animal which could "look up".

They were both watching me. My fists clenched themselves and the perspiration burst out on my forehead. It was an astonishing kind of shame, I think—shame at my inability to say quite simply, "Yes, I will come." There was, too, a degree of anger at finding myself so suddenly pushed up against a wall, held up as it were by some philosophical highwayman with poetry in one hand and astronomy in the other! At last I looked from his flushed face, his expectant eyes, to Mrs Prettiman. She lowered hers and looked at her hands—not the way a seaman does, inspecting his palms, but looking at the backs and the nails. She glanced at her husband.

"I believe you should try to sleep, Aloysius."

I stood up unhandily, swaying against the movement of the vessel.

"I will read to you tomorrow, sir."

He frowned as if the concept were strange to him.

"Read? Oh yes, of course!"

I tried to smile at Mrs Prettiman, but fear it was a sad grimace, and felt my way out of the cabin. I had not shut the door behind me before I heard her murmur to him. I cannot tell what she said.

I told myself that other occasions would occur in which we might renew the conversation, continue what felt like the rising curve of our intimacy. I wished with a spontaneous passion not unlike his that I might be their friend. Yet I saw already that the price was impossibly high. I am after all a political animal with my spark, my—if I may descend to the language fit for sergeants—my *scintillans Dei*, well hidden. I suppose the excuse to be presented to the Absolute is that I did and do sincerely wish to exercise power for the betterment of my country: which of course, and fortunately in the case of England, is for the benefit of the world in general. Let that never be forgotten.

That same night it was, the quartermaster shook me awake a little early. I went to the poop therefore, under a starry sky which was fleeced with moonlit clouds, and waited for Charles to appear. I have to confess that I did scan the sky and was, I think, alive to its transcendent beauty but could not elevate myself to see Mr Prettiman's Good, nor his Absolute. The truth is that while logic compels no belief passion does so quite easily, and it was Mr Prettiman's passion which convinced: so that when he was not there—but why labour the point? His painful presence was needed. Without it I could remember the occasion but not re-create the feeling, the—dare I say—perception. I felt a little rueful I must confess at not being the stuff of which followers are made—and a touch of pain when I felt that Mrs Prettiman had been disappointed in me. I was more than ever glad therefore when Charles appeared. He was cool however. For a time we were silent, standing side by side, each unable to begin. When we did, it was with such a collision that we both burst out laughing.

"After you, sir."

"No, First Lieutenant, after you. We cannot have midshipmen given right of way!"

"I insist."

"Well then—is that Jupiter? Where is the Southern Cross?"

"The Southern Cross will be behind that bank of cloud, I think. In any case it is not necessary to navigation."

"Not even to Mr Benét and his new method?"

"Do not remind me. It makes me—"

"Makes you what?"

"Never mind."

"Jealousy does not become you."

"*Jealousy*? How can I be jealous of a mountebank? That is not—not friendly of you, Edmund."

"I am sorry."

He nodded but was silent, then walked forward to look at the compass. I watched the bank of cloud move away but still could not identify the Southern Cross though Charles had pointed it out to me on other occasions. It is an insignificant constellation when you find it.

Charles came back.

"I am sorry, Edmund, too. I am in the dumps and do not seem able to get out of them."

"I tell you what, old fellow. You need a course of the strangest medicine! A course of the Prettimans!"

"They are witty no doubt. I have little sense of humour."

"Oh, *you*! They would pull you out of the dumps by sheer expansion. Before you knew where you were, you would be discussing things so lofty they make a man forget himself and his petty affairs wholly."

"That has happened to you?"

"While I was with them. Of course no man—except

him—can expect to live at that heat, that height, that intensity!"

"What good is it, then?"

"Try but a single dose!"

"No thank you. We saw the result of that medicine, that concoction at Spithead and the Nore."

"But he is not like that! There is something about him—something which even I, a political creature compounded of equal quantities of ambition and common sense, *while I am there*—"

Charles lowered his voice.

"Do you know what you are saying? Do you know where you are? This is folly! You cannot consort with a Jacobin, an atheist—"

"That he is not!"

"I am glad to hear it."

"You do not sound glad!"

"Oh yes. There is, then, a limit to his infamy."

"That is not fair!"

"You do not understand. I have passed my life in ships, and shall pass the rest of it in them if I am lucky. This is the first ship I have sailed in which is loaded down with emigrants and passengers."

"'Pigs' you call them."

"He received their adulation. He was clever and said nothing that could be construed as an invitation to—"

"To what, for God's sake?"

He muttered.

"I will not use the word."

"Oh, you exasperate me!"

Charles turned, stumped up the ladder to the poop. I stayed where I was, annoyed and hurt at the sudden division between us. I could see Charles back there on the poop. He was grasping the taffrail with a hand on either side of him and staring back into our wake, above which the declining moon shone with an intermittent light. The log was cast and the man reported to Charles, not to me. There was a brief exchange between them. Then the man came down the ladder, went to the traverse board, lifted the canvas and scrawled in a figure seven. It was a repetition of that *snub*—another bit of Tarpaulin—which Benét and Anderson had given me.

So there we were, Charles hunched over the taffrail, I now facing in the other direction and leaning over the forrard rail of the quarterdeck. There was plenty to see, what with the roll of the ship, the rising wind, the mass of sails on our three masts, a whole world of ivory light—old ivory. Seven knots to the east! It was impossible to sulk. I went back, climbed to the poop and stood behind Charles. I spoke as lightly as I could.

"Am I dismissed then?"

To my surprise he did not answer either in the same tone or in anger, but bowed his head between his hands and spoke in tones of extraordinary grief.

"No. No."

"You see he does not talk like that. Why—he was talking, if I understand him aright, of a divine fire up there and down here—"

Charles jerked up his head.

"Here?"

"Well—a metaphor."

"The plates are still hot. There is fire down below there—"

"No, no, no! You mistake me. You mistake him."

"I mistake everyone it seems. Benét is preferred. Anderson addresses me as if I were a, a midshipman. Now you put yourself in danger. Do you not understand? I begin to see how strange a place a ship is. Men have been hanged, you know!"

"For Heaven's sake, Charles! Cheer up! Good God, we are making seven knots to the east, we have sails on all three masts, your frapping keeps us together, all things are well, old fellow!"

"I am confused. I am out of my depth. I believe you to be in danger."

"Don't be such an old woman! I am in no danger. I discuss philosophical matters with another gentleman and would never dream of involving the common seamen in such considerations."

"May I thank you on behalf of us common seamen?"

"Another snub! What is the matter with you? All these pinpricks! Cheer up, man. Look, there is the dawn in the east, there beyond the bows—"

He laughed aloud.

241

"That from the man who wished to become the perfect master of the sea affair!"

"What do you mean?"

"Dawn at this hour?"

"Why, there—no, it has gone, the clouds have covered it. But I tell you, Charles, we are standing eastwards at seven knots into the light! That should be cheering enough for any seaman, common or not, you sulky fellow!"

"Dawn!"

"There, just a little to starboard—one point on the starboard bow—"

He swung round and stared forward where I pointed.

"You can see it clearly, Charles, what is the matter with you? It is no ghost—look there and there—clearer now!"

He was silent for a moment while the grip of his right hand tightened on my arm.

"Heavens help us all!"

"Why, what is the matter?"

"It is ice!"

(18)

"Bosun's mate! Pipe all hands! Messenger, call the captain. Edmund, you must stand aside—"

I moved forward and down to the rail of the quarterdeck. The dull and fitful gleam from the ice which had deceived me into thinking I saw the dawn before us had now disappeared again. The blown spray and fog—perhaps begotten of the ice—the rain and low cloud which wove across our bows like the passes which might go with some sea spell clothed everything beyond the bows in thick opacity.

Captain Anderson's firm step resounded behind me.

"How far was it, Mr Summers?"

"Impossible to say, sir."

"The extent then?"

"Mr Talbot saw it first."

"Mr Talbot, what was the extent of the ice?"

"I saw no end to it, sir, in either direction. I saw ice broad on the larboard bow—at about that angle and ever broader to starboard. It seemed continuous."

"Was it low on the water?"

"No, sir. I think it was a continuous cliff."

My very feet were itching for the captain to order us away from our headlong eastward progress!

"You identified ice on a broader angle to starboard than to larboard?"

"Yes, sir. That may have been the—luck of the fog."

"Mr Summers, was there no call from the forrard lookout?"

"No, sir."

"Have the man arrested."

"Aye aye, sir."

It was unbearably near the tip of my tongue to shout "Alter course, for God's sake!" But Captain Anderson issued his orders in a calm voice as measured as his tread.

"Mr Summers. Bring her round on a broad reach to the larboard."

"Aye aye, sir."

I returned to the rail and held on to it as in an unconscious attempt to halt our violent approach. I even twisted that rail or tried to twist it as if it had been a wheel and I by myself able to turn the ship from her headlong course.

The pipes were shrilling along the deck, the order repeated again and again.

"All hands on deck! D'you hear there? All hands on deck!"

Someone was ringing the ship's bell, not striking out the requisite number for the passage of time and change of the watch but urgently, incessantly. The men came swarming out like bees at an unwonted season from some

ill-judged or accidental blow on the skep. They swarm
and fumble and tumble over each other on the step and
rise in bands to confront the imagined danger. So men
leapt into the rigging, some disdaining the ladders set
for them—one I saw going hand over hand (his rigid
legs held out at an angle) up some vertical rope until the
main course hid him. Men were crowding the fo'castle,
racing along the waist, sliding to a stop by every sheet
and stay. Some came even to the quarterdeck. Few were
tarpaulin'd even in that weather. Some were half naked
or entirely naked just as they had tumbled out of their
hammocks. Now among them and behind them appeared
the emigrants, and below me in the waist, the passengers
crowding out. Mr Brocklebank was shouting up at me but
I could not summon the interest to listen to him. Captain
Anderson was now staring into the binnacle. Throughout
the ship larboard sheets were shrilling in the blocks and
the starboard sheets groaning home.

"Mr Summers."

"Sir."

"Set every sail there is room for."

"The foremast, sir!"

"You heard me, Mr Summers. Every inch of canvas!"

Charles turned and began shouting down into the
waist. I do not think seamen have ever moved more
quickly. Indeed, they obeyed the captain's order rather
than the first lieutenant's, for by the time he had begun
shouting through his speaking trumpet the men were

swarming up the shrouds as if the word "ice" had been instantly audible through every timber of our careering vessel! More sails billowed from the yards and took the wind with a gun's report. Now Charles was hurrying forward. I saw him gesticulating the emigrants out of his way. There were women among them—Mrs East wrapped over her trailing dress with an inadequate shawl she had snatched up in the general panic. The ice remained hidden. It had been the orange moonset in the west which had given us—given me—that deceiving vision of ice to the east through the fitfully opened passages in the smother. Now any passage was more often shut than open.

Anderson spoke again.

"Bring her round another point to larboard."

There were more pipes, orders *sung out* at each mast and repeated up among the glimmering mass of sails. The wheel was spun to starboard, the sheets screamed home! There was a confused shouting of "Light to!" and "Roundly now!" and "Check away!" and "Two blocks on the preventer!" Perhaps I have more than mixed what was mixed already, for I did nothing but will the ship round away from that ghastly cliff. She leaned hugely to starboard, the wind roared over the larboard beam and a mêlée of emigrants with a deal of seawater went cascading into the waist! Our speed increased. Here and there among the sails at their outer edges, the white stuns'ls, those fair-weather sails, began to appear. To wear them spread in this weather was desperate, like our situation,

246

but the captain's order had been specific and peremptory.

He repeated it with his familiar roar.

"Every stitch of canvas there is room for!"

Once more, as in the days of the terrible storm, our masts were bending, but to starboard this time, and more than before, not because we had a storm wind but because we had set a monstrous deal of sail even on those make-shift topmasts! The spray which had deluged us from astern now flew across the ship along the whole length of the larboard side. The billows which had pursued us now struck along that same length. Each wave seemed to heave us bodily sideways towards the direction in which we did not wish to go.

Charles came, climbing hastily up from the waist.

"I caught a glimpse, sir. It seems like no ordinary berg. It lies squarely north and south and there seems no end to it. The cliff which Mr Talbot saw must be somewhere between a hundred and two hundred feet high."

As if to illustrate his words the clouds or fog parted along the starboard beam and bow and the ice glimmered little more than the sails in some strange light which, now the moon had set, seemed to have no source which was identifiable. Foam whiter than the ice climbed the cliff. Then, as we watched, the fog closed yellowly again. Captain Anderson leaned on the forrard rail of the quarterdeck and peered low as if he might be able to see under the smother. Neither he nor Charles, straightening up in defeat, remarked on what was obvious to us all—if we touched the hidden cliff, no man nor woman nor child would live to see daylight. I saw the danger, understood it in every particular and now began to feel it! The chill on my skin below my oilskins and warm clothing was not that of the Antarctic. But all at once the chill itself turned to a definite and perspiring heat, for a sudden and temporary parting of the fog on our starboard bow showed us that not only was the cliff nearer but it rubbed in the point with an appalling act of Nature, which, performed indifferently as it may have been, seemed a theatrical act made for the duration of our glimpse.

"Look!"

Was it I who cried out? It must have been. Before our eyes the face of that part of the cliff which had been revealed fell off, collapsed into a climbing billow. Two huge pieces which must have fallen just before we were permitted to see the action sprang upwards like leaping salmon! They were, I swear, ship-size fragments and falling again as the fog swept all from our sight.

How can a man react who has no service to offer, no counsel to give when he sees such monstrosities and knows that presently, unless there is a miracle, he will be smashed to pieces among them? That more than Antarctic chill became a settled *rigor* which sealed me in my place by the rail of the quarterdeck, careless of wind or spray or green water or anything but our peril. This was a horror of that neutral and indifferent but overwhelming power with which our own ridiculous wood and canvas had nothing to do. We might end as a child's toy, washed up, smashed—

No. The fact has to be experienced. Then, while the rigor still held me, I saw a wave coming at our starboard beam, but out of the fog, a contrary wave from where the unspeakable blocks of ice had fallen. It struck the side and washed clean over us. The bows came up into the wind, the sails thundered, then thumped open like a broadside as the men fought her at the wheel. She danced, losing headway among the contrary waters—

Was my voice among the others? I suppose so. I hope not but I shall never know. Certainly there were voices, shrieks of women and the anguished yelling of men, not merely emigrants and passengers but seamen, cries from aloft, wailing as though we were already lost. The waist below me was a pool of seawater not yet escaped through the scuppers. The black lifelines danced above it and black figures clung and bobbed as the water began to drain away.

Now, below me, a familiar figure in good oilskins waded into the waist! It was Mr Jones, our intelligent self-centred and honest purser. He was wading forward towards his boat on the boom. In his arms, cradled like a baby, he carried Lord Talbot's firkin, that mass of keepsakes and last wishes, last messages which he had sworn to preserve, not knowing that the whole ship had seen it as a joke! He waded forward and the mainmast hid him. The sight made me burst into hysterical laughter.

Charles who had gone somewhere to do something came racing back, splashing through the last inches of the green sea we had shipped. Captain Anderson spoke to him with a new urgency.

"Mr Summers. We must come up more into the wind."

"The foremast, sir!"

The captain roared:

"Mr Summers!"

Charles shouted back in his face.

"I wish to represent that the mast will take no more strain. If that goes—"

"Are you able to propose a better course of action? We are being moved towards the ice."

There was a long pause. Then Anderson spoke irritably.

"Are you *still* attempting to discredit Mr Benét's achievement?"

Charles stood stiffly and answered stiffly.

"No, sir."

"Carry out my orders."

Charles departed. There was more shrilling of pipes and shouting. The leeward sheets were tautened. The sails lost the roundness of canvas bellied by a wind on the beam and flattened. Wrinkles like splayed fingers stretched from every sheet. The sails drummed with tension. Young Mr Tommy Taylor came leaping up to the quarterdeck from below. He took off his hat ceremoniously to the captain.

"Well?"

"The carpenter, sir, Mr Gibbs, sir. He says she is taking

much water. The pumping is continuous. The water is gaining."

"Very good."

The boy saluted again and turned away. The captain spoke again.

"Mr Taylor."

"Sir?"

"What the devil is that fool doing sitting in his boat on the boom?"

I spoke up, for the boy was plainly at a loss.

"It is Mr Jones, the purser, Captain. He is waiting in his own boat for a picked body of seamen to rescue him while the rest of us drown."

"The damned fool!"

"I agree, Captain."

"It is the worst of examples. Mr Taylor!"

"Sir?"

"Get the man down."

Mr Taylor saluted again and hurried away. I lost sight of him almost at once, for the attention was seized by the ice which appeared, perhaps a little nearer, then vanished again. It had been a projection high up and gleaming whiter than before in what must have been the real daylight. Anderson saw it too. He looked at me and smiled that same ghastly smile which he occasionally inflicted on persons near him at moments of extreme danger. I suppose it was brave. I have always been loath to credit him with admirable feelings but neither I nor anyone—except poor, silly, drunken Deverel—has ever doubted his courage.

"Captain—can we not come round a bit farther?"

Appalled, I heard myself, heard my own voice as if it had been that of another, make the presumptuous suggestion. Captain Anderson's smile *twitched*. His right fist, down by his waist, doubled itself and proclaimed to me as clearly as if it had had a mouth, *How I should like to be driven into the face of this insolent passenger!*

He cleared his throat.

"I was about to give the order, Mr Talbot."

He turned away and shouted to Charles.

"Try her another point to windward, Mr Summers."

There was renewed movement in the groups of the crew. Suddenly I remembered Mrs Prettiman and her helpless spouse. I ran quickly down to the lobby and made a rather brusque way through the little knot of passengers in the entry. Mrs Prettiman was standing between the doors of her and her husband's cabins. She was holding the rail lightly. She saw me at once and smiled. I went to her.

"Mrs Prettiman!"

"Mr Talbot—Edmund! How is it with us?"

I pulled myself together and explained the situation as briefly as possible. I believe she paled as she realized the nearness of shipwreck but her expression did not change.

"So you see, ma'am, it is a toss-up. Either we weather the ice or we do not. If we do not we have nothing left—"

"We shall have dignity left."

Her words confounded me.

"Ma'am! This is Roman!"

"I prefer to consider it British, Mr Talbot."

"Oh, of course, ma'am—but what of Mr Prettiman?"

"He is still asleep, I think. How long have we?"

"No one knows, not even the captain."

"Mr Prettiman must be told."

"I suppose so."

Mr Prettiman was awake after all. He greeted us with a great and, if the truth be told, unusual equanimity. I believe he had been awake for some time and with his degree of intellect it was not difficult for him to deduce from the noises and the ship's movement that we were at some crisis. In a word, he had had *time* to fortify himself. In fact his first thought was to get me out of the way so that Mrs Prettiman could attend to the intimate details of his toilet!

"For," said he, smiling into my face, "if they say Time and Tide wait for no man, how much more tyrannical is this mysterious physiology!"

I withdrew, therefore, but was buttonholed by Mr Brocklebank who had a flutter about his lips and who for the first time since the doldrums had appeared without his coach cloak. He was carrying on a quavery conversation with Celia Brocklebank careless of who might hear. As far as I could make out he was imploring her to share the *couch so that they might die in each other's arms*!

"No no, Wilmot, I cannot endure the thought—it is not

congenial! Besides, you have not been there since Christmas when Mr Cumbershum lent you that salubrious book!"

Meanwhile a feeble voice was whimpering from Zenobia's cabin—

"Wilmot!! Wilmot! I am dying!"

"So are we all—I beg you, Celia!"

Has it not been said that in earthquakes and volcanic eruptions the same curious phenomenon of exacerbated sexuality occurs? But whatever the explanation, it gave me a higher opinion of my dear Mrs Prettiman's Roman stance. I spoke with Bowles, pulled the curls of Pike's little girls, suggested to him that a drink would be a good thing—was reminded by Mr Brocklebank there was none remaining, except, as he said, what he had obtained *under the counter* from Master Tommy Taylor. In fact, disappointed in his Celia he retired to the cabin to fortify himself with the bottle, abandoning Celia who showed a marked preference for my company quite suddenly, and I have no doubt that she was in train to find it *congenial* if I had—but Mrs Prettiman returned. I followed her. Mr Prettiman was a little propped up on pillows. He was still smiling with apparent cheerfulness.

"Edmund, we have a thing or two to settle. You will of course look after Letty."

"Of course, sir."

"It is impossible that I should survive in the state in which I find myself. It will be next to impossible for a man in full health. But I, with this leg—therefore, when the end is upon us you must get on deck, the two of you, wrapped in as much clothing as you can wear, and make your way to the boats."

"No, Aloysius. Edmund may do so—must do so. He is young and we are not in any way his responsibility. I shall stay with you."

"Now, Mrs Prettiman—I shall become testy!"

"You will not, sir. Edmund will go, not I. But I would like him to hear this, for I believe he stands in much need of an example—and you know, Edmund, I am a governess! So—now"—and here her voice sank both in pitch and volume and became warmer than I at least had ever heard it—"so now I must make a solemn declaration. In the short span of our married life I have never disobeyed you and would not have done so in the future had there been one, not because I am your wife but because of who and what you are! But we have no future, I think, and I shall stay with you here in this cabin. Goodbye, Edmund—"

"Goodbye, my boy. No woman—"

"I—"

My throat was choked. Somehow I got out of the cabin and closed the door behind me. As I did so the ship became upright, another and I guess contrary wave washed over the waist and burst into the lobby. I waded to the entrance, helped Bowles to his feet and saw him return silent and soaked to his cabin, suggested to the Pike children that it was all great *fun* and got myself into the waist.

"Charles! How is it?"

"I have not time, Edmund. But no one has ever seen a berg like this—like that!"

He nodded to the side, then pounded up to the quarter-deck. There was a little less fog—or rather it had seemed to retreat from us. We had perhaps a quarter of a mile—I should say a couple of cables of open water visible on all sides. Once more the ice was visible fitfully; and now in dim daylight looked harder, colder, more implacable. It seemed clear that we were moving parallel to the face of the cliff and at a great speed. The speed could not be due to our motion through the water but rather to our motion relative to the ice. If the fog cleared for a few moments we seemed to race by the white cliff, but as it thickened again so our speed seemed to slow to what was owing solely to the wind. There was, it was evident, a very fast current racing by the berg from south to north and taking us with it. The sea in fact was as savagely in-different to us as the ice!

I turned to go up to the quarterdeck. Little Tommy Taylor came down it.

"How is the purser, Mr Taylor?"

"I couldn't persuade him to leave the boat, sir. The cap-tain says I will have to tell him he's under arrest."

Tommy went forrard and I continued to the quarter-deck. Mr Benét had the watch with young Willis. The cap-tain stood at the top of the ladder up to the poop, a hand on the rail at either side of the top. He was looking round constantly, at the fog, the glimpses of ice, the confused sea which resulted from the beating of the waves and their recoil from the cliff. As I reached the quarterdeck I heard thunderous explosions behind me where once more there was a cataclysmic fall of ice. Though it was veiled by the fog the noise of the fall was significantly louder.

"Well, Mr Benét, what do you think of Nature now?"

"We are privileged. How many people have seen anything like this?"

"Intolerable meiosis!"

"Understatement? Were you not some time ago the passenger who declared to all and sundry that he would not be anywhere else for a thousand pounds? Mr Willis, contrive to stand up straight and look useful even if you are not!"

"My declaration, Mr Benét, was made *pour encourager les autres*, as you would say."

"And you yourself would *fain die a dry death*, as you would say? Hazleton, you idle bugger, you should turn a rope after you've cheesed it! Captain, sir!"

"Yes, Mr Benét, I see the ice. Mr Summers! Have the longboat ready to drop on the starboard beam."

"Aye aye, sir."

More pipes, more hurry.

"Have you noticed, Mr Benét—"

"Just a moment, Mr Talbot. Mr Summers! Willis—go after Mr Summers and tell him that Mr Talbot suggests filling the longboat with hammocks."

"I did no such thing!"

The captain spoke behind us. It was the only time I ever heard Mr Benét receive even the shadow of a rebuke.

"It will keep some of them busy, Mr Benét, and is appropriate at this time. But you might inform the passengers in general terms that they are still advised not to interfere in the running of the ship!"

Having delivered this relatively mild rebuke to his favourite, the captain retired to the taffrail as if he was embarrassed by his own words. Benét turned to me.

"You heard that, Mr Talbot?"

"I said nothing about hammocks! Nor do I know why the longboat is to be got ready unless it is to ensure the escape of the more valuable persons, in which case—"

"There are no valuable persons, Mr Talbot. We shall all die together. The longboat is to persuade people that something is being done. It is to be a fender between us and the ice—"

"Will that do any good?"

"I think not."

Willis came back.

"Mr Summers says to thank Mr Talbot, sir."

"You are looking green, my lad. Cheer up! When it comes, it will be quick."

"Benét! The ice is nearer—look!"

"We have done what we can. Captain sir. Do we drop the boat?"

"Not yet."

Suddenly the ice was there, close. I could look at nothing else. To my eyes the cliff seemed monstrously high. It was uniformly undercut along the base and the water near it was full of huge fragments which had fallen and which were the immediate danger. I heard the captain shout some Tarpaulin order and saw the longboat drop over the starboard side—saw the thick painter snub as the pull of the water came on the boat. The ice, now gleaming dully white and green, was behaving preposterously. We had swung even farther to the north—I suppose an unordered and involuntary movement made by the men at the helm—and if our heading had been anything to go by should have been moving markedly away from the cliff. But it was evident even to my untutored eye that we were not doing so. For the effect of the earth's rotation which is said to cause that perpetual current round the Antarctic Ocean should have moved the ice as much as it moved us. But for whatever reason, it was not doing so. We were feelingly approaching the ice as *Alcyone* had approached us, beam on or even quarter on. Nor could our sails account for our two movements—the one to the north, the other towards the east and the ice.

I make all this sound too coldly rational! How many times since those dreadful hours have I started up in my bed and *willed* a change in our remembered circumstances! But then, as I clung to the windward side of the vessel, I had no rational appreciation of what was happening, only

the incomprehensible sight of it! How to explain the dis-
organized fury of the sea, the towers, pinnacles, the bursts
of water that had replaced those steadily marching billows
which had swung under and past us for so many days together? For now it seemed that those billows were flung
back at us. Columns of green water and spray climbed the
ice cliff and fell back from it. Wind against wind, wave
against wave, fury feeding on itself—I tried to think of my
parents, of my Belovéd Object, but it would not do. I was a
present panic, an animal in the article of death. The ice was
above us! Ice fell, leapt up monstrously from beneath the
foam, and still we swept in towards that hideous, undercut
and rotten wall. Some of our sails were slack and beating,
some filled the wrong way round and yet we hurried towards and along the wall fast as horses might have drawn
us. If there was anything regular about our situation it was
in the explosive falls of ice from the walls of this mortal
and impregnable city! Then I recognized that Nature—the
Nature which Miss Chumley so rightly detested—had now
finally gone mad. For hours we had been thrust sideways
towards the cliff of ice *downhill*, as Mr Benét had once said,
and at a coaching speed. Now the ice, as if to demonstrate
its own delirium, was performing the impossible. It was ro-
tating round us. It appeared astern, then swung round past
us and went by way of the bows where it had come from.
It repeated the action, then drew in alongside to starboard.
Among all the noises of that situation I heard the longboat
crack like a nut. I do not know if the *coup de grâce* was given

the boat by a floating block of ice or the cliff itself. There was a green road of smooth water close under the ice, only interrupted when the cliff above us spilled some incalculable weight. The blocks that had fallen into the road of green water were going with us at the same speed, crashing and crumbling where they jostled each other or the side of the cliff. A block fell and took a stuns'l off the outer edge of some sail on the mainmast and dropped, comfortably wrapped as it were, the stuns'l yard fluttering behind it like a feather. Another, the shape and more than the size of Lady Somerset's fortepiano, came sideways forward of the mainmast and took the front half of Mr Jones's boat with Mr Jones and Mr Tommy Taylor attached and shot with them through the larboard rail.

But we were now, it seemed, to be introduced even more intimately to the cliff, which arranged itself along our larboard side, careful, as it were, not to touch us.

We were, to use Tarpaulin once more, making a sternboard, or more intelligibly, we were going backwards faster than we had ever gone forwards! The cliff, dropping a few thousand tons of ice by our larboard bow, threw that off to starboard as a boy might thrust a model boat with his foot.

It was a crisis of helplessness beyond seamanship. My brain went. I saw a *mélange* of visions in the ice which swept past me—figures trapped in the ice, my father among them. A cave opened with an eye of verdure at the other end of it.

The last spasm of our ordeal came upon us. The ice moved violently and disappeared before our eyes and we raced *downhill*! It seemed the final sinking, the end of everything.

Only the sinking did not come. We were, it appeared, upright in a windless sea to the east of which a clear white day had spread. Around us in the water, blocks of ice lay still.

I straightened up from my crouched position, unstuck my hands from the rail. Along the decks, people were beginning to move again, but slowly as if they could never be too cautious. We were, after all, turning very slowly in the water. The sails were rustling.

Someone forrard shouted a sentence and there were bellows and screams of laughter and, after that, silence again. I never found out what the joke was or who had made it.

To the west of us lay the yellow fog with here and there a dull gleam of ice in it, some increasing distance away, courtesy, it seemed, of that same circumpolar current which for so many days had been bringing us to the east.

People began to talk.

(19)

It will save trouble if I insert here part of a communication made to me by a member of my old college who wishes to remain anonymous. However, the reader is assured that my old and learned acquaintance is the final court of appeal in matters of hydrology and associated -ologies.

Your description would be well enough for a fiction in the wild, modern manner! Was there not a demented woman screaming curses from the top of your "ice cliff"? Or was there perhaps an impassioned Druid imprecating your vessel before he threw himself down? I much fear it is all too highly coloured for a respectable geographer and if you *do* find someone rash enough to publish your descriptions I must insist on remaining unnamed! The effect of travel on the young, as I have only too often had to notice, is deplorable. It narrows the immature mind to a set of disjunct but gaudy impressions like the window of a print shop! Fortunately, as a man who has had the sense never to travel farther from his place of birth than the metropolis and who for many years has found a college a world in itself, I am able to lend an objective mind to the problems of terrestrial behaviour.

My good sir! If your ice cliff was a hundred feet high it extended seven hundred feet below the surface of the water. That may seem a great deal to you; but my information is that the waters at that latitude are far deeper. It is clear, then, that your cliff was aground and you have discovered a reef to which you should give your name at once if you care for that sort of exhibition. Granted (for a moment) a reef with your monstrous lump of ice on it, the following would be a plausible conjecture. Your ship was hurried towards it by wind and current, only to find as she approached that the current was deflected to the north along the face of the ice, then swirled round the northern end as a chip of wood might be whirled round a corner in the gutter. The constant falls of ice are *plausible* too, for your berg was far north and would be quite rotten.

I come to the major point. If your berg was so long, so vast that it even affected the weather, then it must have stretched so far south that it would be more like a floating continent than a patch of ice! You probably do not realize that an "ice cliff" of necessity implies land on which snow can accumulate, glaciers form and at last slide slowly into the sea where they may set off on such a voyage of destruction as you describe. In fact it implies a vast continent lying over and round the South Pole! As I have spent the greater part of my adult life perfecting a proof that such a continent is *geographic-*

ally impossible you will not expect me to accept your account as other than that of someone tried beyond endurance by a voyage as long as any in the memory of man. I would here (were you sufficient of a geographer to follow the argument) explain my "Principle of Orbital Balance and Reciprocity". Better I think to present you with an argument suited to a layman. I have shown by a simple calculation of the volume of ice contained in your cliff that its formation must date from several thousands of years previous to the creation of the world in the spring of the year four thousand and four B.C.! Pray, when next you write, offer my humble duty to your Lady Mother and her excellent spouse.

We in the ship, I think, could no more credit what we had been through than could my correspondent. Even copying out his letter has distanced me from the event. I believe my first conscious thought was to see if Charles had suffered in any way. He was on the quarterdeck, gripping to the forrard rail and staring down into the binnacle. This made me realize where I was. Somehow I had got out of the lobby and come to the main chains which I had clutched with both hands (an enormous deadeye affording the hold) and hung there like a leaf in a spider's web while all the madness performed itself round us. At my feet, where she had slipped from between my arms, lay Celia Brocklebank in a dead faint! Somehow we had clutched—now I remembered how she had leapt at me and I had seized her in some profound excess of human need and behaviour! But I picked her up again and bore her, wordlessly, back into the lobby while she sighed and rolled her head. I knocked on her hutch. A tremulous voice answered to my knock.

"Who is it? Who is it?"

"Mr Talbot with your wife. She has fainted."

"Pray take her somewhere else, Mr Talbot. I am not fit—I cannot—"

With one free hand I opened the door. The old man was sitting up in his bunk with a blanket covering him to the waist. He was naked, and mephitic. Carefully I laid the girl on him and steadied her head between his fat arm and shoulder. Then I went, shutting the door behind me.

"Mrs Prettiman? It is I—Edmund."

Her voice answered me.

"Come in."

She was sitting by the bunk. They were holding hands—she with her left hand holding his right. I supposed they had been like that ever since I had last seen them. They were both very pale, and the two locked hands lay beside the man in the bunk as if they had been indissolubly knit and then forgotten.

Mrs Prettiman looked up at me.

"We shall live a little longer?"

"It seems so."

She shuddered from head to foot.

"You are cold, Letty!"

"No."

She looked down at the hands and then, using her right hand, freed her left hand delicately from his. I do not know that he even noticed, for he was watching her face.

"Don't cry. It is unworthy of you."

"Come, sir! Mrs Prettiman is—"

"Quiet!"

"I need," said Mrs Prettiman with what I can only describe as rigid control, "a moment or two alone to collect myself."

"I will leave you, ma'am."

"No."

I opened the door for her and she disappeared.

"Tell me what happened, Edmund."

I gave him an account of our adventure as near as I could. I omitted, because I remembered it too little to be able to describe it, the strange way in which Celia Brocklebank and I had found ourselves together. I am sure she remembered it as little as I and I did not think such a passage was relevant to anything which Mr Prettiman would care to hear. I merely remarked that when the thing was over I picked up a woman who had fainted and restored her to her husband.

"Mrs Prettiman would not faint," said Mr Prettiman. "She might cry but she would not faint."

"I think, sir—"

"Well, don't. I will not have you interfering in her education!"

"*Mrs Prettiman?*"

"Do you suppose that if we ever contrive to lead a caravan to found the Ideal City that she can afford feminine weaknesses? I have rid myself of the ones too prevalent among men and she must do the same as a woman!"

"Allow me to tell you, Mr Prettiman, that I have met no woman—No. Yes. I have met no grown woman who has so impressed me with her lack of those same female weaknesses as you are trying to eradicate!"

"You know nothing about it!"

"I revere Mrs Prettiman, sir, and do not mind confessing it! I—value her highly!"

"What has that to say to anything? I am an educationist, sir, and will not have any judgement in that matter questioned. A man who has worked on his own character as long as I have may perhaps be credited with some knowledge of that of others!"

"And pray, sir, what have you done with your own character to so perfect it?"

"Is it not obvious?"

"No, sir."

"This is unendurable! To be lectured by a stubborn boy—it is endurance I have had to cultivate, sir, endurance and equanimity! Get out, before I—Of all the—"

"I am going, Mr Prettiman. But before I do, allow me to tell you—"

"No, Edmund."

It was Mrs Prettiman. She closed the door behind her and went to her seat. Perhaps I was deceived in thinking that her eyes were a little red.

"It is agreeable," she said, "after so much fuss to be able to sit quietly, do you not think so, Aloysius? But we have not invited Edmund to sit down and he stands there obediently. Pray be seated, Edmund. I have looked out of the lobby. We might be in a different world, you know. The sea is smooth and gentle. I would never have believed such a change possible. How do you suppose it happened?"

"I have no idea, ma'am. I have given up any intention of understanding Nature. I am now firmly on the side of those who confine their approach to the world to a wariness of it!"

There was a brisk rapping at the door.

"See who is there, Edmund, will you?"

I had not seen the man since the days of poor Colley! It was, of all people in the ship, Billy Rogers! He stood there, gigantic and smiling cheerfully. My firkin was cradled in his arms.

"Lord Talbot, sir? This here is yourn, I think, my lord, sir."

"Oh yes—please give it to me."

"Begging your pardon, my lord, sir, Mr Summers said I was to take it to your cabin but I dunno—"

"You don't know my cabin, Rogers?"

For a moment the man ignored me. His wide blue eyes were staring past me to where Mrs Prettiman sat in her canvas chair. There was, I thought, a trace of speculation in them. It irritated me and disgusted me. I stepped out into the lobby and pulled the cabin door to behind me.

"In here. Put it down by the bunk."

The man did as I told him, then straightened up and turned to me. He was tall as I and far broader—a giant.

"Will that be all, sir?"

"The men in the boat—Jones, the purser, and the little midshipman, Tommy Taylor—"

"Gone, sir. Davy Jones has them. Didn't have time to holler, as you saw, just took. There'll be many a man aboard this ship what will sleep more comfortable in his bunk or his hammock to know that Jones has made his last demand for payment. Thank you, Lord Talbot, sir."

He knuckled his forehead and rolled away.

Little Tommy Taylor! Gone. Had his last laugh. Aged what? Fourteen? Fifteen? I felt a great desire to speak with someone and express the fact of the complete and irreversible absence of Tommy and I turned to the Prettimans' door. But it occurred to me that Mrs Prettiman had never seemed as amused as I with Tommy's antics. In fact, if I had to hazard a guess I would say that dear Mrs Prettiman, perfect in so many ways and valuing all kinds of people, would make an exception and find herself able to contemplate if not the extinction at least the absence of a dirty-minded little boy with equanimity.

(20)

This, then, if not the end of our voyage, was the beginning of the end. There was a period of some days in which everyone came to believe that our troubles were over—and seldom has a popular belief been so triumphantly vindicated! The weather, though occasionally what we would once have called *rough*, was never uncomfortably so. Mr Summers and Mr Benét argued politely about the longitude. But no one could believe that it was still a matter of importance since the weather was so uniformly clear that it would have been impossible to miss seeing the land even from ten miles away. The middle watch, which I continued to keep with Charles, became a time of enchantment! The stars seemed near enough to touch. Night was a harmony of blue. The sailors seemed to sing the darkness away! During the day all those who could walked the deck, where the Pike children now played regularly and healthily. Mr Brocklebank was to be seen basking in the sun without his coach cloak. I continued to read to Mr Prettiman and once had the privilege of pacing the deck at the side of Mrs Prettiman and was proud of myself—that onetime gorgon now tamed! Indeed, I had hoped that Lieutenant Benét would observe our constitutional and be put in his place by it. But that afternoon when I read to Mr Prettiman, Mrs Prettiman did not stay to listen but excused herself and, I learnt afterwards, took an afternoon constitutional at the side of Lieutenant Benét. An encyclopaedia of behaviour could not have spoken plainer.

One morning Charles told me that I should see an operation worth watching. So it was. I came up on deck and looked round. There were no more than a very few white clouds bulging up towards the meridian. Mrs Pike leaned on the rail by the break of the fo'castle and talked with Billy Rogers as Zenobia had done before she took to her bed. Mr Gibbs with a couple of men was putting the last touches to the repair of the rail where the ice had smashed it. Under the main bitts and near it, Mrs East and the two small Pike girls were holding a dolls' tea party! But now there was a whole series of orders from Captain Anderson and the dolls' party was interrupted by the need to use some ropes made fast there as the ship was *hove to*. (Please consult Falconer, for I shall not.) Men stationed themselves all along the larboard side with sheaves of line in their hands. There was a boom rigged outboard with a lead suspended from it—a much heavier lead than the hand-lead which one man can manage. Mr Benét in the waist shouted "Let go!"; down went the lead with a pfutt! The line was abandoned all along the

side of the vessel—another length lifted and at once abandoned—another and another—

"Take up the slack!"

"Charles—what is this about? Will it tell us where we
are?"

"No indeed—" He paused for a moment, then smiled.
"You might say it tells us where we are not."

Now the line was no longer up and down but leading
out to an angle towards the northwest.

"There is your circumpolar current, Edmund. I suppose
it is the only direct evidence anyone ever had."

"You are talking in riddles."

"Mr Summers, would you suspend your conversation
long enough to bring her over the lead?"

Charles smiled wryly. He went off and bade the parties
of men alter the strain on various sheets, easing some
so that their sails rounded their bellies a little, and a
rustling and tinkling of water now sounded from our travelling bows. Captain Anderson smiled his brief yellow
smile down at me. Well, what captain would not be happy
on such a day of sunlight and whispering, chuckling, delighted water?

"Hand over hand and roundly now!"

"Up and down!"

"A hundred and ten fathom, sir."

There was a pause while the vertical line was hauled in.
At last the dripping lead itself broke the surface.

"Bear away, Mr Cumbershum. Northeast true."

Mr Benét hailed from the waist.

"The lead is inboard, sir. Sand and shell, sir!"

The captain nodded as though he had expected this information. I turned to the first lieutenant.

"That was all very interesting. What does it signify?"

"Why, that we are in soundings. Benét had his own ideas about our longitude and the captain too. So have I and so has Cumbershum. In this visibility it does not matter much."

He went off, about the ship's interminable business.

"Mr Talbot. A word with you."

I turned. Mr Brocklebank had emerged from the lobby. Once more he was massive in his wrapped coach cloak.

"What can I do for you, Mr Brocklebank?"

The old man drew close.

"I fear I did not appear at my best, sir, during the late emergency—"

"Well, you are old and cannot be expected—"

"It was not age, Mr Talbot, not decrepitude but sickness. I feared a syncope, a sudden failure of the vital organ."

"The ship seemed almost certain to sink and that was about to settle all our problems."

"Better without a syncope than with one. I fear the enemy within more than the sea without! You remember when *Alcyone* lay alongside us?"

"Indeed I do!"

"Oh, but now I remember—you was in your cabin,

which was what she must have been crying about—"

"She?"

"The young lady. I was interrogating the surgeon from *Alcyone* when he came from your cabin but he brushed me aside! There's a medical man for you! He went back to his ship and the women crowded round him—I understand now! They wanted to know how you went on."

"Oh, it was Miss Chumley! It must have been!"

"Imagine that—a strong fellow like you monopolizing the surgeon, let alone the women—Good God, there never was such a consultation as I had then while two ships were parting! I hallooed him and they implored him and orders were shouted and there was such a groaning and a creaking—and that silly young woman crying, *'Mr Truscott, Mr Truscott, will he live?'* and Lady Somerset crying, *'Marion, Marion, not before the sailors. Oh, this is so affecting'*—and so much *'Cheerily, my hearties, roundly now'* —so much noise from the sails and the surgeon—can you imagine it? Just bawling back at me, *'What do you want?'*— and I crying, *'I wish for a regimen'* and he— *'Less of the pipe, none of the bottle, less of the trencher and none of the couch, you fat old fool'*—and the young one flinging her arms round Lady Somerset's neck with a cry of *'Oh, Helen!'* And it sheered off, *Alcyone*, I mean, so I have had to do the best I could without proper medical advice, which accounts for my indifferent performance when—"

"She really cried out, *'Will he live'*?"

"The young woman? Yes, or words to that effect. It may

275

have been '*I suppose he will live*' or '*He may live*'—"

"It must have been '*Will he live?*' She would not have cried out the surgeon's name twice had she not been distracted!"

"Yes. Well. She may have cried it twice, '*Truscott, Truscott*', or perhaps it was '*Oh, Truscott!*' or '*Mr Truscott*'!"

"Oh, God."

"I remember it clearly. Pipe, bottle, trencher, couch. I ask you!"

"Oh, if she did not cry his name twice I am the unhappiest of men!"

"Mr Talbot, this is unlike you! I was simply explaining my conduct during the late crisis. She may have cried, '*Truscott, Truscott, Truscott*'—or more. And the worst of it is, under his regime I let more wind than I did when I was eighteen stone of solid man!"

"But she did cry out!"

"How else could I have heard her?"

"Charles had seen her the night before staring through the side of the ship—"

"So did the surgeon cry out, '*No pipe, less trencher, no bottle and no couch*'? Or was it '*less couch*'? By which he would have implied an occasional healthy recourse to the connubial. He would not have said no bottle and no trencher—and here I have been living all these weeks chaster than a nun! Women are so cruel. '*You go right out on deck, Wilmot,*' she says. '*I cannot endure your horrid smells. Besides, I believe it is bad for my complexion.*'"

"And Miss Chumley expressed the deepest concern for my welfare!"

I waited for a reply, but the old man, one hand on the bulwarks, his feet spread wide, had lapsed into a state of concentration on his interior. I withdrew quickly.

So I added yet another atom of comfort and torment to the cobweb-thin collection of yearnings and surmises that bound me to her.

There is, I suppose, only one moment of drama towards which the reader is still looking. When, after this year-long or nearly year-long voyage, did we sight land? I sympathize with the reader's suspense. It has been, it still is, a difficulty to me too. The truth is that our first sight of land was about as undramatic as it could well be. I have thought now and then of ways round this dull patch. I had thought of introducing the slapstick, the low comedy of Nature making fools of everyone in sight. I pictured a misty morning, a slight air; and the moment at which someone on the ship, preferably a woman or child, realizes the ludicrous truth. There are gales of laughter from the crew and sheepish grins from our navigators. We are aground in still water, which sinks away slowly to leave us high and dry—and what is more, as the mist is drunk up by the sun, we see that we are able, by the use of ladders, to step ashore! But a certain *synaesthesia* with our noble vessel tells me that in such a case there would have been three dreadful reports as the weight came wholly on

Charles's frapping and the hull subsided into its own weed and ballast and spread like—anything that melts in the sun!

Then again, I thought of preserving the truth but *sharpening* it a little. There was, for example, a hole in the bulwarks under the main chains, and examining this with Mr Askew, the gunner, I learnt about the dreadful art or craft of cannon-ball rolling. A disaffected sailor is able to lift a cannon ball out of a shot garland and allow it to decide for itself what damage it will do. Mr Askew—he muttered the information, for it is not to be spread throughout the lower deck of a ship—informed me that as a ship *works*, such a cannon ball, in an unfortunate case, is able to fly the full length of the vessel and take apart the random target as brutally as if it had been shot from a gun. But the hole had not been made by a cannon ball or there would have been damage to the main chains as well. Perhaps the ice did it, though I myself am inclined to rats. But build up the suggestion of disaffection, detect a mutter here and there, and you have your high drama to take the place of the low comedy. There is a confronta-tion. The crew and the emigrants inch out of the fo'castle threateningly. Captain Anderson is proud and defiant. The men move forward. One is about to strike a—

But the cry rings out from the crosstrees of the fore-mast.

"Deck there! Land ho! Land ahead and on the larboard bow! Deck there! Land ho!"

It will not do, of course. I do not mean because this is an autobiography, for I have come to think that men commonly invent their autobiographies like everything else. I mean it would be too stagey.

The truth in a way was subtler and more amusing. On a morning of perfect visibility, when Mr Summers handed the captain his folded paper with the computed latitude and longitude, the captain examined it with raised eyebrows and compared it with the other folded paper which had been given him by Mr Benét. His only comment was to order the ship's course to be maintained. We sighted land some hours later.

What a novelist could not have foreseen and the autobiographer must make as interesting as he may was the complete reversal of expected attitudes. The crew, which might have rolled cannon balls, or made protests, or grumbled and sent deputations *before* we sighted land, were quiet, good-humoured and obedient until the low-lying coast was there before them. Only then was there murmuring and the clear voice of dissent. They thought we should disembark at once on this land of milk and honey, pausing merely to select ourselves the slaves of our choice from the eager applicants!

It was at this time that Mr Prettiman had some kind of—revelation is the only word I can find for it. He confessed that he now believed there was a profound mystery (rather than secret) at the heart of the cosmos to which man would be admitted. He was made extraordinarily happy. I myself had a premonition of his death which like all the premonitions in my life proved to be mistaken. In brief, I learnt from a few words what I had no business to know. I have to own, it was moving and—confounding, even if he was, as he must have been, deluded.

On that day as I entered his cabin I saw that his eyes were closed and I paused, for in his pain, sleep was very precious to him. I wondered if I should go away again but as I stood there, he spoke, or rather muttered in what I can only describe as a tone of awed astonishment.

"*I am able to bless*—!"

Yes, I should have gone there is no doubt about that. But in a strange embarrassment I did nothing but utter an involuntary, and I fear silly, laugh. His eyes opened and looked straight into mine. A positive tide of crimson seemed to consume his face. I got out of the cabin, shut the door and only then was able to feel the extraordinary difference between these few humble words and the rarified concept of the Good which we were too often prone to discuss. My mind plunged back to that early interview when I had read to him from Voltaire's *Candide* the strange words of *le bon vieillard* "We have no need of priests—we are all priests"!

I went away confounded for a time and have thought since that it was one of several occasions in my life when I have felt myself to be on the brink of a mystery which through character, upbringing and education I am wholly unable to penetrate. But at the time, when I came to myself, I reflected that after all, the "good old man" had been one hundred and sixty five, and even *he* blushed as he spoke openly of the religious mysteries of El Dorado!

The day after that we sighted land, as I have said.

"Land ho!"

It was land indeed and visible at an astonishing distance. But the truth is that the diamond nature of the air in those climes has to be experienced to be believed so I will not labour the point. As for the longitude, it at once pleased and irritated all our navigators; for Charles and Benét had kept their workings to themselves like card players and revealed them only to the captain. He in his turn, with a sense of humour which I had not suspected, kept his own counsel—the longitudes were the same except for a mile or two! The Benét–Anderson method, therefore, might be good or bad. Nothing was proved or disproved. Charles, by rejecting the palpably wrong reading of one chronometer and relying on the other two, which were fairly close together—he added the readings and divided them by two—had achieved the same result. Luck must be considered to have favoured both parties. The land was where they said it was. So everyone and no one was satisfied.

Our adventure was now running down. We obtained fresh meat from one settlement and a quantity of vegetables from another. Beans we had always with us. It must be confessed that with the sight of land that common sense which is a useful though grey component of my nature gradually reasserted itself. There were changes among us all. Mr Prettiman returned to his customary state of excitement and anger. It rendered him more amusing than awesome. The emigrants, too, were a source of amusement to me. They appeared to think that we should steer straight for the nearest bit of land and disembark there! The rigid system of separation which had once obtained in our vessel had been so moderated by time and adventure that I could now walk among them without comment. They thought that one might walk round the coast to Sydney Cove, the weaker members riding in the wagons with which the aboriginals would provide them! Here, they thought, was a land of freedom, where crops and flocks grew themselves, black men and women were eager to learn and serve and every white man was a little king with a gang of chastened convicts to keep the blacks in order!

Winter had worn its worst away when we sighted the north point of Flinders Island and altered course to move up the east coast! We were held up by contrary winds for a while between there and Cape Howe. But we were cheered, I think, by moving among names which were familiar so that the bald points seemed to cry us a welcome in our own tongue. Despite all the increase to my reading and thinking which I got from the Prettimans, I cannot but be a patriot! I have been brought to see—and not only by them—the defects of England. I will not subscribe to the furious rubbish of "My country right or wrong!" But nevertheless, when I search my heart, among all the prejudices of my nature and upbringing, among all the new ideas, the acceptance of necessary change, the people, writers and artists, philosophers and politicians—even the wild-eyed *social philosophers*—the deepest note of my heart-strings sounds now as it will to my dying day—"England for ever!" So seeing those bald lumps of land and hearing their names, King Island, Flinders Island, Cape Howe, I felt, even if I did not cry, "England for ever!"

(21)

From Cape Howe, I believe it was, we had what Cumbershum irritated Oldmeadow by describing as a "soldier's wind", meaning one so conveniently on the beam that even a soldier could take the ship there and back. Oldmeadow replied with some nonsense about "a sailor on a horse" but by now I was bored to distraction by their service dislikes and rivalries. Oh, the restlessness in that ship! The ladies! I have the word of both Mrs Prettiman and Mrs Brocklebank that they were *dying to get their stuff out of the hold and have everything clean*! Even the cleanest of us were dirty, I believe. After all, it was now months since we had been able to use anything better for washing than saltwater soap! I had in fact wondered whether or no I should entitle my three volumes nothing less than *Saltwater Soap* but alas—owing to the pusillanimity of English book publishers, the occasion has not arisen. So we came at last to Sydney Cove and our little world burst wide open. We were brought alongside the new quay and the ship was invaded, for the articles we had brought in our hold were long awaited. No one took much notice of the few passengers. Iron railings were of more account. Anderson left the conduct of the ship to Mr Summers and hurried ashore with Mr Benét (the *image* of a flag lieutenant).

I did not chuse to go with them, for it appeared that the governor, Mr Macquarie, was absent, visiting an island even more drearily penal than the Cove. Some of our passengers fought their way ashore through the agents, porters, bales, boxes and noise. Miss Zenobia Brocklebank was carried on a stretcher, hustled on every side and with only the tip of her nose showing. Mr Brocklebank stopped by me.

"Goodbye, Mr Talbot. I hear you propose to publish an unillustrated account of the voyage. I advise against it. Nothing you can ever write can match the success of your medical practice."

"I beg your pardon?"

"Have you not half cured our good friend Mr Prettiman? In fact, sir, I believe you should abandon the Muse for Aesculapius! Good day to you."

"Mrs Prettiman—Mrs Prettiman! I will not say goodbye but *au revoir*! Surely we shall meet again!"

I could not hear what she said for the noise, nor get near her because of the mob on deck and the opened hold. It was a distracted parting. Mr Prettiman was half sitting up on the stretcher and peering at the quay. Two or three men detached themselves from a crowd and pressed aboard. He was expected! He was borne off without a backward glance and Mrs Prettiman followed him docilely. I was about to run after her but the stretcher of

285

the senile midshipman Martin Davies got in my way. The Pikes followed with the Easts in attendance, as if they were their servants! Mrs Brocklebank came running back—had she left her yellow shawl—oh no, she had been wearing it all the time—how silly! But she came very close to me and declared that she had quite forgotten what happened when we so nearly missed the ice—I could not tell what she meant then and cannot now.

"Farewell, dear Mr Talbot. Believe me, our secret is safe with me!"

Charles came up from the fo'castle.

"Edmund. You have not gone. I thought we had said farewell in the middle. This is insupportable."

"What sort of man do you suppose the governor is?"

"This gentleman seems to have business with you. God bless you!"

The gentleman had indeed. It was Markham, one of the entourage! He welcom'd me, took me straight off to, as he said, "wet my whistle". The phrase was a mixture of the *knowing* and the *common* which I found fairly representative of the junior members at the Residency. An English inn does not transplant well, but I have to acknowledge that the settlers had done what they could. I was startled to find that a general air of piety was required in the governor's presence. However, Markham said we were "safe for the time being", though the governor's deputy was only marginally less pious than the governor himself.

"Captain Phillip is a naval man?"

"Oh, indeed. He and your captain will be discussing the fate of that old hulk of yours—not hard to settle, I should judge by the look of her!"

"We lost our topmasts and had the devil and all to do."

"You ain't a naval man, by any chance?"

"God forbid. Our captain does not carouse."

"Neither does Phillip. 'Goodbye, Mr Markham. I shall see you tomorrow at divine service.'"

"Good God!"

"It's tolerable here when you get used to it. The flies are the devil. Good riding and shooting. By the by, there's a pack of letters for you at the Residency."

"Letters!"

"Came in the bag."

"I must go."

"Hey, wait a minute! You have to report to Phillip, you know!"

The upshot was that we went back to the ship, the state of which was indescribable, for already they were unloading from her as much of her stores as were immediately required on shore. I changed into reasonable clothes.

My interview with Captain Phillip was not long. He accepted my credentials without comment, hoped I would be happy in what he was pleased to call "the family", hoped my godfather was well, then asked in a voice little above a whisper for a paper on Mr Prettiman. I had to reply that I had not committed anything to paper. The man was now a cripple and married. I was convinced that he represented

287

no danger to the state. Phillip looked up at me under his brows but said nothing.

"Sir—there is another matter!"

"Yes?"

"The ship, sir. What will happen to her?"

"I am told she cannot go to sea again. She will become our guardship. The additional space for offices is very welcome."

"And her officers?"

"That scarcely concerns you, Mr Talbot."

"With respect, sir—"

"Mr Talbot, I make every allowance for the conduct of a young man in what amounts to the first few moments of an entirely new situation to any he has known hitherto, but you are a very junior officer and must be made aware of that fact at once!"

"I am aware of it, sir, and only the very deepest feelings of my heart could impel me to speak at such a moment. But, sir, as a naval officer you must have known many voyages, many commissions—must know how close friendships may become and how—passionately involved one may find oneself with the affairs and the future of a, a shipmate!"

The deputy governor regarded me for a moment or two in silence. Then his lips twitched into a smile.

"That is all true. I remember—but that is not to the purpose. Well. Captain Anderson is aware that continued command of a permanently moored guardship in this harbour is not possible for a post captain. He will return to England. Lieutenant Benét—a most unusual young man—goes with him."

"I was not thinking of the captain or Lieutenant Benét, sir."

Captain Phillip leaned back in his chair and regarded me solemnly.

"You interest me, Mr Talbot. Proceed."

"I was hoping to find, sir, that you would use your vast experience of things naval to reach down and promote a man who is not only my friend and a fine seaman but what is more a convinced and devout Christian!"

Captain Phillip leafed through the papers I had presented to him. Again the smile dawned round his lips.

"You not only interest me, Mr Talbot. You surprise me."

"Thank you, sir!"

"I offered command of the ship to Lieutenant Benét. But as I expected, after five minutes with him, he declined it. I hope the Navy does not lose him. He, with an address which seems natural to him but might be though impertinent in another youngster, pressed the claims of Lieutenant Summers."

"Good—Heavens!"

Captain Phillip smiled broadly.

"Captain Anderson had already done so. He said with emphasis that Lieutenant Summers was admirably suited to the charge of the ship."

"So Lieutenant Summers will be a captain!"

"Who said so?"

"I thought—"

"On the other hand, it is possible, of course. His duties would include King's Harbour Master with the emoluments from that position, for we have lost the one we had."

"I am sure emoluments are the last thing in Mr Summers's mind. He desires only to serve his God and his King."

"He said so, perhaps."

"Indeed. It was an injunction laid on him at the start of his career by Admiral Gambier in person and it has been his guiding star."

"Gambier is a good man. A pious man."

"It was my hope, sir, that my first letter to my godfather might contain a description of my joy at being able to represent to Governor Phillip the propriety of promoting a man of strict Christian principles—"

"'Governor Phillip.' Yes. Well. Who knows? So you want Summers made a captain, eh? You know of course that Governor Macquarie will have to confirm? And then the promotion will have to be confirmed from Home? However. Yes. I'll do it."

"Thank you, Governor, a thousand times!"

"You'd better get him here as soon as possible. And now about your affairs, my boy. We won't work you too hard for a while. Take a week or two to settle in. Look round you. When you write to your godfather you might include—no. One doesn't want to seem to be—"

"It will give me great satisfaction to mention your kindness, Governor. I hardly like to ask—but would it be possible—could I take the good news to Captain Summers myself?"

"Handsomely, lad! I haven't even signed an acting commission! Good Heavens, we cannot go about a serious matter like promotion in such a scimble-scamble fashion!"

"I beg pardon, sir."

"No, no. By the by—isn't your mother a FitzHenry?"

"Yes, sir. My father—"

"We have the forms here, you know, printed quite in the modern manner. After all, it is only 'acting'. It isn't as if His Royal Highness's signature was required—*that* must wait to come out from England if it ever does."

"Yes, sir. A little more delayed, I suppose, in peacetime."

"Charles Summers, lieutenant—any middle name? No—of the ship—being—to acting—signed—deputy governor."

"I can't thank you enough, Governor!"

He was regarding me curiously.

"Anything for yourself?"

"For me? I—could I take the commission to him?"

The deputy governor looked a little startled. But then he burst into hearty laughter.

"It has indeed been a long voyage! Oh, I should not say that—but Benét and Summers, Cumbershum, is it? And Anderson—now you—I tell you what, my boy. That is—that must have been far and away the happiest ship in the service!"

"Do you have communication with India, Governor?"

"The Bag, of course. Anything you want sent, let Markham know. He oversees it."

"Thank you, Governor."

"And, Talbot—the entourage is expected to set a good example, you know."

"Yes, Governor."

"I'll see you at matins."

He lifted himself an inch or two off the seat and gestured in the direction of the door. It was all much unlike the rosy anticipations with which I had set off from England. But in my delight with the paper I held in my hand I could not be sorry. I went with winged feet towards the ship, a Glaucus with a gift of gold or bronze—and there was Charles, standing at the forrard rail of the quarterdeck. Two carts full of luggage were bumping away along the cobbles and Anderson and Benét were strolling by them! They had lost no time.

But the ship was in a turmoil. All the hatches had been broken up. Booms were swaying up burdens of every sort, casks were being rolled, bales piled, dust rising—

"Charles! Charles!"

I jumped the gap between the quay and the ship. Later, when I saw how wide it was, I took myself to task for attempting anything so silly.

"Here!"

He glanced at the paper, then back at the work in progress.

"Not now, Edmund! If I take my eye off the unloading there'll be a fight, before you blink!"

"Read it, man! You must read it!"

He glanced at the form, then back at the work in hand; then swung round and faced the paper squarely. He seemed prepared to look at it endlessly, his mouth open and his eyes anxious. I unrolled the paper and held it so he could read. The colour drained from his face, he put out a hand and sat down heavily. So that was my golden armour!

I found, when Charles had recovered and we were sitting by a bare cot in the captain's deserted quarters, that a junior captain's status is signified by one epaulette worn on the right shoulder. The dear old fellow was very bashful in his confession but finally told me that he did in fact have a single epaulette stored away—stowed away—which I thought a quite extraordinary and touching indication of what *had* been a modest yet hopeful character! He was changed by the voyage, as we all were, and I could only hope that time would restore to him the simplicity and amiability which had once been so evident in him. I begged him to come ashore but he would not.

"Before you know it they would be playing pranks or truant. The men would get careless and then somebody would have a bale dropped on him. There is more in this unloading than you dream of. I can only be thankful the

293

voyage was so lengthened that we have no strong drink left in her."

I wondered for a moment whether to tell him that Benét and Anderson had both recommended him for his present position but dismissed the idea at once. Instead, I bullied him until he consented to put on his single epaulette for me. As far as I was concerned it was an anticlimax. The wretched ornament had been so long in store it was permanently crumpled and the gilting turned to something suspiciously like brass. It looked as if a large bird, an eagle or a vulture, had muted from a mast on his shoulder.

"I am most impressed, Charles! I may still call you Charles? You will not mind the involuntary word 'captain' escaping from my lips now and then?"

"It is a dream."

"Well—let us celebrate it ashore."

"No. I will see the governor tomorrow. But today—"

He fell silent and I wondered if the requirement of his religion had come before him. But then I saw that he was stroking the bare wood of the side of the bunk—the way, I thought suddenly, a man or woman might stroke the side of their onetime bridal bed! He stood up, went to the bulkhead and stroked it—stood by the great stern window and rubbed the mist of his breath from the glass—

"What is it?"

He came back, sat down by me on the bunk again.

"You will not understand me, Edmund. That time after

294

I was made a midshipman and got my hands on a sextant. Then later when the board called me before them and told me I had passed for lieutenant—and now! Captain? Yes—but I have a ship, my ship!"

"Oh, come. You will do better than this! Captain!"

"You would not understand."

I left him at last, to take up residence in the spare bedroom which Markham had kindly loaned me. I went, with a sense I could not at first define, of disappointment. I did finally track it down to Charles's delight with a moored and superannuated vessel!

Markham had not returned from some assignation. I thought then that my sense of greyness and disinclination for anything but sleep was from short commons and nothing to drink. I went therefore to the only inn in the vicinity which looked respectable—and felt lonely. Then I remembered the letters—paid my shot and hurried to the Residency. My letters were in a tied bundle on Markham's desk. I sat there and opened one which I recognized by the straggling direction as from my father. In his usual ill-spelt and indeed ungrammatical hand he told me without any preamble that my godfather was dead. He had rejoiced at the fall of the Corsican Tyrant too well and died of the consequent apoplexy. My future fell in ruins round my feet.

That was the beginning of a strange time for me. I was given no work and was supposed to be "familiarizing" myself with the situation. In fact I was avoiding it and

came slowly to recognize that I was missing *my friends!*
Those friends, I now saw, were the people with whom I
had passed the best part of a year and whom I knew as
well if not better than I knew my own family! Oldmeadow,
Brocklebank, Mrs East, Mrs Pike, Pike, Bowles, Smiles,
Tommy Taylor, Prettiman, dear Mrs Prettiman—before I
knew what I was doing I found myself moving in pursuit
of them! But they had vanished! My friends had vanished!
Charles was in the course of vanishing in his new obses-
sion with that hulk!

The next morning I went to the Residency and tried
to find out what had happened to them all. Prettiman was
not in hospital, but they had taken rooms, it was thought.
Oldmeadow had marched his men up river in pursuance of
orders. It was not clear what had happened to the Brockle-
banks—

And so on. Charles came to the Residency, epaulette
and all, and was closeted with Captain Phillip for a time.
He came out, burning with enthusiasm for the job of improving the buoyage system in the harbour! I walked back
with him to the ship as if I had never left her, but once
there found he was happily preoccupied with Mr Cumbershum in the business of ridding the ship of her guns and at
the same time ensuring that the balance was kept as even
as the eye could measure it. I wandered round, therefore,
a revisiting ghost. I found my first cabin and my second
cabin with the marks of suicide driven into the deckhead.
I walked on the poop where I had dared those monstrous

walls of black flint at the tail end of the tempest. My hand on the rail felt a roughness in the palm and I looked down. My hand had lain on the very place where Deverel's sword had nigh on cut the rail through!

There was a lump in my throat as if the memory had been happy. I could not understand what was happening. I stood with Charles and Cumbershum and they spoke of whips and timber-hitches, differed in some arcane detail of ropework, until Cumbershum stumped away muttering "Different ships, different long splices". Even then Charles seemed far away and regarding me as a speck on the horizon while he had himself his eye on a business of the utmost importance—though it was but the working of the decayed vessel alongside a sheerhulk where all her rigging but the stump of the mainmast was to be lifted out of her!

I found the Prettimans. Mr Prettiman was being fitted with a kind of harness or strapping which would enable him to walk with crutches and perhaps in time hobble on two sticks. Mrs Prettiman was already busy with papers and arrangements for meetings. She consented to give me half an hour. When I tried to describe my state she laid down her pen, put off her pince-nez and lectured me.

"You need employment, Mr Talbot. No. You cannot help here. In fact, you should not be here at all. It will do you no good up at the Residency. The voyage has been a considerable part of your whole life, sir. Do not refine upon its nature. As I told you, it was not an Odyssey. It is no type, emblem, metaphor of the human condition. It is, or rather it *was*, what it was. A series of events."

"I think there has been death in my hands."

"Stuff and nonsense. Goodbye, Mr Talbot. For your own good—do not come here again."

That was on the eve of the King's Birthday. I was still in a state bordering on the morbid. Mr Macquarie had not yet returned from his island; Markham and Roberts, the other two secretaries then resident, were kind but distant. The news of my godfather's death had reached them and Captain Phillip too.

Charles had our old ship towed out to the sheerhulk and moored alongside her. As far as I could see, he never moved out of her but was visible occasionally through the telescope which stood on the veranda of the Residency, his epaulette flashing in the eternal sun.

The King's Birthday intensified my loneliness if any-thing. There was a great dinner given by the deputy governor to those he thought deserved it, and this included, I am told, a number of discharged convicts, some of them wealthy. It began in the late morning and continued into the dusk. Captain Phillip had had some idea of controlling the number of healths drunk but he was unsuccessful. In fact, I believe that Edmund Talbot was the soberest man in Sydney Cove! I grieved for my friends the Prettimans, not really knowing which of the two meant the more to me—I grieved anew for Miss Chumley, that bright and unattainable star in the distant north—I grieved for Charles, who wore my golden armour and was so sure of my affection that he ignored me. Indeed, the fireworks had begun and the still waters of the cove redoubled them when I left that riotous company and went to stand by myself on the veranda, where I could stare at the sea and sky until they numbed me.

A little breeze brushed a shadow across the water. The myriad vessels—merchant, fishing, whaling, company or war—turned slowly to hang all one way on a single anchor. Our old hulk and the sheerhulk and the powder barge on the other side of her turned with them. There were red and blue and yellow stars over the water and the excited cry of children from beyond the hedges of the Residency garden.

I brooded on the disaster that had befallen me. Like Summers in the early years I should now have to *work my passage.* I should not be able to pass on a mention of the governor to my godfather, should not be able to press in high places for Charles's temporary promotion to be made permanent. No, indeed. It was no Odyssey, no paradigm, metaphor, analogue—it was the ridiculous sorrows of Edmund Talbot, whom life no longer spoiled as if he were its favoured child.

I went to the telescope and looked at the sheerhulk. Our—I have written our!—the foremast and mizzenmast of Charles's command lay on the sheerhulk's deck. All that remained standing of the mainmast was the lower portion as far as the fighting top. I found myself looking into the dark entry to the lobby and half expected to see Mr

Brocklebank emerge with his so-called wife huddled next to him under the dirty coach cloak. But all was emptiness.

There was something strange about the forrard part of the vessel, something odd about the bows. The huge anchor hung motionlessly suspended above the water—fairly by the hawse, did not seamen call it?—so as to be let go at a moment's notice, the crown so near the surface I could see a reversed anchor hanging below the real one.

What was odd?

It was as if a mist was forming round her bows, rising, so faint a mist that only a man who had been examining the whole ship for so long—there was an acrid odour in my nostrils. It was the fireworks, of course, sheaves of them now ascending above the darkling water. The land breeze was beginning and the upside-down anchor had vanished.

Charles appeared on the quarterdeck—came stumbling out of the entry to the captain's quarters! He leapt down the ladders, ran full tilt along the deck and vanished into the fo'castle. Behind him, a column of mist rose through the hole in the deck where the foremast had been. Charles appeared on deck again. He rushed to the mainmast, worked at it, then came away with a great axe in his hands. He ran up to the fo'castle and began to hew at the ropes which held the hulls together. He raced aft through smoke which was beginning to rise now from the whole length of the ship, was on the quarterdeck striking out again! There was a gap of water—a yard, no more—between the two hulks—all along the side of the sheerhulk which had the powder barge nestling next to it! Suddenly the hole in the deck, where the foremast had been, turned red. A single flame stood up through the hole into the open air. Charles came racing back. He sprang to the belfry, beat the bell into a furious jangling. Slowly the burning ship, smoke billowing up from her everywhere, moved out under the impulsion of the breeze into the roadstead with its swarm of anchored craft. Still the bell, and again the bell! I turned the telescope on the nearest merchantman and saw men gathering in the fo'castle round the anchor cable. Beyond her a small schooner began to haul up her staysail—farther out, still another let her squaresail drop and swell on the topmast as she made a sternboard out of the path of the dreadful vessel. Charles dived into the fo'castle but came staggering out almost at once. He raced the length of the deck, dived into the lobby and disappeared. The entry to the lobby vibrated with a dim but furious light. Over the harbour, but now no higher than a rising column of smoke, the rockets banged and crackled.

Quite suddenly I understood that Charles was in deadly danger! I did not know if he could swim, but most sailors cannot. Without thinking I began to run, down through the gardens, over cobbles, through an alley and came out panting between the godowns on this side of the quay. I ran in a panic to the landing place where a gaggle of dinghies and ships' boats lay to their painters, climbed down—saw one had oars, cast off the painter, leapt in and set myself to row. I am no oarsman and was unhandy. Nevertheless I kept on, for all that the burning vessel seemed hopelessly beyond my reach; and then it was apparent that I could catch her, for she slewed to starboard and stopped, the tide running past her as she lay, slightly canted and aground. Wherever the ports had been open the smoke poured out of her sides, and despite the smoke I could see how she glowed below decks. I ran the dinghy hard against her, close by the aftermost of Charles's frapping—a huge cable that ran up her side and vanished onto the deck. I clambered up her tumblehome, got myself over the bulwarks and fell on the deck coughing out curses and smoke.

"Charles!"

He had gone into the lobby. I tore off my neckcloth and bound it over my mouth and nose, then dived into the smoke.

"Charles!"

One foot stepped on nothing and I fell—it was the hole where the mizzenmast had been—and I was hanging half over it. I got up and could not tell where the ladder was. I found myself holding a rail, then a door handle. It was the cabins. I felt along them, seemingly for ever. I could not remember clearly why I had got out in the middle of the night—and then thought, of course, that it was to stand the middle as usual.

"Charles! Midshipman Talbot—"

He was nowhere, it seemed. I pawed at doors and rails: and then my feet perhaps having a better memory than my head, I found myself at the entry to the waist; and after that my feet took me up the ladder to the quarter-deck where the watch was changing.

"Talbot!"

Charles was nowhere to be seen. My head cleared a little and I remembered how he had dived into the fo'castle. It was possible—I ran down the ladders.

"Talbot, you fool!"

There was a fearful explosion almost under my feet and the frapping burst, went flying in the air, and at once there were two other explosions, one after the other. I saw the deck split open from my feet right to the fo'castle itself. The whole ship opened and sent up a tower of bright flame in the midst of which what was left of the mainmast fell thunderously. A mighty tide of sparks rushed up to over-take the fire which hung above us.

"Jump, you silly bugger!"

My hair went in a burst of flame. I turned to climb the stairs but they had gone. I went to the bulwarks but they were on fire.

"The larboard side, for Christ's sake!"

That was downhill. There was enough left of the deck round the wheel for me to cross. It did not seem to matter. But my face was hurting and my hands. I reached a stretch of bulwark where there was no fire. I looked over into cool water which even the reflections of the burning world could not heat. I let myself fall into it.

Cumbershum got me by the collar, for I could not help myself. Somehow they lifted me into the boat; and it was there that I began to feel my pain; and until they got me to the hospital I had much ado to stop myself crying out. They stripped me and bound me with lamb's-wool and poured the sickly laudanum into my mouth.

I will not detail my sufferings. Did they pay for anything? I think not. But there came a time when my body was well enough to let me understand the situation. My godfather was dead. Charles was dead. All those people were gone from me as surely as if they had stayed and been consumed in the burning ship.

No trace of Charles was ever found. At low water the wreck had disintegrated and displayed her bowels for all to examine who would. He was gone. A service of remembrance was held and Charles praised as a devoted servant among those who have no memorial but have vanished away as though they had never been. I was praised far more than I deserved, but I knew grief feelingly. I dreamed of him and them and the dead ship. I woke with tears on my face to endure yet another day of harsh, intolerable sunlight. It was in the driest and emptiest of interior illuminations that I saw myself at last for what I was, and what were my scanty resources. I got up, as it were, and stood erect on naked feet. The future was hard and full. Nevertheless I girded myself and walked towards it. But I firmly believed that whatever might happen to me in the future, this was the unhappiest period of my life.

(22)

Truth, being stranger than fiction, is naturally less cred-ible. An honest biographer, if such there be, will always reach a point where he would be happier if he could tone down the crude colours of a real life into the delicate tints of romance and legend! Such was my reflection only the other day when I reread some of the bald account which I have rendered of our antarctic adventures.

I have always been embarrassed for such authors as Fielding and Smollett, to say nothing of the moderns, Miss Austen, for example, who feel that despite all the evidence from the daily life around them, a story to be veridical should have a happy ending—or rather I *was* so embarrassed before my own life took a turn into regions of phantasy, of "faerie", of ridiculous happiness!

One day, still sorrowing, I was standing on the veranda of the Residency and wondering what interior power it is which keeps the majority of men from committing sui-cide, when a distant *thump* made me look up. A ship had come in through the heads, and as I saw her I jumped in good earnest, for our saluting gun answered from below the veranda with a bang and an immense cloud of white smoke. She was a warship, then. I went to our telescope and focused it on the stranger.

I believe even then something told me that a fairy story had begun! The ship was flying a signal—her number, I suppose—and other flags which might mean anything. Under her bowsprit there was a complicated glitter. I could make out a crown, a red centre surrounded by blue, and caught my breath as I saw it might well be what a dockyard would make of a crowned kingfisher, a blue bird, a halcyon, an *Alcyone*! I went quickly to the office and was very nearly hit by the wad from the next explosion of our answer to her salute. Daniels and Roberts were in the office and just abandoning the paper darts with which they had been conducting the affairs of the colony. Markham, coming through the other door, said it was His Majesty's Frigate *Alcyone* and now we should get some news we could believe instead of rumours from drunken merchant captains. I told myself that the most I could expect was a letter from Miss Chumley to answer the many I had sent to India by any ship going that way. But Sir Henry would have news of her. I remarked that I was acquainted with her captain and would stroll down. I went before anyone had the opportunity to offer me company and waited by the telescope until the small group that had gathered there had looked their fill. *Alcyone* was coming in quietly with all but her tops'ls clewed up, as was natural in such a crowded roadstead. But she was a warship and so we were signalling her into the new quay.

My turn came. I saw immediately Sir Henry Somerset on the quarterdeck and all aglitter in his full-dress uniform for a call on the governor. The reader may perhaps guess at the positive convulsion—no, I remember! My heart was all smashed as you might break an egg into a frying pan! What was my confused delight when I found myself gazing at the image of Miss Chumley! She stood by Lady Somerset on the quarterdeck, just *astern* of Sir Henry, who was busily issuing orders. The two ladies had their heads together, watching him, I think, and obediently silent as the ship turned in the channel. Now Sir Henry was examining the Residency with his telescope—we were eye to eye! He turned and said something laughingly to Miss Chumley. Now she was begging him for his telescope—a young officer was offering his own—he was holding it for her—she was making an adjustment—I took off my hat and waved—Miss Chumley abandoned the telescope and positively flung herself on Lady Helen's breast! They embraced, Miss Chumley stood away—seemed confused, distraught almost—she ran quickly to the companionway and disappeared! Suddenly I was aware of the unkempt appearance we were accustomed to present in the early morning—better than the positively *farouche* appearance of the generality of men in Sydney Cove but the difference was little—and hurried away to put myself straight. By the time I was shaved and dressed as I ought, *Alcyone* was tied up alongside. I raised my hat to Sir Henry, who was coming up the Residency steps as I went down them, but I believe he never noticed me. He was followed by a midshipman who carried a large *portefeuille*. Sir Henry was red in the face and puffing.

By the time I reached the quay, *Alcyone* had established her berth. Her after and forrard gangways were down, with sentries at them and quartermasters. Already she was taking in water and supplies. Despite the bustle on the quay, Lady Somerset was standing on it in a space which seemed sacred to her. Miss Chumley was not to be seen. As I approached Lady Somerset I took off my hat, but she instantly begged me to resume it. After India it was quite disconcerting to see a gentleman without his hat. I stammered a compliment on her appearance but she would have none of it.

"Mr Talbot, you have no idea the straits to which poor females are reduced in a frigate! But at least we did not suffer as this place appears to from flies—faugh!"

"One does not become accustomed to them. Lady Somerset, I beg you—"

"Now you are going to ask to see poor Marion."

"Poor Marion? Poor Marion?"

"She cannot abide the sea nor become habituated to it. She will even prefer the flies, I don't doubt."

"Lady Somerset—if you only knew how I have longed for this meeting!"

"I am a romantic at heart, Mr Talbot, but the care of a young female has gone some way towards curing me of what I begin to think an aberration. Your letters went far beyond what I proposed for you when I consented to a correspondence. Are you trifling, sir?"

"Lady Somerset!"

"Well, I suppose not. But a—what are you? Fourth secretary? And your godfather is dead, we hear."

"I fear so. Oh, it was so unfortunate!"

"For you, perhaps. Him too, we must believe. Though as far as the country is concerned—"

"She is coming!"

Indeed she was! Miss Chumley, in the time since we had been eye to eye through telescopes, had changed entirely! Where was the cloak of dull green which had hung from her shoulders? This radiant vision was dressed in white with a scarf of Indian gauze lying across her shoulders, then hanging from both arms. Her gloves buttoned to the elbows. A wide-brimmed straw hat was tied on lightly by another scarf which nestled under her chin. Her face glowed in the shelter of a rosy sunshade. Her other hand held a fan with which she attempted, not with entire success, to keep the flies away. I swept off my hat.

"Mr Talbot—your hair!"

"An accident, ma'am, a trifle."

"Marion dear, I believe we should invite Mr Talbot to come aboard, but tomorrow perhaps—"

"Oh, Helen! I beg of you! The land is unsteady but wonderful! It appears of such an extent, with trees and houses and things! Oh, Helen, they are English houses!"

"Well. You may stay for a while. I shall send Janet to you. Do not leave the quay. Mr Talbot will look after you."

"Indeed, ma'am, I ask nothing more than to be allowed—"

"And do not allow any of the natives, the aboriginals I believe they are called, to approach her."

"Of course not, ma'am."

"Nor convicts, naturally."

"No, ma'am. May I advise? We do not use that word here. They are 'government men'."

Lady Helen curtsied minutely, turned and went on board again. Miss Chumley and I continued to look at each other. She was smiling delightedly and shaking her head as if in disbelief and then fanning away flies—I suppose I was grinning like an idiot or laughing like one—behaving, in fact, very little as a secretary from the Residency should behave within ten yards of a surely amused audience! We spoke but as people in trances. By the magical properties of Mind so little understood, she and I could remember later what neither of us heard consciously at the time.

"Mr Talbot, you are quite, quite bronzed!"

"I apologize for it, Miss Chumley. It is not permanent."

"I fear I am weather-beaten."

"Oh, ma'am—an English rose! You have been in the rains, a monsoon or something."

"We have been at sea."

"Not all the time!"

"I did not know there was so much, Mr Talbot, that is the fact of the matter. One sees maps and globes but it is different!"

"It is indeed different!"

"Most of it you know, sir, is quite unnecessary."

"Quite, quite unnecessary! Away with it! There shall be no more sea! Let us have a modest strip between one country and another—a kind of canal—"

"The occasional ornamental lake in a prospect—"

"A fountain or two—"

"Oh yes! Fountains are of the utmost importance!"

It was at this moment, I believe, that we both became aware of the absurdity of our words and laughed, or rather giggled, at them. I began to reach out with my arms in a quite spontaneous gesture but I saw valuable Janet appear at the after gangway and dropped them again.

"Miss Chumley, we are both much put upon by the ocean—but surely you reached India?"

"Oh, yes. We were in Madras for a while and then Calcutta. But my cousin—after the death of poor Rosie Aylmer—all that talent, that goodness, her beauty—so tragic and so *frightening*, for she was little older than I am! My cousin thought me too *green* to last out the epidemic. Lady Somerset brought me away again and what must Sir Henry do but fall in with the admiral?"

"Kind fate has brought us together. I have maligned the universe!"

Miss Chumley laughed deliciously and—if I may so express it—more collectedly.

"The universe? Fate? Say rather that the Corsican Tyrant contrived our meeting! Well, it is no wonder, for many people and particularly the French have found it difficult to distinguish between him and Fate."

"Napoleon!"

"The wretched man has escaped from Elba and landed in France. We are at war again. The news came overland to the admiral in the Red Sea, so that when he met us off Cape Comorin he was able to order us here with *utmost despatch* and what is more, I suppose, we shall leave with the same desperate haste."

"I cannot endure it! You put me at once in the seventh heaven and in anguish!"

"Poor Mr Talbot! I believe any young person would do whatever—but I should not say such things!"

"Miss Chumley—oh, Miss Chumley—Miss Chumley!"

I became aware that Miss Oates, Lady Somerset's *valuable Janet*, was standing behind Miss Chumley. I took my hat off and bowed to her, she curtsied and we returned to our conversation but in less passionate tones.

"As you know, Mr Talbot, Lady Somerset has kindly taken me in charge."

"A precious responsibility that any—"

"There is a kind of agreement between us that I may not answer the question—that is—"

"Oh, Miss Chumley!"

"Young persons are generally thought to be too

313

ignorant to be allowed to dispose of themselves in a proper direction and must have an elder to do it for them."

"I had thought her a devotee of Nature."

Miss Chumley fanned flies away from her face. Then, in a gesture which moved me inexpressibly, she leaned forward and fanned the flies away from mine.

"One should be a Shakespearean heroine, Mr Talbot, and take care always to be at Act Five. I mean the comedies, of course."

"Oh indeed! What have we to do with crookbacks and angry old men with wicked daughters?"

"Nothing, of course. But what was in my mind was that straightforward offering of the hand as if a young person were in fact a young man in disguise—"

"Miss Chumley! Like Juliet you would, I swear, teach the torches to burn bright! The air, the sun however bronzing—colour—forgive these tears—and flies—they are flies—tears, I mean, of joy!"

Impulsively I thrust out my hand. She allowed the fan to fall the length of its string from her wrist and laid her hand in mine, laughing.

"Dear Mr Talbot! You have quite swept me off my feet!"

At length—and how unwillingly!—I released her hand.

"Forgive me, Miss Chumley. I fear my nature is too ardent."

She flicked the fan back into her hand and busily cleared the flies from before me. In the space cleared momentarily her glowing face came near. Lady Somerset appeared beyond it. Miss Oates was nowhere to be seen. Miss Chumley turned quickly.

"Helen! Where is Janet?"

"She fled below when the sailors began to laugh. You should resume your hat, Mr Talbot."

"Sailors, ma'am? Laughing?"

"That went near to being *public*, Marion!"

"I am sorry for it, Helen. But as I told Mr Talbot he quite swept me off my feet, and what is a young person—"

"You should go below now."

"But, Helen—"

"Lady Somerset—"

"You shall see him tomorrow if we are still here—but on a lungeing rein, mind!"

She watched the girl out of sight.

"You have my sympathy, Mr Talbot, but nothing more. Your godfather's death will delay your rise to fame and fortune, I imagine."

"I have an allowance sufficient for a young man—too little I agree for any larger establishment. My father—"

"A junior secretary cannot marry even if he has private means. Until I came on deck—Mr Talbot, it was *too familiar*! Well. You are wholly eligible except in the article of fortune. I am vexed, Mr Talbot, caught between my care of a young female—"

"She is the most beautiful lady in the world!"

"A proper sentiment on your part, sir. She is also all

wit, which will outlast beauty and is worth a lot more, though gentlemen can never be brought to think so. The remainder of her character, Mr Talbot, is compounded of determination and—until this episode I would have said—of common sense!"

"She was—we were—made for each other."

"In Calcutta she was besieged."

"I can believe it. Oh, God!"

"I am a romantic after all, it seems. You may see her to-morrow morning."

"I beg of you, ma'am, allow me to take her driving! Between now and sunset—"

"Tomorrow. Today we go to engage rooms in an hotel if there be one proper for us. Indeed the case is so desperate I believe we must make use of one even if it is not quite proper."

"Lady Somerset, I cannot believe you!"

Lady Somerset fixed me with a bold eye and spoke swooningly in her deep contralto.

"Since you expect to be a married man, Mr Talbot, you had better know the worst. Baths, sir, hot baths. It will be news to you, perhaps, but ladies require them just as much as you do!"

With that and the indication of a curtsey she returned to the ship. I hurried off and wrote a note requesting the privilege of driving Miss Chumley on the morrow. Back came an answer within an hour. Lady Somerset presented her compliments to Mr Talbot and consented to his driving Miss Chumley and *Miss Oates* on the morrow for an hour or two in the morning. Mr Talbot would be expected on the new quay by ten o'clock.

Lady Somerset may have expected a barouche. It was, however—and I was lucky to find it—an Indian buggy, with a rumble seat facing *aft* for Miss Oates and two seats facing *forrard*. This was brutal for poor Miss Oates—but love demands sacrifices from us all! I and the buggy were at the ship by a quarter to ten in the morning. It was already so hot that walking the horse was not merely unnecessary but inadvisable. I became once more an object of curiosity and—I think—amusement to the crew of the vessel.

Lady Somerset appeared first. She fanned disgustedly at the cloud of flies which surrounded both me and the horse.

"Good morning, Mr Talbot. That seat is dedicated to Miss Oates, I suppose. Your horse is small. At least he will not run away with you."

"The difficulty, ma'am, is to get him to move."

Lady Somerset signified her agreement. I had almost said "nodded"; but with her, the movement was as little of a nod as the bowed assent of Almighty Zeus.

"She will be here directly. You have no idea the number of times—ah! Here they come."

I cannot remember what I said or she said or they said—

(23)

And then?

I forgot so much these days, that is the trouble. Not that it matters, of course. None of these volumes is able to be published until we are all forgotten. In any case, journals tell so little. I leafed through these and found myself able to do no more than sample here and there. I shall not re-read them. Letters too. Only the other day one reached me at the Foreign Office from—of all people—Lieutenant, or I should say Mr Oldmeadow. He has a grandson, of course, and wants this and that. He himself turned in his commission long ago and took up a land grant, then bought more. He is now lord, he swears, of a bigger estate than Cornwall! That, and the lanky boy with his strange way of speaking, had me dwelling on the glimpses I had of Australia. It was mostly a memory of the birds, green swarms of them, or white ones with a yellow crest. I suppose it all happened, the voyage too. Only the other day the Prime Minister himself said, "Talbot, you're becoming a deuced bore about that voyage of yours."

Oldmeadow's letter did afford me a glimpse of my

friends the Prettimans. They came towards the interior by way of his estate. He gave a vivid picture of them—she leading in her trowsers astride a mettlesome steed, he just *astern* of her but riding side-saddle with his legs on the off-side as he had foreseen! A handful of immigrants and freed *government men* and one or two savages followed them.

Oldmeadow said—now what the devil did he say? Of course! He tried to persuade them that to go on was sheer insanity. But they rode off into the back of beyond, no matter what he could say to them. As he said in his letter, not a hair nor hide of any of them has been seen since. I hope they reached some sort of place. And then again, there was the letter years before that, from what's his name, Old Mr Brocklebank. He claimed to be prospering in his paint shop. Zenobia (his elder "daughter"!) had died only a month or two after leaving the ship. She had a message for me, he said. It was something like "Tell Edmund I am crossing the bridge." Devil take it, there were no bridges anywhere near Sydney in those days and our old tub wasn't a steamship!

But of course, I remember now. Miss Chumley appeared, followed by Miss Oates. I handed her up, Miss Oates fairly scuttled into the rumble seat. I do not know how she managed it. By the time I looked round she was seated and staring into the air, both hands gripping the handles on either side of her.

"Are you settled, Miss Oates? Miss Chumley?"

"I am very comfortable, sir. May I suggest?"

"Anything!"

"May we move away from the water? You know my aversion for the sea."

"Of course, ma'am. We shall drive inland."

We were off. I cannot say the drive was exhilarating as far as skill in driving is concerned. The small and sullen horse was perhaps more accustomed to funerals than to parties of pleasure. I did encourage him into a trot once, but it was not the "fast trot" and he soon gave up, clearly feeling that three passengers were more than enough. I thought so too, though for a different reason. Granted, however, that you are forced to be a threesome, Miss Oates was an ideal chaperon. I asked her if she was comfortable, Miss Chumley invited her to admire the extraordinary whiteness of a tree trunk and after that she might not have been with us at all!

"I divine that you are taking me to view a prospect, Mr Talbot. If I dare suggest—"

"Anything, of course!"

"Have you not a prospect of trees, woods, forests, fields at our disposal? An oak, now, or beech—"

"Our only proper road goes out to Paramatta. Our principal view or prospect is thought to be the harbour with its shipping. In the circumstances, I do understand your disinclination for it. What else? Our buildings, as you see, are not metropolitan. I might take you by way of the foundations of the new church past the place where services are sometimes held in the open air—"

Miss Chumley fanned the flies vigorously from before the small portion of her face which straw and gauze did not cover.

"I have had a great deal of religion, you know, sir," she said. "You can hardly conceive of the care which is lavished on the orphans of the clergy."

"You sound wistful, Miss Chumley. I suppose there was no chaplain in *Alcyone* nor no random parson such as we once had. I quite see that might be an additional hardship for a young lady."

"Yes. I suppose it was. Oh, what pretty birds!"

"We must go this way. There are savages down *there* and their appearance is not to be borne, the women in particular."

"It is a great thing that Helen has allowed you to take us off like this."

"It is a great compliment that Lady Somerset has confided you to my protection. No man ever had a more precious responsibility."

"Do not have too high an opinion of me!"

"It is impossible that I should—but why should I not?"

"Because, because it is my ambition never to—be a disappointment! I hope that was prettily said, but fear—"

"It was exquisite. It moves me to distraction—oh, Miss Chumley!"

"Janet—are you comfortable? You would not care to change places with me for a while?"

I mastered myself.

"Would you not care to sit by me here, Miss Oates?"

But it was plain that Miss Oates would not care to sit anywhere but where she was, facing backwards and petrified.

"Here is some country for you, Miss Chumley."

"Mr Talbot—those men! Are they—"

"Government men? Yes."

She spoke in a whisper.

"They are not restrained!"

"They will not harm us. As for restraining—to what end? That wild country, those blue distances, may extend for all we know for three thousand miles!"

"You are quite, quite sure?"

"I would not have brought you this way had I not been sure! Only the violent or hopelessly depraved ones are restrained. If they are really wicked, then they are sent off to an island and beaten too. I was beaten myself at school and thanked the master afterwards! It was the making of me, I believe. Of course, as the Greeks said, you know, 'Never too much.' Our country is very high-principled and we ought to be proud of the fact. These fellows have found this shore in no way fatal to them! Why, a few days ago, on the King's Birthday, I dined at the same table as a time-expired 'government man', a rich and successful one! Foreigners condemn us for what they call 'slavery'. This is not slavery, not the galleys, the dungeons, the gallows, the torture chamber! It is a civilized attempt at reformation and reclamation. Do not look to your left. There are some aboriginals in the bush."

Miss Oates squeaked. Miss Chumley spoke over her shoulder in a voice which I had not heard before.

"Do collect yourself, Janet! Mr Talbot assures me that the creatures will not harm us. But I am overcome with the strangeness of things—the trees, the plants, the air—Oh, what a butterfly! Look, look! And what flies!"

"One endures them, that is all, I am afraid."

"One should live in a city after all. This craze for Nature must pass and society come to its senses!"

"Did you not have a great deal of Nature about in India, Miss Chumley?"

"Calcutta is a city, of course. But we spent some days ashore at Madras with the collector before proceeding to Calcutta. Devoted as I am to dry land, I do not know that the experience was valuable. There were so many directions in which the collector positively forbade us to go!"

"Because of the natives?"

"Oh no! They are harmless. He said he could not permit us to approach a heathen temple—yet he himself, I should have thought, was hardly a deeply religious man! Have you ever seen an Hindoo temple, Mr Talbot?"

"I believe not. I have read about them though."

"I cannot see why buildings devoted to the practice of another religion, or superstition, shall I call it, should be out of bounds to a young person. In Salisbury, you know, we have many buildings devoted to Nonconformity and even a Quaker meeting house!"

It was too much for me.

"You are adorable!"

"I do not think I am, but am glad that you think so, though you should not say so, I believe. In fact, I would wish you to remain in that opinion for—I think our horse is going to stop."

"This is agony, Miss Chumley—"

"Helen said we should take the collector's advice, though I think myself that he meant it as an order! But then, Helen is not at all intimidated by old gentlemen, you know!"

"Not even by beautiful young gentlemen like Lieutenant Benét?"

Her answer was a peal of laughter.

"Oh, Mr Benét! He had such a *tendre* for Helen—the whole ship talked of nothing else!"

"And you, Miss Chumley—you?"

"We talked a great deal of French. I am always happy to talk French. Do you speak French, sir?"

"Not the way Mr Benét does."

"I think your ship saved his reason, for he was most unhappy at the end. He had begged for an *entretien*, a tête-à-tête—oh, I should not talk like this!"

"Please continue!"

"Janet, you are not to listen. Sir Henry was quite unreasonable. I was to stand outside the door *upwind*, because anyone who entered would naturally come that way. Mr Benét rushed through. He fell on his knees before her and seized her hand, all the time reciting his verses—then

324

the ship rolled and there they were, positively *entangled*. Then, as luck would have it, Sir Henry, against all custom, did come in through the *downwind* door! It was like a play."

"And then?"

"He was so angry! Sir Henry, I mean! He was angry with me too. Can you understand that?"

"Perhaps. But I could never be angry with you myself."

"Even Mr Benét was angry with me for a while, though not long. I threatened to tell Lady Somerset that his name rendered him conscious even to blushing. Which is why he altered the—"

"I do not understand."

"It is complicated, is it not? You see, his father started the French Revolution but then had to flee from the guillotine, leaving their estates and everything—and took the new name in a kind of self-mockery, which is very French, I think."

"So *that*—is why our quarrel boiled over—why Mr Prettiman was—why Mrs Prettiman—she called me—"

"I suppose he will change his name back when the war is over."

I blurted it out.

"Miss Chumley—how old are you?"

Miss Oates squeaked again and Miss Chumley looked a little startled, as well she might.

"I am—I am seventeen, Mr Talbot. Nearly eighteen. You do not think that—"

"That what?"

We were looking at each other eye to eye. A positive tide of pink suffused what was visible of her face.

"You do not think me too young?"

"No, no. Time—"

"Come! I will not have you grieving!"

"I—"

"You are not to be sad, sir! Mr Benét will recover. Sir Henry is no longer angry with me. Does that satisfy you?"

"It does indeed. More than you can know."

Did I say so? Did she? Was she really as anxious, so innocent or ignorant, and was I ever so moved by her? It is the emotions of later life which are roused by these partial memories, memory of her extreme youth and beauty—and my youth too, lanky young fool with everything to learn and nothing to lose. We spoke something like that. I think we felt something like that.

"I believe, Mr Talbot, the episode is to be forgotten with no harm done. We shall treat it the way Mr Jesperson who instructed us in the Old Testament would sometimes tell us to go on. 'Young ladies, you need not examine verses 20 to 25 too closely and Chapter 7 is to be omitted altogether!'"

"It is sometimes advisable."

"India, you know, is not a biblical country. I am sure of that, because when we were in Calcutta I looked it up in my cousin's copy of Cruden's *Compleat Concordance to the*

Old and New Testament. It goes straight from INDEED to INDIGNATION, with nothing in between."

"A depressing thought!"

"I do not wish you to be sad!"

"Dear Miss Chumley, life is all sunshine and flowers. Who cares if tomorrow the clouds come?"

"It is well enough for gentlemen to be bronzed, for they are fortunate in not finding themselves hedged as we do. But a young person—you see how high these gloves button and I must hold a parasol every moment I am in the sun. The brown natives of India—they sometimes look quite elegant—the natives are positively awestrook like the angel in *Comus* when they see an English lady! We must not be *bronzed*, you know, or our influence for good among them would quite disappear. My cousin says that by the end of the century the whole of the Indian peninsula will be Christian."

"All owing to the complexion of our English ladies."

"Now you are laughing at me!"

"Never!"

"Janet, you are not to listen. Mr Talbot, my little note which I slipped into Lady Somerset's letter to you—you discovered it?"

"I did indeed!"

"Believe me, the very moment it was sent off I would have given anything to have it back, for I seemed then to have presumed, to have made such a frank declaration—you did not find it too—too—?"

"Oh, Miss Chumley! It kept me—restored me to sanity, I would say! I treasure the little paper and could repeat the message to you word for word."

"You must not. But you did not find the words too—"

"They are sacred."

"Janet, you may unstop your ears now. Janet!"

I turned in the seat. Miss Oates had her bonnet pushed up and her hands pressed to her ears inside it. Her eyes stared back the way we had come. They were bolting like a hare's. An aboriginal was following us. He was stark naked and he carried a wicked-looking spear. I shouted at him repeatedly and at last he turned aside and vanished into the scrub. I do not think it was because I shouted. I think he had lost interest in us, as they do after a while.

"I believe we should turn here."

How the wretched horse pricked up his ears and trotted! He knew where he was going and went there for all I could do. He sketched out, as it were, the *mores* of his owner or the person accustomed to "drive" him. Who needs to stop by a particularly fine tree and then successively at two houses, a well and a boatyard? In the end, when my wrists were sore from unavailing persuasion, we came out to a slightly raised promontory with the harbour in full view. A wooden seat had been set there for weary travellers and I welcomed it, though an aboriginal stood by it, gazing out over the harbour as if he owned the place! The horse stopped by the seat. The native wandered off without a backward glance.

"My apologies for the wretched animal. Miss Oates, I will hitch him here and leave him in your charge."

Her answer was the expected squeak. I handed Miss Chumley down and led her along the verge, over the water. Presently I stopped and faced her.

"Miss Chumley—I have said that you and I have been the sport of Neptune as much as ever Ulysses was. The ordinary rules of behaviour cannot apply to us. The many letters I have written to you—"

"I treasure what I have received!"

All this conversation was breathless but in a strange way distracted. Something spoke which was not either of us.

"Miss Chumley—You must understand how instantly I knew my fate—how deeply I am attached to you? Tell me—what I cannot believe—that your affections are engaged elsewhere and I will retire to nurse a broken heart. But, oh, ma'am, if you should be free and disposed to receive my addresses not unkindly—in short, if you was to regard me in the light of more than a friend—"

Miss Chumley faced me with smiling lips and sparkling eyes.

"A young person, Mr Talbot, could not receive addresses more calculated to please her!"

"Oh, I could proclaim it to the whole world!"

"I promise you, Mr Talbot, the whole ship shall receive incontrovertible proof of our understanding before it leaves the harbour—Why, what is the matter?"

The tide was low. There, a mile or two away but clear as an etching in that diamond air, the black ribs of our poor old ship stood out of the water. I remember the impossibility of speaking about it to Miss Chumley. We stood there silent while the whole history of that voyage flooded me and started out under my eyelids so that I had to disguise the effort to wipe the water away as an attempt to rid myself of the eternal and infernal flies! For she knew nothing, none of the people, nothing of the terror, horror, savagery, devotion, boredom and mortality which yet seemed to cling round those distant baulks of timber.

"Miss Chumley—what happened to Lieutenant Deverel?"

"He left the ship and took service with a maharajah. He was made a colonel, though they did not call it that. He wears a turban and rides an elephant."

And then—

"Mr Talbot! That flag!"

I turned and looked to the right. Less than a mile away *Alcyone* lay alongside the quay.

"I very much fear, ma'am, it is the recall. The Blue Peter."

We turned and looked at each other.

I pass over the mutual declarations, the farewells and promises. They are able to be found in a thousand romances and why should I add to their number? In the end, of course, I had to take her—them—back to the ship. I hit the wretched beast harder, I imagine, than he had ever been hit before and was able with difficulty to prevent him running over the little cliff. At least he got us to the quay more quickly than we had left it. Miss Oates scurried to the gangway as if someone were chasing her. I handed Miss Chumley down. The ship's company was preparing for departure, there was no doubt about it. They showed considerable interest in us, there was no doubt about that either. I even heard the shouted order—"Eyes in the ship, curse you!" and the crack of a starter. But what was that to do with us? She turned to me with a smile.

"You have my word, sir, I will wait—if necessary for ever!"

"And I am yours for ever—there's my hand on it!"

Impulsively I thrust out my hand. Laughing now, she laid her hand in mine.

"Dear Mr Talbot! Once more you have quite swept me off my feet!"

Her glowing face came near. I snatched off my hat, and careless of propriety, and indifferent to the furtive glances of the seamen, seized her in a firm embrace. We kissed. I believe I have never, except when occasionally disguised by drink, made such a public exhibition of myself. It occurred to me even in that moment of delirium that the whole ship now knew exactly where we stood. Miss Chumley had done precisely what she knew had to be done.

Then the ship sailed, taking my heart with it.

*

My dear readers—for I am determined we shall have more than one descendant—may now imagine that they have the "fairy tale" to the end. They may suppose a steady rise in the ranks of the colonial administration—but no! The fairy tale was about to begin!

It was only the next day that Daniels remarked that the bag brought by *Alcyone* was a heavy one. He invited me to fetch my letters which were cluttering up his desk. I was too absorbed in my loss and my happiness to pay much attention. Letters from England at that time interested me but faintly. Indeed, it is a melancholy truth that letters commonly brought more bad news than good. It was therefore two days after *Alcyone* had left that I bothered to collect them. I read first a letter from my Lady Mother, who seemed, I thought, quite extraordinarily joyful for no detectable reason. Why was she "so comfortable"? Why did she refer to my dead godfather as a "dear, good man"? He had seldom merited such a description in public or private life! I turned to the letter from my father. My godfather's will had been read. He had left me nothing but had bought up the mortgages and left them to my Lady Mother! Though we could not be called wealthy or even rich, we were now in comfortable and what my father described as "suittable" circumstances!

More than this—dear readers, I beg you to suspend your disbelief as willingly as you can contrive—but concentrate rather on the well-known example of Mr Harrison, who was elected to Parliament without his knowledge and only discovered the pleasing intelligence when he chanced on an English news-sheet which was loaned him by a traveller in a Parisian brothel! By agreement one of the incumbents of my godfather's rotten borough had asked for the Chiltern Hundreds and I, Edmund FitzHenry Talbot, had been elected! Beat that, Goldsmith! Emulate me, Miss Austen, if you are able! The most striking expressions of astonishment are inadequate in the face of such a nearly unique experience! I read the joyful news over and over again—looked then at my mother's letter, which now made complete and indeed what I could only think of as "suittable" sense! My first impulse was to communicate the interesting facts to the Fair Object of my Passion! My second was to request an immediate interview with Mr Macquarie.

He was very understanding. I had scarcely told him the news and shown him the relevant portion of my father's letter when he besought me to regard him less as a governor than a friend.

What is there to add? Mr Macquarie pointed out the difficulties in the way of providing me with immediate transport. As soon as a ship should be available, of course—meanwhile, he thought that in view of this signal display of Divine Providence we should give thanks together. I humoured him. Indeed, good fortune and happiness seem to me much more compelling towards the Great Truths of the Christian Religion than their dreary opposites! Mr Macquarie, when we had risen from our knees, asked me humbly enough whether I would chuse to regard myself as entirely outside the ranks of government ("We are a happy family, Mr Talbot") or whether in the interim I would, as it were, loan the Colony my talents? I put myself at his disposal at once. He had, he said, many reasons for wishing a closer *liaison* with the government at home. He thought I would be interested to view what he had accomplished in the short time which had been available to him. Such knowledge would be of inestimable value to one of our legislators!

My letter to Miss Chumley grew to immense length. The sloop *Henrietta* put in but needed much attention to her rigging. There now occurred exasperating delays which were no one's fault in particular but endemic to the naval service in time of war. I transferred my gear to another ship, which incontinently left without me but with my gear and letter. *Henrietta*—but why should I elaborate? I followed hard on my letter but was delayed at Madras, which proved to be a fortunate circumstance since it gives me an opportunity of allowing the reader a glimpse of Miss Chumley's epistolary genius. I had, of course, in my own letter proposed matrimony formally. The words in which the Dear Object of my Passion consented to make me the happiest of men must be forever sacred to me. However, she consents to my copying some of the rest of that letter here.

The climate continues oppressive. Oh, for an English day! Well, I am busy counting my blessings, of which the greatest—but I shall not flatter you, for that would be the worst of beginnings, would it not? Let me turn rather to the "Draft of my Maiden Speech", which you was kind enough to include and invite me to criticize. Dear Mr Talbot, I found it truly admirable! When you declare "I accept election by the route of what has been called a 'Rotten Borough' solely that I may devote myself to the reform of an insane and unfair system!" my very heart cried out—*This was noble!* By the way, who is Mrs Prettiman?

Will you think me too oncoming if I refer to our proposed journey home together? My cousin (you know he is in the Church) has some reservations on the subject and I enclose a letter to you from him. I do so agree with you that we should attempt on the way to visit the great Centres of Civilization. The Pyramids! What excitement among all the others! But should we not get you to your important Parliamentary Duties as quickly as possible?? The Holy Land—you know of course how the Hallowed Places must shine in the heart of any young person! But I have always found it difficult to love the Israelites as I should! There! I have confessed it! I am sure they were a most estimable people, for they lived on manna, did they not, and a wholly vegetable diet is so lowering as to render a person young or old incapable of energetic wrong-doing. But when their diet changed—all that smiting hip and thigh, whatever that means—I am sure it is very violent! Of course, I would not dare to criticize the Great Founder of our Religion and do not mean to: but following that Sacred Career in the very Footsteps of the Master would be too painfully affecting for a young person to contemplate. In short, sir, may we not, as Mr Jesperson would say, "omit the Holy Land altogether"? But naturally I shall in all things be guided by you and my only wish is to stand by you in what you call "this momentous translation from Fourth Secretary to a Member of the most powerful Body of Legislators in the world!"

My readers may imagine with what joy I read and reread this tender missive! I turned at last to the letter from Miss Chumley's cousin. It was no lessened joy to find that he was a churchman indeed, for he was a bishop and signed himself "Calcutta +".

What more is there to say? So must end this account of Edmund Talbot's journey to the ends of the earth and his attempt to learn Tarpaulin! Yet I divine in my unborn readers an unease. Something is missing, is there not? The bishop could not consent to our journeying from India to England while still unmarried. It would be an extremely bad example set in a part of the world only too open to licence of every kind! He himself very cordially offered to perform the ceremony! So, my dear readers may rest contentedly assured: there did come a day when I leapt ashore in India from a pinnace. A "young person" under a rosy parasol stood, as it might be, twenty yards away. Valuable

Janet was behind her and a group of dark servants. Above the rosy parasol a greater was held and spread. But she took no heed of the sun when she saw me. I swept off my hat—she broke into a run—and your great-great-great-great-great-grandmother fairly sprang into my arms!

(24)

After I read Oldmeadow's letter I went for a walk, remembering all those old acquaintances—enemies who in
retrospect now seem to be friends. They came up one by
one, some I had forgotten entirely—Jacobs, Manley, yes,
Howell. I seemed to touch them all with my mind, one
by one, Bowles, Celia Brocklebank, Zenobia, little Pike,
Wheeler, Bates, Colley—and so on, from Captain Anderson down. It was a curious exercise. I found that I could
remember them without much emotion—even Lieutenant
Summers. Even Mr and Mrs Prettiman. That night I had
a kind of dream. I hope it was a dream, for dreams in any
event are mysterious enough. I do not mean their content
but the very fact of them. I do not wish it to have been
more than a dream: because if it was, then I have to start
all over again in a universe quite unlike the one which is
my sanity and security. This dream was me seeing them
as it were from ground level, and I was seeing them from
ground level because I was quite comfortably buried in
the earth of Australia, all except my head. They rode past
me a few yards away. They were laughing and chatter-

ing in a high excitement, the men and women following them with faces glowing as in a successful hunt for treasure. They were high on horses—she leading, astride with a wide hat, and he following, side-saddle, since his right leg was useless. You would have thought from the excitement and the honey light, from the crowd that followed them, from the laughter and, yes, the singing, you would have thought they were going to some great festival of joy, though where in the desert around them it might be found there was no telling. They were so happy! They were so excited!

I woke from my dream and wiped my face and stopped trembling and presently worked out that we could not all do that sort of thing. The world must be served, must it not? Only it did cross my mind before I had properly dealt with myself that she had said, or he had said, that I could come too, although I never countenanced the idea. Still, there it is.

The novels of William Golding

ff

Lord of the Flies

A plane crashes on a desert island and the only survivors, a group of schoolboys, assemble on the beach and wait to be rescued. By day they inhabit a land of bright fantastic birds and dark blue seas, but at night their dreams are haunted by the image of a terrifying beast. As the boys' delicate sense of order fades, so their childish dreams are transformed into something more primitive, and their behaviour starts to take on a murderous, savage significance.

ff

The Inheritors

This was a different voice; not the voice of the people. It was the voice of other.

When the spring came the people moved back to their familiar home. But this year strange things were happening – inexplicable sounds and smells; unexpected acts of violence; and new, unimaginable creatures half glimpsed through the leaves. Seen through the eyes of a small tribe of Neanderthals whose world is hanging in the balance, *The Inheritors* explores the emergence of a new race, *Homo sapiens*, whose growing dominance threatens an entire way of life.

ff

Pincher Martin

Drowning in the freezing North Atlantic, Christopher Hadley Martin, temporary lieutenant, happens upon a grotesque rock, an island that appears only on weather charts. To drink there is a pool of rain water; to eat there are weeds and sea anemones. Through the long hours with only himself to talk to, Martin must try to assemble the truth of his fate, piece by terrible piece. *Pincher Martin* is a terrifying and unforgettable journey into one man's mind.

ff

Free Fall

Somehow, somewhere, Sammy Mountjoy lost his freedom, the faculty of freewill 'that cannot be debated but only experienced, like a colour or the taste of potatoes'. As he retraces his life in an effort to discover why he no longer has the power to choose and decide for himself, the narrative moves between England and a prisoner-of-war camp in Germany. In *Free Fall*, his fourth novel, William Golding has created a poetic fiction, and an allegory, as moving as it is unforgettable.

ff

The Spire

Dean Jocelin has a vision: that God has chosen him to erect a great spire on his cathedral. His mason anxiously advises against it, for the old cathedral was built without foundations. Nevertheless, the spire rises octagon upon octagon, pinnacle by pinnacle, until the stone pillars shriek and the ground beneath it swims. Its shadow falls ever darker on the world below, and on Dean Jocelin in particular.

ff

The Pyramid

Oliver is eighteen, and wants to enjoy himself before going to university. But this is the 1920s, and he lives in Stilbourne, a small English country town, where everyone knows what everyone else is getting up to, and where love, lust and rebellion are closely followed by revenge and embarrassment. Written with great perception and subtlety, *The Pyramid* is William Golding's funniest and most light-hearted novel, which probes the painful awkwardness of the late teens, the tragedy and farce of life in a small community and the consoling power of music.

ff

The Scorpion God

Three short novels show Golding at his subtle, ironic, mysterious best. In *The Scorpion God* we see the world of ancient Egypt at the time of the earliest pharaohs. *Clonk Clonk* is a graphic account of a crippled youth's triumph over his tormentors in a primitive matriarchal society. And *Envoy Extraordinary* is a tale of Imperial Rome where the emperor loves his illegitimate grandson more than his own arrogant, loutish heir.

ff

Darkness Visible

Darkness Visible opens at the height of the London Blitz, when a naked child steps out of an all-consuming fire. Miraculously saved but hideously scarred, soon tormented at school and at work, Matty becomes a wanderer, a seeker after some unknown redemption. Two more lost children await him, twins as exquisite as they are loveless. Toni dabbles in political violence; Sophy, in sexual tyranny. As Golding weaves their destinies together, his book reveals both the inner and outer darkness of our world.

ff

The Paper Men

Fame, success, fortune, a drink problem slipping over the edge into alcoholism, a dead marriage, the incurable itches of middle-aged lust. For Wilfred Barclay, novelist, the final unbearable irritation is Professor Rick L. Tucker, implacable in his determination to become The Barclay Man. Locked in a lethal relationship they stumble across Europe, shedding wives, self-respect and illusions. The climax of their odyssey, when it comes, is as inevitable as it is unexpected.

ff

Rites of Passage

Sailing to Australia in the early years of the nineteenth century, Edmund Talbot keeps a journal to amuse his godfather back in England. Full of wit and disdain, he records the mounting tensions on the ancient, sinking warship where officers, sailors, soldiers and emigrants jostle in the cramped spaces below decks. Then a single passenger, the obsequious Reverend Colley, attracts the animosity of the sailors, and in the seclusion of the fo'castle something happens to bring him into a 'hell of degradation', where shame is a force deadlier than the sea itself.

ff

Close Quarters

In a wilderness of heat, stillness and sea mists, a ball is held on a ship becalmed halfway to Australia. In this surreal, fête-like atmosphere the passengers dance and flirt, while beneath them thickets of weed like green hair spread over the hull. The sequel to *Rites of Passage*, *Close Quarters*, the second volume in Golding's acclaimed sea trilogy, is imbued with his extraordinary sense of menace. Half-mad with fear, with drink, with love and opium, everyone on this leaky, unsound hulk is 'going to pieces'. And in a nightmarish climax the very planks seem to twist themselves alive as the ship begins to come apart at the seams.

ff

Fire Down Below

The third volume of William Golding's acclaimed sea trilogy. A decrepit warship sails on the last stretch of its voyage to Sydney Cove. It has been blown off course and battered by wind, storm and ice. Nothing but rope holds the disintegrating hull together. And after a risky operation to reset its foremast with red-hot metal, an unseen fire begins to smoulder below decks.

ff

The Double Tongue

Golding's final novel, left in draft at his death, tells the story of a priestess of Apollo. Arieka is one of the last to prophesy at Delphi, in the shadowy years when the Romans were securing their grip on the tribes and cities of Greece. The plain, unloved daughter of a local grandee, she is rescued from the contempt and neglect of her family by her Delphic role. Her ambiguous attitude to the god and her belief in him seem to move in parallel with the decline of the god himself – but things are more complicated than they appear.